Peter A. Flannery lives in the S[...] wife and two sons. Afte[...] college before changing [...] horticulture. After sever[...] he switched again, setting [...] toy and hobby industry. It [...] [...]sign studio in Edinburgh that [...] [...]om sculpting to writing, producing background stories for the company's models and games. He is now a self-published author working entirely on his own material.

Other books by Peter A. Flannery

First and Only
A fast paced thriller about the world's first true psychic and the deranged killer who stalks him.

Battle Mage
A classic coming-of-age fantasy epic in which a young man must overcome guilt, grief and physical weakness in order to fulfil his destiny.

Decimus Fate

and the
Talisman of Dreams

Peter A. Flannery

BLACKHEART BOOKS

Decimus Fate
and the
Talisman of Dreams

ISBN: 978-0-9570919-6-2

First published by Blackheart Books in 2020

Contact:

Twitter: @TheFlanston

Website: www.peterflannery.co.uk

To Logan and Callum, my two amazing boys.

To Judith who suggested the idea of a fantasy
whodunnit during a chat over the garden fence!

And to Julie who reads my waffle many times,
spots numerous mistakes and always
helps me stay on track.

Author's Note

I want to say a huge thank you to all the readers who have supported me over the last few years. Whether you bought one of my books or downloaded a free copy during a promotion, I want to thank you for taking a chance on a new author.

And if you left a review, or took the time to send me a message, then you are totally awesome and I am in your debt! I would love to buy each and every one of you a beer or a coffee, or an ice cream cone with a chocolate flake on top!

Some writers have wonderful publishing houses to help and support them. All my strength and motivation comes from you, the reader.

Thank you.

Decimus Fate

and the

Talisman of Dreams

The Blue Tile

The Blue Tile

The artisan felt sick with fear. He had no idea why the emperor's sorcerer had summoned him, but he was terrified that it might have something to do with the 'blue tile'. For the last two years he, and twenty other mqagical artisans, had been working to complete a bowl shaped chamber that was designed to absorb the magical energy of anything placed within it.

Built into the floor of a marble hall, the chamber was lined with thousands of blue tiles each one imbued with magic and set in place with binding spells. All the thousands of tiles were identical, except for one.

It was almost a year ago when a stranger had stopped the artisan on his way to work at the palace. The artisan had found the man's presence unsettling and began to walk past him until the stranger spoke.

'I know how to save your son.'

The artisan stopped.

'What do you know about my son?'

'I know that you have tried everything to save him, and that all your efforts have failed.'

'How do you know this?' asked the artisan. 'Are you a physician?'

'No,' said the stranger. 'But I know of a cure if you are willing to pay for it.'

'But I have no money. I have given everything I have, and still my son is going to die.'

'Not if you do something for me,' said the stranger.

The artisan's eyes grew narrow with suspicion. Many people had made tempting promises, but this man seemed different.

'What do I have to do?'

'A simple thing,' said the stranger and, reaching into his robes, he drew out a blue tile that looked identical to those being used in the palace. He handed the tile to the artisan. 'All I want you to do is set this into the chamber as you would any other tile.'

'Is it dangerous?'

'No,' said the stranger. 'No one will even notice that it's there.'

As the artisan turned the tile over in his hands he noticed a design etched into the back... three parallel lines joined together by a series of overlapping diagonal lines.

'Can you really save my son?'

'Yes,' said the stranger and, with a sigh, the artisan tucked the blue tile into his clothes.

That was almost a year ago and the stranger had been true to his word. How he found a cure the artisan did not know, but that did not matter. All that mattered was that his son was alive. But now the artisan was about to pay the *real* price for saving his son's life. He was certain that his interference had been discovered. However, as he continued, he noticed other artisans making their way to the palace. By the time he reached the chamber the entire compliment of workers was there.

'Thank you for coming,' said a powerful voice and the artisans looked up to see the emperor's sorcerer standing on the crystal disk of the recepticule. Tall and slender with grey hair and dark green eyes, the man walked down the steps and into the base of the chamber.

'Come, please,' he said, inviting the artisans to join him.

Still uncertain, but somewhat relieved, the artisan joined his fellow craftsmen as they made their way down into the voluminous chamber. It really was an awe-inspiring sight; a great bowl of enamelled blue tiles rising around them in a shimmering wall that formed a full three quarters of a sphere.

'Magnificent work,' said the emperor's sorcerer. 'A true credit to your art.'

The artisan breathed a sigh of relief. He was not about to be punished. He and his fellow craftsmen were here to be thanked.

The emperor's sorcerer moved among the men, shaking hands and patting shoulders. Slowly he moved through the group and climbed back up the stairs to address them.

'The emperor is delighted,' he told them. 'And as a final reward your families will each be paid a stipend of five silver coins a month for the rest of their lives.'

The faces of the artisans lit up with pride.

'What you have created here is unique and impossible to replicate.' The sorcerer's green eyes shone with satisfaction as he stood on the recepticule and reached out to the activation column where three stone spheres sat in gold cradles. Moving slowly, he picked up the first of the spheres, each of which was marbled with gold.

This first sphere activated the chamber's containment field and the sorcerer's form seemed to shimmer as he placed the sphere in the white marble housing of the column. As he did this, the artisans began to shift and murmur. They were now trapped in the heart of the chamber.

'You have given us a way of increasing the emperor's power,' said the sorcerer as he lifted the second of the marbled stone spheres.

And now the artisans began to panic. Placing that sphere would harmonise the magical energy that each of them possessed. With a single voice of anguish they cried out as the sorcerer set down the second sphere. Some dropped to their knees as the arcane essence was drawn out of their bodies until it filled the chamber with glowing light.

The third sphere would vaporise the artisans in a blinding flash of energy that would be absorbed by the tiles before being channelled into the recepticule on which the sorcerer now stood.

The artisan watched as the sorcerer raised the final stone sphere. He and his fellow craftsmen had been used, and now their magical energy would be harvested to make a powerful sorcerer even more powerful. All around him, his fellow artisans wailed in terror, but not him. His thoughts were of a secret blue tile and of the beloved son who was alive because of it.

Looking down into the chamber, the sorcerer gave a smile of triumph as he lowered the final sphere into its niche. The cries of the artisans were suddenly cut off as the chamber flared with a blinding white light and the sorcerer gasped as his body was filled with a surge of magical power.

As the light faded the sorcerer drew a breath. The device had worked perfectly, but then he frowned. No… not quite perfectly. As the plasma of vaporised souls slowly dissipated, he became aware of a flaw in the perfection of his new device.

Rushing down from the crystal disk he entered the chamber where the air was filled with the smell that follows a lightning strike. Face tight with outrage, he whirled about. Focusing his mind, he scanned the device with his magical perception, trying to determine exactly what had been done, but he sensed nothing.

Was one of the tiles damaged or misplaced? He swept his gaze over the myriad of tiles but could see nothing but perfection. The sorcerer ground his teeth and magical flames surrounded his fists as he let out a primal cry of rage. Something had been done to his beloved creation and he had just killed the only people who could tell him what. Slowly the rage went out of his body...

It didn't matter, he told himself. The device worked. So long as he did not try to do too much, he could increase his power until no sorcerer in the world could match him. Feeling calmer he walked out of the chamber and returned to the crystal disk. Finally he dismissed the invisible flaw as irrelevant and his lip curled in a sneer. He was the emperor's personal sorcerer, the most influential magic user in the world, and his name was Oruthian Bohr.

Back in the chamber, thousands of blue tiles tinkled softly as they cooled. They looked identical. There was nothing to tell one of them from another, except that the back of one tile was etched with a design known to mystics as the Web of the Wyrd. To others, this design was known to have a different meaning; to them it was known as the ancient symbol for fate.

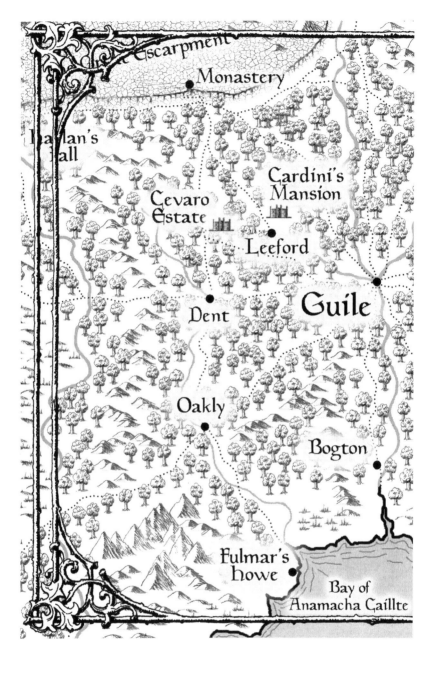

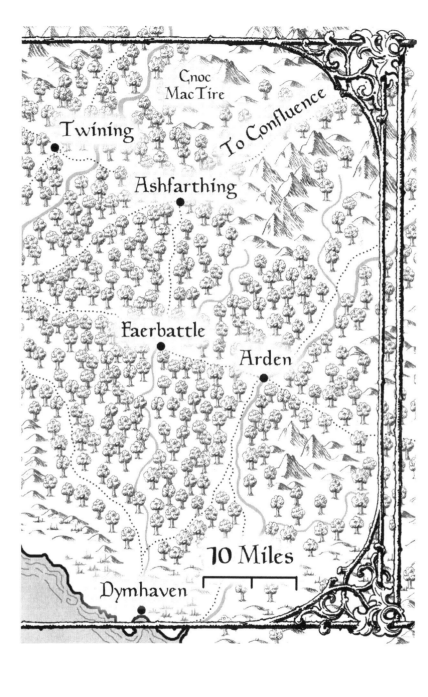

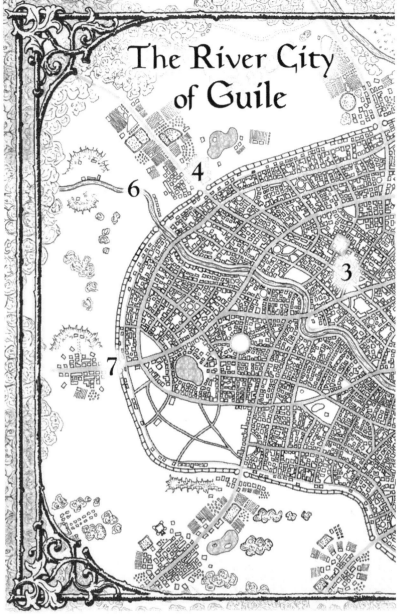

The River City
of Guile

1. Blackfell House   3. Abnoba Temple

2. The Fool's Hope Inn   4. Northwest Gate

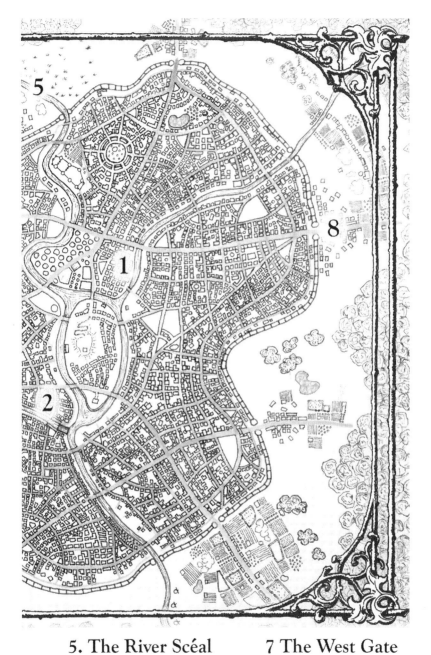

5. The River Scéal   7 The West Gate

6. The Norward Canal   8. The East Gate

1
The Tutor

The merchant knew he was being followed, but he had no choice except to push on through the narrow streets of Guile. It was almost midnight and the air was thick with the sickly sweet smell of hops from the brewery at the end of Cooper's Row. Veils of mist hung over the road forming yellow haloes around the few oil lamps that burned in this, the poorest quarter of the city. The ramshackle buildings rose three storeys high, looming over the road and punctuated by narrow alleyways that ran between them.

Leading his mule, the merchant hurried along. It was a damp night and cold, but the merchant was sweating. Every dark alleyway seemed to be filled with menace and his heart was beating so fast it left him breathless. Madam Carletta of the Fool's Hope Inn had advised him to hire protection but he had baulked at the cost.

'No one would dare attack a member of the merchant guild within the city walls,' he had told her, but the landlady of the Fool's Hope had not been so sure, and now he bitterly regretted not taking her advice. He kept glancing backwards but he never saw the black man in the dark clothes who came after him.

Turning in the direction of his home, the merchant pressed on. The crossroads ahead of him were lit by one meagre lamp where normally there would be four. The open space was dark and forbidding but still more appealing than the menacing presence he sensed in the streets behind.

Grabbing his mule's bridle he started forward then stopped as a young man stepped out in front of him. The man appeared to be in his early twenties with a narrow face, dark hair and a pointed nose that had clearly been broken at some point in the past.

'Not so fast, my friend,' said the young man.

The light from the solitary oil lamp glinted off a thin-bladed dagger and a glowing sigil on the back of his hand marked the young man as an apprentice mage.

Trying not to panic, the merchant pulled his mule to the right then stopped again as another figure emerged from the shadows. He turned, only to find two more young men blocking his way while a further two now stepped up behind him. Unlike the apparent leader of the group, these young men had the broad shoulders of those accustomed to physical work. They were dressed in moleskin breeches with the waxed cotton jerkins worn by the ferrymen who plied the rivers of Guile. All of them were armed with knives or the long machetes used for hacking through the thick reeds that grew along sections of the river. It was clear that they had been waiting for him.

'You can't attack me,' said the merchant. 'No one attacks a member of the merchant guild. Not within the city walls.'

The leader gave a mocking laugh.

'Don't worry,' he said. 'They won't find your body in the city.'

The merchant started as one of the young men stepped up behind him. Using his knife he cut the straps on a saddle bag and drew out a metal chest about two hands wide. There was no visible lock or keyhole, only an engraved plate lying across the join where a normal lock would be.

The young man took the chest to the leader of the group who cradled it in the crook of his arm. He placed his right hand on the engraved plate which began to glow causing him to wince and remove his hand as if it had been burned.

'I'm told,' he said, now tapping the engraved plate with the tip of his knife, 'that only your hand can open this chest.'

'You don't understand,' said the merchant. 'You can't force me… The chest will only open if I want it to.'

The leader gave a wicked smile. 'Oh, you'll want it to,' he said. 'By the time we've finished with you, you'll be begging it to open.'

The merchant was now sweating profusely and shaking with fear.

'Please!' he cried. 'I promised to pay Master Veleno his share.'

'Ah,' said the youth. 'But we don't work for Master Veleno.'

'Then he'll kill you!' gasped the merchant. 'He'll kill you if you defy him.'

'But who's going to tell him?' said the leader. 'You'll be dead and I don't see anyone else around.'

The merchant's eyes darted around the crossroads. The streets were empty. There was no one to witness the attack. Turning back to the leader he drew a breath to plead for his life then stopped as a second street lamp suddenly flared into life. Everyone turned, and there, standing beneath the newly lit lamp, was a dark and imposing figure.

The man was tall with the ebony skin of people who hail from the Southern Isles. He was dressed in black leather breeches and a black leather doublet with articulated plates of hardened leather on his right arm and shoulder. A bandolier of throwing stars angled across his chest and a slender shortsword hung at his waist. He stood with a relaxed stance that spoke of confidence. He was not heavily built and yet he possessed the kind of physical presence that would give any man pause. The man's stern features were gathered in a frown and even in this meagre light they could see that his eyes were blue.

'Oh, but you boys have made a terrible mistake.' The man shook his head as if he were truly sorry for the fate that awaited them.

'There's been no mistake,' said the leader of the group. 'This just means we bury two bodies in the forest tonight.'

The stranger smiled as if he found the threat endearing.

'You still have time to walk away,' he told the leader. His voice was deep and warm but with a hard edge that was distinctly intimidating. 'If you return the chest and leave, Master Veleno might not learn of what you did tonight.'

'I don't think so,' said the apprentice mage and with a jerk of his head he directed his companions to attack.

Knowing they would be severely punished if Master Veleno heard of their attack, four of the young ferrymen rushed forward. Two were armed with knives and two with machetes, but the black man in the dark clothes did not back away. Instead he stepped forward to meet his attackers. One of them raised his machete to strike, but the stranger closed in quickly. He grabbed the young man's arm and spun him around, forcing him into the path of the other three assailants. With a savage twist the stranger flipped the young man onto his side and he screamed as one of the bones in his arm broke with an audible 'crack'.

4

Two knives now flashed towards the stranger as a third man hefted a machete. With impressive speed the stranger disarmed his first opponent before delivering a backhanded blow that broke the young man's nose. Arching away from a knife-thrust, the stranger caught his second attacker's wrist, removed the knife from his hand and flipped him onto his back. Then, with agility that belied his size, he spun about, landing a roundhouse kick squarely on the jaw of the last attacker who had just raised his machete to strike. The man's knees gave out and he dropped his weapon as he stumbled to the floor.

Still holding his downed opponent's knife, the stranger turned to face the leader of the group. The fight had taken all of ten seconds and the stranger had not even drawn his sword.

Two of the original gang remained standing. The ferryman to the left had not attacked and he stood with his knife trembling in his hand. The leader was clearly shocked by the speed with which the stranger had defeated his companions, but he also looked surprisingly confident. Still holding the merchant's chest he reached into his tunic and pulled out a small crystal sphere that was filled with a swirling green light.

'So you know how to fight,' he said in a mocking tone. 'Let's see how tough you are when you're breathless and paralysed.'

The black man glanced at the glowing sphere and his brow gathered in a frown.

'I'm warning you,' he said. 'This is your last chance to walk away.'

For a moment the young man hesitated then he smiled as he threw the crystal sphere at the stranger's feet. The sphere shattered and a glowing green gas flowed towards the stranger and the ferrymen lying close by. The magical fumes seemed to seek them out, engulfing their torsos and swirling about their heads.

The youths on the ground began to writhe and choke as if their limbs were frozen and they could not breathe, and the leader smiled. He had stolen the sphere from his master's workshop and he was glad to see that it had been worth the risk.

The stranger seemed to stagger and the leader smiled, but then a magical light sprang up beneath the stranger's doublet as if the skin of his chest was glowing. The light was fierce, like fire, and the green smoke began to dissipate.

The leader stared in disbelief as the stranger stepped clear of the smoke and walked towards him. The magical fumes in the sphere were strong enough to fell a draught horse, but the black man in the dark clothes seemed unaffected and now he stood there as calm and intimidating as ever.

The leader looked down at the stranger's chest where the neck of his black doublet had been pulled open to reveal the edge of a tattoo that glowed faintly in the man's dark flesh. The leader's eyes widened as he recognised the tattoo of a demon hunter. Originally formed to combat demons that broke through into the human world, this elite unit of warriors had become a weapon to be used against those who opposed the emperor. For a moment the apprentice mage paused in fear then, with a snarl of frustration, he turned to run still cradling the merchant's chest in his arms.

Still holding the knife he had taken from one of his attackers, the stranger drew back his arm and threw it. The leader was barely twenty paces away when the knife took him in the back of the leg. With a cry he fell forward and the chest went skidding from his grasp. With the knife still sticking out of his leg he tried to get to his feet as the stranger advanced towards him.

The magical green smoke had now lifted from the other youths and with much groaning and choking they picked themselves up from the ground. The stranger walked past the injured leader to retrieve the chest from the street before looking down at the young man.

'You were foolish to ignore Veleno's decree on the merchant guild,' he said. 'But I will keep my silence if you promise to leave the city.'

'Silence!' spat the leader of the gang. 'It should be you asking me to keep silent.' With a grunt he pulled the knife from his leg and staggered to his feet. 'I know what you are,' he said, pointing a finger at the stranger's chest. 'I know why the magic didn't harm you.'

He paused, wincing with pain.

'You're a deserter, and I think Master Veleno will be very interested to know that one of your sort is holed up in the city.' Even though he was pale and sweating, the young apprentice mage smiled. 'In fact I'm sure he would pay handsomely for such information.'

The stranger's blue eyes suddenly hardened.

'Silence would be the wiser course.'

'Silence be damned,' said the leader. 'Maybe this night will prove worthwhile after all.' With that he jerked his chin at the members of the gang and together they limped away into the night.

The stranger watched them go then he gave a heavy sigh and turned back to the merchant who was still standing beside his mule. The merchant drew a shuddering breath and watched as the stranger returned the chest to his saddlebag.

'I'll see you home,' said the stranger. 'But next time don't ignore the advice of one of the wisest people in the city.'

The merchant was still in shock, but he gave a nervous nod. He now remembered seeing the stranger in the Fool's Hope Inn, but the merchant did not move in magical circles and so *he* had not heard the story of the dark-skinned man with blue eyes and a tattoo on his chest that protected him from magical harm. Had he heard such stories he would know that the young apprentice mage was right...

The stranger had once been a demon hunter in the service of the emperor. That was before he rebelled against his oath and paid a terrible price for his disobedience. Now he lived the quiet life of a hired sword, taking on whatever protection work he could find.

His name was Alexander Teuton, but the patrons of the Fool's Hope knew him only as the Tutor.

2
The Sage of Blackfell House

It was almost midnight in a more affluent part of the city where three people were engaged in a desperate battle to save a young girl's life. There was the lawyer, his wife, and a tall man in charcoal grey robes.

The bedroom was bathed in candlelight as the girl's choking breaths filled the air. Her head was strained backwards, her neck bulged and the tracery of veins beneath her skin shone with a sickly purple light. The furnishings in the room spoke of wealth, but no amount of money could help the girl, and the lawyer's hands were slippery with sweat as he held his daughter down.

'Hold her tight!' said the man in the charcoal grey robes as he strode to one side of the room and used a slender dagger to scratch an arcane symbol into the wall.

Similar marks were now scrawled upon numerous items in the room. The man had used soot to write on curtains and used his dagger to carve symbols in the dressing table and floor boards. He had even cut his arm so he could use his own blood to paint mysterious characters on the window. Every time he wrote something down the girl's suffering seemed to increase as wisps of purple smoke emerged from her mouth and tendrils of magical energy radiated from her body. The glowing tendrils passed through the lawyer's clothes and burned his skin and he gritted his teeth as he tried to maintain his hold.

The magical strands also sought out the man in the charcoal grey robes, but he seemed oblivious to the searing pain. His attention was focussed entirely on containing the curse that had been cast upon the girl. If he got it wrong the curse would re-establish itself more strongly than ever and the girl was not strong enough to endure a second attempt to free her.

Standing at the foot of the bed, the lawyer's wife was deathly pale as she clutched her hands to her throat.

'You must be ready to comfort her,' the man in the charcoal robes had told her. 'You must be calm and strong. No matter how you feel you must make her believe that she is safe and loved. If she doubts you, she will die.'

Terrified but resolute, the woman could only nod.

And so it had come to this. The lawyer and his wife were beyond themselves with worry, but this was their last hope. They had tried everything but no one had been able to help them until a local healer suggested they try the man in the charcoal robes, the man known to some as the Sage of Blackfell House.

Exhausted and sick with anguish, the lawyer snatched a glance at the man who had come to help them. Tall and slim, with broad shoulders and shoulder length hair, he struck an imposing figure. His features were strong, almost hawkish, with prominent cheekbones and a full mouth that was now clamped tight with concentration. But it was his eyes that gave one pause. Those eyes were so dark as to be almost black and yet they glittered with flecks of gold. Such gold flecked eyes were the mark of a feral mage and yet the man in the charcoal robes insisted that he did not use magic.

'How can you save her if you don't use magic?' the lawyer had asked.

'Curses like this can be broken with certain symbols and patterns,' said the Sage. 'Magic would make it easier but the correct placement of the symbols should suffice.' He paused. 'But the process puts great strain on the body. Your daughter may well die in the attempt.'

'She is dying already,' the lawyer had said.

'Then we shall try.'

That was two hours ago and the girl did indeed look close to death. Her eyes had rolled back in her head and her body convulsed each time the robed man added a new set of symbols.

'We're close,' he said. 'But this curse was designed to resist interference. The more I constrain it the more dangerous the energy will become.'

Dropping to his knees he scratched a series of characters in the corner of the girl's bedside table before stepping back to survey all the marks he had made. The lawyer and his wife glanced at each other then tensed as their daughter's body was caught in a spasm of magical force.

'Esme!' cried the mother and the lawyer groaned as glowing skeins of magic engulfed his arms, but the man in the charcoal robes merely frowned.

Magical energy had begun to surround the girl's body in a writhing nimbus of light that was slowly expanding outwards. Each time it encountered one of the marks it shrank back as if it were probing for weakness and the Sage gave a snarl of frustration. The arcane symbols might contain the curse, but without actual magic they were not strong enough to break it. His only hope was to focus the malicious force in one location. Turning to the mother he barked out a demand.

'I need something to write on,' he snapped. 'Something hard but easily broken.'

The magical force had found a gap in the confining circle and was now growing in strength as if it could breathe through it, but still the terrified woman just looked at him.

'Quickly!' said the man.

His harsh tone brought the woman to her senses and her eyes swept around the room.

'Here,' said the mother, passing him a comb from the girl's dressing table.

The man turned it over in his hands. The comb was made from bone and the spine was flat and smooth. If he kept the characters small it should do. Holding his dagger by the blade he began to write. He needed to get the characters just right or it would not work. Within a matter of seconds he had finished and he placed the comb in the gap between two of his previous marks.

Immediately the glowing energy began to probe this new inscription and to the mother's horror it seemed to grow in strength. The marks on the comb started to glow while those scratched into the floor boards on either side began to dissolve as if they were formed from nothing more than dust. In a matter of moments all the Sage's work would be undone.

The mother glanced at the tall man who was now focussed entirely on the comb. For a moment she thought he had failed, but then his expression took on a distinct note of satisfaction and the gold flecks in his eyes seemed to glow.

'Yes!' he cried, and with a suddenness that made her start, the man fell to his knees, took the magic-infused comb in his hands and snapped it.

A burst of magical light exploded around his hands and the comb was reduced to dust. For the first time, the man cried out in pain and his fingers curled into claws as the burning energy surged through his flesh.

The woman might have gone to help him, but the sound of her daughter's cry captured her attention. Turning round, she saw her husband release his grip as their daughter began to weep. She was no longer straining from the torment of the curse, she was simply frightened and confused. Slowly they helped her to sit up and some of the fear seemed to fade from her eyes.

'I had the most terrible dream,' she said, her voice hoarse and quiet.

'I know,' said the mother. 'But it's over now. You're safe.'

With that she drew her daughter into her arms and held her close.

Still holding his hands out in front of him, the man in the charcoal robes got to his feet. For a moment he watched the family come together on the bed. Raising his left arm, he adjusted a charm bracelet on his wrist until a tiny pewter wren hung down. For a moment he watched the charm as if he were waiting for it to give him some sign then, seemingly satisfied, he relaxed his arm. Finally, he reached out with his senses, but no trace of the curse remained. It was done.

Without a word, he walked quietly away and slipped out through the bedroom door. At the stairs, he reached for the banister and winced. His hands still burned with incredible pain, but that would pass with time. Slowly he made his way down to the ground floor of the house. He had just opened the front door when he heard the lawyer's voice.

'Sir!' said the lawyer. 'Sir! Please wait!'

The man in the charcoal robes turned, his hawkish face illuminated by the oil lamp that burned in the porch.

'My friend,' said the lawyer, 'How can we ever thank you?'

'No thanks are necessary,' said the man.

'Surely…,' began the lawyer, but the man in the charcoal robes raised a hand to cut him off.

13

'I take it you know the person responsible for the curse.'

The lawyer's expression darkened. 'I have my suspicions.'

'And I take it they are still at large.'

'Yes,' said the lawyer and the man in the charcoal robes gave a sigh. A curse like this used to be quite rare, but in recent years they were becoming more common.

'Maybe it's time for you and your family to leave Guile,' said the man. 'You might want to try the mage city of Confluence. The council there still exerts a degree of control and the use of such malicious magic is frowned upon.'

'I will consider it,' said the lawyer. 'But for now, please allow me to…'

'Goodnight,' said the man and before the lawyer could finish he swept out of the door and off into the night. He wanted no payment and he did not deserve their thanks. The spell that had tormented this family was a painful reminder of the curses he had cast when he lived under the thrall of magic. He had not cared if the target was worthy of such punishment, only that he got paid. And unlike the spell cast on the lawyer's daughter, *his* curses had not been so easily broken.

The man walked on through the empty streets of Guile, but every shadowed alleyway seemed to be filled with the ghosts of his past. There *had* been a time when he lived for magic and power; a time when his very name struck fear into the richest and most powerful people in the land. Now only a handful of people in the city knew his true identity and he was happy to be forgotten.

He was no longer a notorious sorcerer, no longer *the man who slew the Demon of the Vale*. He now used his knowledge of the arcane arts to help people where he could.

He was the man in charcoal grey robes.

The Sage of Blackfell House.

And his name was Decimus Fate.

3
The Fool's Hope

Even as Fate and the Tutor headed for home, two monks entered the river city of Guile. One was male and the other female and both had the dark hair and bronze skin of the Shīku people. Dressed in golden yellow robes, they provided a splash of colour in the dark streets of the city. The man was of medium height with a lean build that spoke of discipline and physical fitness. By contrast, the woman was small and slender. Her long hair was gathered into a knot and held in place by a pin of polished cherry wood. The man's gaze was hard and alert, while the woman looked about her with an air of curious serenity.

As they passed through the northwest gate, they were approached by several people offering them a place to stay for the night. The woman met these offers with a smile, while the man dismissed them with a stern wave of the hand.

Moving beyond the disgruntled faces they approached a group of grubby children gathered against the wall. They were squatting round a small pot filled with burning embers and each of them held a crude lantern tied to the end of a stick. They watched the strangers approach then jumped to their feet as the male monk held up a coin.

'We are seeking a particular inn.'

'I'll take you anywhere in the city for two coins,' said one boy of about ten.

'I'll do it for one,' said a girl of similar age.

The male monk held the coin as if he were considering his options until a slightly older boy stepped forward.

'I'll do it for a blessing,' he said and the twinkle in his eye made the female monk smile.

'What is your name, my son?' she asked, her voice surprisingly deep and melodic.

'They call me Weasel.'

'Is that because you're good at getting out of trouble?'

'No,' said the boy. 'It's because I can take down prey more than twice my size.' He gave a little laugh at his own cleverness and the female monk's smile grew a shade warmer.

'Very well, Weasel... Convey us safely and the blessings of the Inja will be yours.'

The other children looked on sourly, but Weasel simply grinned and crouched down to light his lantern from the embers in the pot.

'So where's it to be?' he asked.

'The Fool's Hope Inn,' said the male monk.

'The Fool's Hope it is,' said the boy and with that he led them off into the twisting streets of Guile.

*

It was after midnight when the Tutor finally returned to the Fool's Hope Inn, a large two-storey building of plaster, brick and timber. The sign over the door depicted two hands, one reaching down to the other in an act of kindness.

Many of the patrons had long since left for home, but the Tutor could still see candles shining through the dimpled windows and he could hear the low murmur of late night conversation. The Fool's Hope was not your typical bawdy drinking house. There was a limit to the kind of behaviour that Madam Carletta would allow in her establishment. Those who overstepped the mark were 'asked to leave' by Victor, Madam Carletta's massive

17

doorman, or the Guillotto sisters, who might be a good deal smaller, but were no less scary when it came to a fight.

Dressed like men, in leather trousers and quilted doublets, the two sisters were standing in the recessed doorway of the inn. Gizelda was the older of the two with green eyes, short auburn hair and an athletic build. Her younger sister, Megan, was very similar in appearance, except that she wore her long hair in a braid. Neither woman was known for their small talk so the Tutor merely dipped his head in acknowledgement.

'Was Madam Carletta right about the merchant?' asked Gizelda as he reached for the door.

The Tutor paused and gave a wry sniff of amusement. When was the landlady of the Fool's Hope not right?

'So who attacked him?' asked Megan.

'Ferryman thugs,' said the Tutor. 'Just youngsters, really.'

'Idiots,' said Gizelda. 'Veleno'll have their hides.'

The Tutor could only nod in agreement.

'Safe home, though,' said Megan and the Tutor smiled.

'Safe home,' he said, and with that he opened the door and passed into the reassuring warmth of the inn.

There was the familiar odour of wood smoke and beer, and the Tutor's mouth watered at the lingering smell of roasted meat. He wondered if there was still a chance of getting some food from the kitchens.

The few remaining patrons looked up as he passed a series of wooden pillars on his way to the bar. He stepped over the outstretched legs of an enormous man who was sleeping in a winged chair beside the dying embers of an open fire. It was Victor, Madam Carletta's doorman. He did not wake up, but he gave a low snarl and briefly raised an arm as if to ward off some annoyance in his dreams. Victor was a permanent fixture of the Fool's Hope Inn and the Tutor smiled with amusement as he continued to the bar where a woman was leaning on the polished wooden counter. With her high cheek bones and strong jaw line, she was a handsome woman with grey hair and a distinct spark of intelligence in her deep brown eyes. Known as Madam Carletta, she was the owner and landlady of the Fool's Hope Inn. She gave the Tutor a quick appraising look, and although nothing was said, it was clear that she was relieved to see him back safe.

As the Tutor reached the bar, she stood up straight, took the cork from a bottle and poured a golden liqueur into a short glass before sliding it towards him.

'You have visitors.'

'Oh?' said the Tutor as he lifted the glass and turned to look around the inn.

'One Abbess Shimitsu and a Master Ando,' Madam Carletta went on. 'Shīku monks by the look of them.'

The Tutor frowned as he recognised the names. What on earth was Abbess Shimitsu doing in Guile?

'I put them in the snug,' said Madam Carletta and the Tutor gave a distracted nod.

With a distinct sense of unease, he downed his drink and set the glass on the counter.

'I assume the merchant got home safely?' asked Madam Carletta as he began to turn away.

'He did.'

'No trouble?'

'A little,' said the Tutor, and Madam Carletta arched an eyebrow at what was clearly an understatement.

'Go on,' she said. 'Your visitors are waiting.'

With nothing else to be said, the Tutor set off towards the cosy room at the far end of the inn. The Shīku monastery was perched on the edge of the Great Plateau and the Tutor wondered what could have happened for Abbess Shimitsu to make the long journey to visit him in the middle of the night. Filled with concern he pushed open the door and, sure enough, there was Master Ando and Abbess Shimitsu sitting in the upholstered seats of the snug. Their golden yellow robes looked bright and cheerful, but this did nothing to alleviate the Tutor's fears. Catching sight of him, the two monks got to their feet.

As the Tutor approached, Master Ando gave a shallow bow of greeting. His smile was warm if a little subdued, whereas Abbess Shimitsu's smile was an open expression of joy.

'Alexander,' she said as she reached out to take the Tutor's hands.

Her dark brown eyes shone as she held him at arm's length. Abbess Shimitsu was the leader of the Shīku monastery and the most kind-hearted person the Tutor had ever met. He could see the joy in her eyes, but he could also see that she was not well. Her deep bronze skin was paler than normal and the slender woman had lost weight since he last saw her some eighteen months ago.

'What are you doing here?' he asked. 'What's wrong?'

Abbess Shimitsu did not answer at first. Instead she reached out to touch a jade pendant that hung around the Tutor's neck.

'You still wear it.'

'Of course,' said the Tutor.

Abbess Shimitsu's smile took on a note of sadness and both their minds were cast back to a night almost three years ago when he had first arrived at the monastery. The Tutor remembered little of that night while the abbess recalled it with painful clarity.

She remembered how the Tutor had appeared at the monastery gate, wounded, grieving and close to death, but even in his weakened state the monks had been reluctant to let him in. The Tutor's clothes were torn and they could all see the complex tattoo on his chest. They recognised it as the mark of a demon hunter and were fearful of the dangers that might follow such a man, but Abbess Shimitsu refused to turn him away.

'She told me to come,' the Tutor had muttered, his voice cracked and choked with grief.

'Who told you to come?' asked Abbess Shimitsu.

The Tutor had not answered, only held out his hand to reveal a circular pendant with a small sapphire set in a circle of silver, which in turn was set in a vibrant disk of jade.

'Worlds within worlds,' breathed one of the monks.

Abbess Shimitsu stared down at the pendant and her heart clenched with sorrow. The pendant symbolised a person with Faerie blood who had chosen to live in the human realm. She remembered giving this pendant to a childhood friend and now she looked with great sadness upon the man who had won her friend's heart.

'Bring him inside,' she had breathed, and from that moment the monks had cared for the Tutor and nurtured him back to health.

The Tutor had remained at the monastery for over a year, slowly recovering his strength and learning to live with the grief that had threatened to crush him. Now he stood in the Fool's Hope Inn, strong and hale but with a hole in his heart that the monks had been unable to fill.

For a moment, Abbess Shimitsu's fingers lingered on the pendant then she withdrew her hand and the Tutor tucked the jade disk beneath the neck of his shirt.

'Please,' he said. 'Tell me what's wrong.'

For the first time Abbess Shimitsu's smile faltered as the three of them took a seat. She placed her slender hands on the table and took a breath.

'It's the monastery,' she said at last. 'There is a sickness there. I fear our brothers and sisters are dying.'

The Tutor frowned and glanced towards Master Ando whose dour expression confirmed Abbess Shimitsu's words.

'Tell me everything,' said the Tutor and she did.

She told him how it had begun almost two months ago with a general feeling of malaise. How the monks had begun to suffer from headaches, tiredness, upset stomachs and aching limbs.

'At first we thought it was the water,' said Abbess Shimitsu. 'The monastery wells are deep and we wondered if the aquifers had become contaminated.'

The Tutor nodded. The water would certainly have been his first thought.

'But the water's fine,' Abbess Shimitsu went on. 'We tried isolating patients for fear of contagion. We even wondered if the grain stores had been affected by some kind of poisonous mould, but we found nothing.'

The Tutor could hear the desperation in Abbess Shimitsu's voice. She was an incredibly capable woman and it was clear that the sense of helplessness was tearing her apart. She gave a wan smile as Master Ando placed a hand on her shoulder.

'All we know is that our brothers and sisters keep getting ill,' she continued. 'They retire to their beds and seem to improve, but no sooner are they feeling better than they start to decline once more. And with each bout they grow weaker. We are all growing weaker.'

The abbess paused as Madam Carletta appeared with a tray of hot drinks and a plate of food for the Tutor.

'I thought camomile tea might suit the lateness of the hour,' said the inn's landlady and Abbess Shimitsu gave her a smile of thanks. She was about to leave when the Tutor drew her back with a question.

'Have you heard of any strange diseases or illness in the area?'

Madam Carletta shook her head. 'There was an outbreak of morbilli in the spring, and the reservoir above Faerbattle was tainted with swine soil, but apart from that, no, nothing out of the ordinary.'

The Tutor put a hand to his mouth as he considered the problem.

'And Sister Hīra hasn't been able to help?' he asked, for Sister Hīra was the monastery's most experienced healer.

'She's helped with the symptoms,' said Abbess Shimitsu. 'But she has no idea as to the cause. No one does. We've consulted physicians, apothecaries and even a sorcerer familiar with curses, and all to no avail.'

The Tutor's gaze took on a darker edge. The Shīku's entire existence revolved around helping people. He could not imagine why anyone would want to hurt them with a curse.

'I've tried everyone I can think of,' said Abbess Shimitsu. 'But it seems that no one can help us.' She paused and the desperation in her voice was painful to hear. 'Finally, I wondered if you might know someone…'

The Tutor had never seen the abbess so despondent and he would do anything he could to help. He began to run through the healers and physicians he knew in the city, but they were more familiar with the more mundane infections and the injuries that normal people might sustain. He was beginning to get a sense of Abbess Shimitsu's helplessness when Madam Carletta spoke.

23

'There is someone who might be able to help,' she said. 'He's a bit mysterious, and there are some dark rumours about his past, but people say that he can help when no one else can.'

The Tutor and the two monks looked up at the landlady of the Fool's Hope.

'I don't know his name,' said Madam Carletta, 'but people refer to him as the Sage of Blackfell House.'

4
Fate

Fate woke to the resonant croak of a raven. Perched outside the first floor window, the bird flew away as Fate's housekeeper opened the curtains of his bed chamber.

'One of the finest mattresses in the city and still he sleeps in a chair.' The disapproving voice came from a small hunchbacked woman. 'Not that *I* care if your clothes are crumpled and your supper is ruined.'

With her wrinkled skin, wild dark hair and piercing black eyes, she was like the caricature of a witch from a children's story, although the creases at the corners of her eyes spoke of humour rather than cruelty. Hobbling over to another window she drew open a second set of curtains.

Fate squinted against the daylight as the woman turned to look at him.

'Good morning, Motina,' he said as he sat up straighter in the chair and rolled his head to ease the stiffness in his neck and shoulders.

'Barely,' replied the woman. Her full name was Varna Motina, an exile from the eastern province of Karuthia. 'Another minute and you'd've been woken by the midday bell.' Even as she spoke there came the chimes of a bell tolling over the city. The woman raised a finger and arched her eyebrows as if to say, 'See!'

Moving away from the window she picked up a tray containing bread, cheese and grapes, with a white porcelain cup and a small silver teapot. Motina's gait was uneven and the tray tilted ominously, but somehow she managed to convey it safely to a small table beside Fate's chair.

'I take it you saved the girl,' she said as she set the tray down.

'How did you know?' asked Fate as he helped himself to a grape.

'Because you slept,' said Motina. With one gnarled finger, she held the lid of the teapot in place as she poured him a cup of tea. 'You'd still be wide awake and pacing if she'd died.'

Fate glanced at the woman who had kept his house in order for the last nine years. She might be diminutive in stature, but she was as shrewd as a pin.

'Bergamot tea, hot,' said Motina. 'Just as you like it.'

'Thank you,' said Fate. He reached for the cup and winced at the lingering pain in his hands.

'Are you all right?' asked Motina.

'It's nothing serious. Just some spasms from the curse last night.'

The housekeeper frowned and started towards him, but Fate waved her away. Flexing his hands he took hold of the cup and breathed in the herbal aroma as he raised the cup to his lips.

With a lingering air of concern, Motina moved away and turned down his bed despite the fact that it had not been slept in. 'Veleno's men called again last night.' The housekeeper's tone made it clear that this was not good news.

Fate narrowed his eyes.

'I told them you were indisposed and they were *not* happy.'

Fate stared through the steam rising from his cup as Motina crossed to the fireplace. With a groan of effort she knelt down before the hearth, pulled over a basket of firewood and arranged a few pieces of kindling in the grate.

'I think the 'Lord of the City' has finally run out of patience.' She spoke the title with a heavy dose of sarcasm. Choosing a larger log, she broke off a piece of dry bark and crushed it between the palms of her hands. 'You can't avoid him forever,' she said. 'And he won't be happy when you turn him down.'

Motina stole a sideways glance at Fate, but the master of the house said nothing. With a sigh, the housekeeper reached out her hand and began to sprinkle the crushed bark onto the kindling. At the same time she spoke a few whispered words in a foreign language and the crushed pieces of bark burst into flame.

Stereotypes notwithstanding, Varna Motina was, in fact, a witch.

The magic embers ignited the kindling and Motina added two larger logs before standing up from the fire. She was about to speak again when they heard the jangling sound of a bell coming from somewhere outside. Fate raised an eyebrow as his housekeeper turned to look at him.

'That's the gate bell,' said Motina. 'It's not like Veleno's men to be so polite. Normally they just throw stones at the main door until they get an answer.'

Moving to the window, she could see three people standing at the gate in the perimeter fence. One was a tall black man with broad shoulders and a narrow waist. He was clearly of the fighting type. The other two figures were dressed in golden yellow robes, and one of them was a woman.

'They look like monks,' said the housekeeper. 'At least, two of them do.'

Fate gave a weary sigh. He might have slept through the morning, but sleeping in a chair was not ideal and he still felt drained from the previous day's exertions.

27

'Shall I send them away?' asked Motina.

'No,' said Fate. 'Give me a few minutes and I'll see them in my study.'

Getting to his feet he moved to a washstand in the corner of the room and removed the charcoal grey longcoat that he had fallen asleep in. In daylight, one could see the faint shimmer of arcane symbols woven into the fabric.

As Motina moved to the door, she glanced at the man she had served for almost ten years. She watched as he unbuckled his black belt with its two dragon-handled daggers and its collection of small leather pouches. She opened the door as he removed his silver-trimmed tunic and white undershirt to reveal a pale torso decorated with a series of magical symbols and a litany of scars. She herself had given him one of those scars; a burn on his chest, like a many-pointed star. Lowering her eyes, she smiled at the memory of her foolishness and how he had saved her in spite of herself. Shaking her head, she stepped out of the room, closed the door and went down to see who had come to request the help of her master today.

*

'I don't like this,' said the Tutor as Master Ando stepped back from the bell hanging beside the main gate of Blackfell House. The tattoo on the Tutor's chest was designed to protect him from magical harm and right now he felt it humming like a swarm of angry bees.

'Are we in danger?' asked Master Ando but the Tutor shook his head.

'No...' he said. 'I think we're fine, so long as we don't try to force our way in.'

Master Ando turned to Abbess Shimitsu. 'Do *you* sense anything?'

28

Abbess Shimitsu paused as she stared through the wrought iron railings.

'I sense many things beyond this gate,' she said. 'But nothing to suggest we are in imminent danger.' Her own powers of magical perception were more subtle than the tattoo on the Tutor's chest, but she knew better than to ignore his concerns.

'We should go,' said the Tutor. 'Find someone else who can help us.'

Abbess Shimitsu considered his reaction for a few moments before asking him a question.

'Do you trust the landlady of the Fool's Hope?'

The Tutor looked at her as if the question was absurd. 'Of course I do.'

'Then we shall proceed,' said Abbess Shimitsu and the matter was effectively settled.

A few minutes passed before a small hunchbacked woman emerged from the main door of the house. Upon reaching the gate, she introduced herself as the master's housekeeper and took their names as she opened the gate to let them in.

The Tutor trusted Madam Carletta, but he could not suppress a growing sense of unease as the hunchbacked woman led them towards the house. The housekeeper made no attempt to make them feel welcome until Abbess Shimitsu remarked on her accent.

'It sounds like you're a long way from home.' The housekeeper gave her a sideways glance as Abbess Shimitsu continued. 'I've heard the pine forests of Karuthia are filled with the most wondrous scent.'

'You've a good ear,' said the housekeeper and Abbess Shimitsu gave a modest smile.

'A pilgrim once brought me a bottle of spirit distilled from the resin of Karuthian pine trees,' she said. 'We drank it as we discussed the philosophy of Vinkas Kurdika.'

The hunchbacked woman suddenly stopped. 'And what was your conclusion?'

'That things would have been better if the leaders of Karuthia had followed his teachings instead of hunting down those who practised magic.'

For a moment the housekeeper held the abbess with her piercing black eyes, then the croaking call of a raven sounded over the garden and she smiled.

'It would appear that the wisdom of the Shīku people matches their reputation.'

Abbess Shimitsu inclined her head and any tension between the two women seemed to evaporate like an early morning mist.

The Tutor shook his head in amazement. It seemed there was not a person alive that Abbess Shimitsu could not relate to in one way or another. The housekeeper noticed his reaction and, with an amused smile, she turned away and continued towards the house.

Built from some kind of dark granite, Blackfell House lived up to its name. Set in a square plot of land, the house was surrounded by a waist high wall of stone, topped with wrought iron railings. The gardens were not lavish, but the lawns were trimmed and the flower beds were not overgrown. A herb garden to one side of the house seemed to be the only area that benefitted from any real enthusiasm, while the trees that lined the main driveway all appeared to be dead.

Standing about fifteen feet tall, they were not large, but their branches were contorted and leafless like something from a gothic fairytale. They stood like sentinels along the gravel driveway and the Tutor was relieved when he emerged from beneath their overarching boughs.

The house itself was well proportioned with leaded windows and pitched roofs on either side of the main door. There were just two main storeys to the house with attic windows in the gable ends and a crenulated tower in the south west corner. It was the house of a wealthy nobleman and the Tutor questioned why such a man would have a reputation for helping people. He began to wonder just how much this 'help' would cost.

The housekeeper led them towards the main door, the stone lintel of which bore the unsettling inscription...

WOE TO THOSE
WHO TRESPASS UNINVITED

Abbess Shimitsu appeared not to notice the inscription, but Master Ando certainly did and the expression in his hard brown eyes told the Tutor to be on his guard.

The interior of the house was decorated with quality furniture and ornaments that seemed to have been collected from every corner of the world. The oak floorboards were covered with a series of fine carpets and the walls were softened by various tapestries and wall hangings. Some depicted historical scenes while others featured arcane patterns and magical scripts that the Tutor did not recognise.

They moved through a reception hall and down a short corridor before passing through a doorway into a high-ceilinged room, the walls of which were largely obscured by books.

In the far corner of the room was a large desk covered with various papers and all manner of obscure items, including a rack of glass vials, a jeweller's eyeglass, and what appeared to be the taloned foot of an eagle. Sitting behind the desk, and currently staring out of the window, was the man they called the Sage of Blackfell House.

He was clearly a tall man with dark shoulder length hair and strong, hawkish features. He was dressed in the charcoal grey robes of a sorcerer and the Tutor's sense of apprehension surged to new heights. There was something about this man's appearance that struck a chord in his memory.

The man seemed distracted as they entered the room. On his left wrist he wore a bracelet made from some dark polished metal and hanging from the bracelet were a number of charms. The Tutor could just make out a few of the small shapes: an hourglass… a key… a tiny dagger wreathed in smoke… As they drew closer, the man turned from the window as his housekeeper announced them.

'May I introduce Abbess Shimitsu and Master Ando, from the Shīku monastery of Tan Jit Su, and 'the Tutor', currently of the Fool's Hope Inn.'

The man acknowledged the two monks with a bow of the head, but at the mention of the Tutor his gaze sharpened and all trace of weariness and disinterest was gone.

For a moment, the Tutor was taken aback by the directness of his gaze then he noticed the gold flecks in the man's dark eyes.

'And this is…' began the housekeeper, but the Tutor cut her off.

'I know who he is,' said the Tutor in a harsh tone that surprised Abbess Shimitsu. 'His name is Decimus Fate,' he continued without taking his eyes off Fate. 'He's a sorcerer… an assassin… a murderer.'

Fate did not lower his eyes and the tension between them mounted, until he smiled.

'One shouldn't believe every piece of gossip and rumour.'

The Tutor bristled at this flippant remark and his hand dropped to the hilt of his sword. The gold streaks in Fate's eyes marked him as a feral mage, someone who could wield magic without the need of words, gestures or props. Such individuals were extremely rare, and extremely dangerous, and Decimus Fate was considered to be among the most dangerous of them all. However, it was also said that he had saved scores of people when a powerful demon had broken through into the human world.

The demon had unleashed an explosion of fire that killed half the people in the village, and it would have gone on to kill the remaining half had it not been stopped by a sorcerer in dark grey robes; a sorcerer that came to be known as 'the man who slew the Demon of the Vale.'

This was Fate's reputation... ruthless, powerful, dangerous.

Fate saw the recognition in the Tutor's gaze, but he had no desire to antagonise the man and so he broke eye contact and gestured towards the three chairs that had been set out for them.

'Please,' he said. 'Take a seat.'

Abbess Shimitsu was clearly surprised to learn of his identity. She had heard of the great Decimus Fate and was aware of the stories associated with his name. However, she maintained her composure as she and Master Ando slowly took a seat.

The Tutor remained standing.

'Are you saying it isn't true?' he demanded. 'Are you saying that you haven't murdered people for money and power.'

Fate sighed. 'I'm saying that things have changed.'

The Tutor raised a sceptical eyebrow and waited for him to continue.

'It is true,' Fate went on. 'There was a time when I killed people who deserved to live, and took payment from people who deserved to die.'

'So what's changed?' demanded the Tutor and the gold flecks in Fate's eyes shone with a dangerous light.

'Let's just say, that I now take payment from people who deserve to live.'

The two men stared at each other, but slowly the ominous light faded from Fate's gaze and he turned to address Abbess Shimitsu.

'Now, Revered Mother,' he said. 'What can I do to help the monks of Tan Jit Su and a man who rebelled against the demon hunters?'

The hint of a smile returned to Fate's eyes as he looked up at the black man with the blue eyes.

Yes, the Tutor recognised Fate, but Fate also recognised the Tutor.

5
The Lord of the City

The following morning was misty and cold as the Tutor led Abbess Shimitsu and Master Ando back to the main gate of Blackfell House. The two monks had come to Guile on foot, but the Tutor insisted that horses would be quicker and Madam Carletta had been happy to lend them three good-natured mares from the Fool's Hope stables. The landlady had also supplied them with rations, bed rolls and waxed cotton tarpaulins in case it rained. Now they dismounted before the gate and Master Ando pulled the bell chain to announce their presence. As the jangling chimes rang out they saw movement at one of the windows of the dark stone house. A tall figure in grey robes was looking out towards them.

The Tutor's gaze hardened as he stared at the partially obscured figure. He had been surprised when the sorcerer agreed to help them and even more so when he said he would be able to leave with them the following morning.

'So long as I'm back within a week,' Fate told them. 'Until then it would suit me to be out of the city for a few days.'

The Tutor knew there was something he was not telling them and this only added to his misgivings, but he tried to conceal his uncharitable feelings as Abbess Shimitsu came to stand beside him.

'I'm sensing an unhealthy level of hostility,' said the abbess.

'I don't trust him,' replied the Tutor. 'He's hiding something.'

Abbess Shimitsu looked up at the figure in the window.

'If what you have told me is true, I suspect he is hiding a great many things.'

*

Even from the window of his study Fate could feel the Tutor's suspicion. The man was dangerous and, just for a second, Fate wondered if he had made a mistake in taking this case. Could there be a more sinister reason for the Tutor coming to find him?

No...

He remembered the genuine look of surprise on the demon hunter's face when he saw who the Sage of Blackfell House really was. No... their motives were clear and he would do what he could to help the abbess in spite of the Tutor's suspicions.

He turned away from the window as Motina entered the room.

'Jonas has your horse ready in the courtyard.' The small hunchbacked woman held out a grey long-coat as Fate crossed the room towards her. 'You do know that Veleno won't forget about you just because you leave the city for a few days.'

'I know,' said Fate. 'But the artificer should have finished the device I commissioned by the time I get back. I'm hoping that will be enough to satisfy Veleno.'

'A device to conjure a few ounces of gold is not the same as having the great Decimus Fate at your beck and call.'

'I was never at his beck and call.'

'But he got used to the power you gave him,' said Motina. 'He won't want to give that up.'

'Things have changed,' said Fate.

'Indeed they have. But I don't think the Lord of the City appreciates your change of heart.'

'Then he'll just have to accept it.'

'Or he might just kill you.' The housekeeper smiled as she handed Fate his coat, but she was not joking. 'Veleno might be charming, but he's accustomed to getting what he wants, and you can't defend yourself as you once could.'

'Is that concern, Motina?' said Fate. His lightness of tone seemed to dismiss her warning, but Motina noticed how his hand drifted to the charms on his bracelet. 'I thought you'd rejoice in my demise. It would free you from the drudgery of service.'

'I am already free,' she said, suddenly serious. 'Besides,' she added in a lighter tone. 'I've got used to you, the way a person gets used to the smell of dung when they work in a stable.'

Fate gave a soft snort of amusement as his stern features were softened by a smile. 'I'll see you in a few days.'

'And if Veleno calls?'

Fate paused as he reached the door. 'Tell him I've gone on a pilgrimage.'

*

The Tutor watched as Fate appeared from behind the house leading a handsome grey horse along the driveway.

'Good morning,' said the sorcerer as he opened the gate to join them.

'Inja's blessings,' replied Abbess Shimitsu with a bow of the head.

Master Ando gave a bow of greeting, but no sound got past the tightness in the Tutor's jaw. His distrust was palpable but, rather than being offended, Fate seemed mildly amused. He could feel the Tutor's eyes upon him, but his only reaction was the faintest hint of a smile.

'Looks like the weather is set to improve,' said Fate in a conversational tone.

Banks of mist still hovered around the buildings of the city, but it was already beginning to dissipate and the emerging sunlight gave the promise of a fine autumn day.

'I want to thank you again for agreeing to help us,' said Abbess Shimitsu as Fate adjusted a strap on his horse's bridle.

'You're welcome,' he said. 'Although it remains to be seen whether I can help you or not.'

'Intention is more important than outcome,' said Abbess Shimitsu but Fate was not so sure.

'Sadly, that is not always the case,' he said.

The Tutor concurred and the fact that he agreed with Fate annoyed him intensely. 'Come on,' he said. 'It's two days' ride to the plateau. If we leave now we should reach the monastery before sunset tomorrow.'

Without further ado, they mounted their horses and headed north along a road lined with tall poplar trees. Being unfamiliar with the city, Master Ando held back with Abbess Shimitsu, leaving Fate and the Tutor to ride together.

'So, how did you come to know the monks of Tan Jit Su?' said Fate and the Tutor felt his annoyance increase. He was in no mood for small talk and yet it felt rude not to answer.

'They helped me when I was in need.'

'That was after you betrayed the demon hunters, I take it.'

The Tutor glanced sharply sideways.

'Oh, I know,' said Fate. 'Refusing to carry out orders is not what most people would call betrayal, but the Emperor is not *most people*.'

The Tutor turned his gaze back to the road. 'You don't know what you're talking about.'

'I know that you almost paid with your life,' said Fate. 'And I know they killed your wife and daughter.'

The Tutor's horse gave a snort of protest as he forced it into Fate's path. Calming his own horse, the sorcerer looked down at the slender sword that was now pointing at his chest. Slowly he raised his eyes to meet the Tutor's icy blue gaze.

'You will not mention them again,' said the Tutor, and for a moment they stared at each other while Master Ando and Abbess Shimitsu looked on with concern.

'Forgive me,' said Fate. 'I should have known better than to trespass on such tender ground.'

'Yes,' said the Tutor. 'You should.' Lowering his eyes he sheathed his sword and straightened his horse on the road. They continued in silence, following the road west towards the River Scéal, the main river around which the city of Guile was built.

Another mile and the road rose up towards a walled bridge that spanned the river in four broad arches, each wide enough to allow two river barges to pass each other with room to spare. A growing number of people were now using the road and a series of street traders had set up their stalls on the bridge itself.

The flow of people suddenly slowed as a crowd began to gather against the north wall of the bridge. They were pointing up river and muttering in anxious tones. Looking in that direction, the Tutor could see two river barges moving slowly towards the bridge. The barges were some way off, but it was clear that they were sailing very close to each other.

However, whatever was happening, it was none of their concern. The Tutor began to lead them past the growing crowd until he found their way blocked by a line of six men. Each of the men had a shortsword and an iron-bound cudgel hanging from their belt, and each was wearing a blue shirt and a black leather waistcoat, the unofficial 'uniform' of Master Veleno's nefarious gang.

Looking beyond the line, the Tutor noticed two young men being held by more of Veleno's thugs. Both were bound and gagged, and the Tutor's heart quickened as he recognised one as the apprentice mage from the attack on the merchant two nights ago. Maybe the young man had told Veleno about him. He was just wondering if the crime boss was here for him, when a voice rang out and the line of men parted to reveal the self-styled Lord of the City himself.

'What a pleasant morning for a stroll along the river, wouldn't you say, Lord Fate?'

Standing in the middle of the bridge was Master Veleno, a well dressed man with silver-grey hair and a carefully manicured goatee. A half smile softened his grey eyes, the way a leather sheath might soften the outline of a lethal blade. Dressed in a blue velvet doublet with a double row of gold buttons, Veleno was feeding lumps of sugar to a beautiful black stallion, and even the metal fittings on the horse's tack appeared to be made of gold.

'Bedrolls, tents and travel bags!' said Veleno as he stroked his horse's nose with a finely gloved hand. 'Surely you weren't going to leave the city without telling me!'

Only now did the Lord of the City look up and his gaze settled squarely on Fate.

'Good morning, Veleno,' said Fate. His tone was one of weary resignation rather than fear.

'Going far?'

'Just a few days,' said Fate. 'No need to come and see me off.'

Veleno laughed. 'As it happens, I had other business on the river this morning. Meeting you on the road is but a happy coincidence. Now... aren't you going to introduce me to your friends?'

'No,' said Fate and Veleno smiled. No one else spoke to him like that and for some strange reason the Lord of the City liked it.

The Tutor had never met Veleno in person but, like everyone else in Guile, he knew that he was one of the most dangerous men in the city. No other gang leader had as much power or influence as Master Gianni Veleno. Even Captain Monetti of the city guard was reluctant to lock horns with the Lord of the City.

The Tutor kept his eyes low as Veleno cast his gaze over him and the two monks. He did not know what kind of trouble Fate had with the gang leader, but he had no wish to get involved. For a moment, Veleno's eyes lingered on the Tutor, but then he handed the reins of his horse to one of his men and walked forward to stand beside Fate.

'Did you think I wouldn't notice you sneaking off before we had the chance to cement our agreement?'

'There is no agreement,' said Fate.

'Come now... Let us not begin the day with unpleasantness.'

'I've no wish for unpleasantness, but I will not work for you.'

Veleno cast another glance over the sorcerer's companions. 'But I can pay a hundred times what these fine citizens will pay you.'

'I don't need your money.'

'Ah, yes,' said Veleno. 'The secret vault of Decimus Fate! Maybe it should be you paying me.'

'And I will,' said Fate. 'As I said before, I have commissioned a device to furnish you with gold.'

'Hmm,' said Veleno, looking less than impressed. 'Your contraption sounds impressive, but I have found someone who can provide me with ten times as much.'

Fate frowned with suspicion. He knew of several people in the area who were capable of conjuring or transmuting gold, but he did not know of anyone who could produce the amount that Veleno was talking about. Even for the most powerful practitioners, the magical production of gold was notoriously difficult. There *were* ways to produce more, but these came with grave risks.

Veleno gave Fate an apologetic look.

'You would need to match that, and more, for me to be tempted by offers of payment,' he said. 'So let us return to the matter of your services.' Moving closer he laid a hand on the neck of Fate's horse. 'The job I have in mind is no great challenge for a man of your talents. And I promise this will be the last time I call upon you. We might call it your last hurrah!'

'And still I must decline.'

Veleno's playful expression suddenly hardened and Fate tensed. Veleno could be charming, but he could also be utterly ruthless. Fate knew he could be killed simply for turning the crime lord down.

'In that case…' said Veleno. Turning away, he gestured to a figure that had been standing further back. 'I'm sure you remember our good friend, Xanda.'

As the new figure came into view, the Tutor glanced at Fate and it was clear from the sorcerer's face that things had taken a serious turn for the worse.

The man wore full length magician's robes in the deepest shade of purple. His left hand was covered by a black silk glove that came up to his elbow, but it was his

42

face that caught the Tutor's attention. The entire left side of his face appeared to be formed from some kind of smoky black glass. There was no clear distinction between normal skin and glass. It was as if one blended into the other.

The smoky glass was smooth, but it was also covered with a mass of tiny fractures and cracks. A small bead of blood oozed from one of the larger cracks and Xanda wiped it away with a handkerchief he took from his robes. The man's jaw was clenched as if fighting against constant pain and his eyes were different colours; one dark brown, the other a hard and frosted white.

'And of course, our crystal mage still remembers you,' said Veleno. He raised a hand to Xanda's face although he refrained from actually touching it. 'But then, how could he forget, considering the affliction he suffered at your last encounter?'

'He suffered the effects of his own spell,' said Fate.

'Only because you reflected it back at him!'

Fate shrugged. 'He shouldn't have tried to kill me.'

'There is that,' conceded Veleno. 'But now I find myself in something of a quandary. If I let you refuse me without consequences then every rogue in the city will think he can do the same. I can't have people turning me down willy nilly. Not without paying me an inordinate amount of gold,' he added with a smile.

Fate's gaze moved to Xanda.

'Oh, don't worry,' said Veleno. 'Lord Xanda is not about to make a second attempt on your life. But we have found a list of people who might.'

With that, Xanda unfurled a roll of parchment containing a list of about a dozen names. The names were enclosed by lines of arcane script and the scroll pulsated with a magical watermark, a circular design of flames coiling around a set of scales.

Walking over to Xanda, Veleno leaned in closely to read from the parchment.

'Ah, yes. Here it is,' he said as he focussed on a particular sentence of the document. '*For those hereby named to be notified in the event of accident, injury or any other circumstance that weakens, or makes vulnerable, the sorcerer known as Decimus Fate.*'

'What an impressive tribute,' Veleno continued. 'That so many people would like to see you dead.' He stood back from the scroll and looked up at Fate. 'This scroll was created to inform people of any vulnerability or weakness in your condition. Is that correct?'

'It is,' said Fate.

'And now you tell me that you have given up magic,' said Veleno, stroking his beard as if in thought. 'I think that would count as a state of vulnerability, wouldn't you?'

The gold streaks in Fate's eyes glowed as Veleno turned to Xanda.

'And how is such a scroll activated?' he asked the mage.

'You burn it,' said Xanda, and with a quick gesture he produced a writhing tongue of flame in the palm of his right hand. Holding the scroll with his gloved hand, he brought the magical flames close to the parchment.

'Shall we do it?' asked Veleno. 'Shall we let these people know that you have surrendered your greatest weapon?'

'Do what you must,' said Fate and, just for a moment, Veleno's face hardened with anger. The Lord of the City was not accustomed to being denied. He was about to say something else when one of his men leaned in close and pointed to the river.

'Aha!' Veleno exclaimed. 'Saved by the barge!'

With his good humour seemingly restored, Master Veleno turned away and moved to the side of the bridge where the two river barges were now approaching.

'Oh, do come and watch,' he called back to Fate. 'A gang of young ferrymen attacked a merchant who was under my protection,' Veleno explained. 'So I let the ferrymen decide a suitable punishment. Now come. Let's see how the first of these scallywags has fared.'

One of Veleno's men held the bridle of Fate's horse as he dismounted and moved to stand with the crime lord who was now leaning against the north wall of the bridge.

The Tutor gestured for Abbess Shimitsu and Master Ando to stay where they were before getting down from his own horse to see what was happening. It was at this point that the bound apprentice mage recognised the Tutor and the young man began struggling as he tried to get Master Veleno's attention. The man's eyes strained in the Tutor's direction as he tried to make himself understood through the gag in his mouth.

'Hmmm,' he grunted, nodding towards the Tutor. 'Hmm's a hemon humher!'

'Will someone shut that brat up!' said Veleno. 'He is spoiling the mood!'

There followed a series of blows and the apprentice mage doubled over in a heap. As Fate went to stand beside Veleno, the Tutor also moved to the north side of the bridge. A murmur had now risen up among the watching crowd and he heard someone say hulled... 'They've been hulled.'

The Tutor's heart sank as he looked down at the two river barges that would soon pass under the bridge. He

45

could now see why the barges were so close together. Tied between the barges were the pale and lifeless figures of two young men.

Being 'hulled' was a ferryman term for a severe form of punishment where the victims were tied between two barges that would then make their way down the river. If the barges came too close, the victims would be dragged through the water and possibly crushed between the heavy vessels, too far apart and they would be stretched as surely as being on the rack. Dislocation of limbs was common and it was not unheard of for someone to lose a hand or limb entirely, not to mention the risk of drowning.

The men piloting the barges did their best to keep the vessels at a certain distance. Far enough apart to keep the victim out of the water, but not so far that they were pulled limb from limb. However, the barges were unwieldy and the river currents made this almost impossible.

As the barges reached the bridge, the ropes were replaced by boarding planks and the two vessels were tied up to the stone pilings of the bridge. The victims were untied and brought on deck where their condition was examined. One of the pilots bent over the young men. After a few seconds he stepped back and gave a dour nod.

'They've survived!' cried Veleno with apparent joy. 'The young scoundrels!' He clapped Fate on the shoulder and turned to the other two captives who were being held nearby. 'Now let's see how *these* two fare on the next leg of the river.'

The Tutor felt sick to his stomach. He had told the young men to flee the city, but it appeared that only two of them had taken his advice. He watched as the apprentice mage and his unfortunate companion were dragged to a gap in the wall where a set of stone steps led down to a landing platform under the bridge.

The young ferryman was the first to be taken down, but as the apprentice mage was dragged towards the steps he managed to free the gag from his mouth.

'He's a demon hunter!' he cried. 'I told you he was!'

'Wait!'

Veleno's men stopped in their tracks.

'Bring him here,' said Veleno, his eyes narrowing with a mixture of interest and suspicion.

Veleno's man hauled the young man back onto the bridge and deposited him at Veleno's feet.

'I told you I wasn't lying,' he cried. 'I told you he was a demon hunter.'

'Who?' asked Veleno.

'There,' said the apprentice mage. 'The southerner in the black clothes.'

The Tutor tried to sink back out of sight but it was too late. The Lord of the City was looking directly at him, a smile of satisfaction spreading across his face.

'Well… What a morning this is turning out to be.' With a wave of his hand he directed his men to secure the Tutor.

For a moment the Tutor considered jumping into the river, but that would only delay the inevitable. Raising his chin, he allowed himself to be brought forward.

'This is none of your concern,' said Fate, trying to place himself between Veleno and the Tutor. 'This man is merely trying to help the monks of Tan Jit Su.' But Master Veleno waved a hand and Fate was drawn to one side. Then the Lord of the City looked into the Tutor's hard blue eyes.

'Is it true?' he asked. 'Are you a demon hunter?'

'No,' said the Tutor. 'It is not true.'

Veleno gave a suspicious 'Hmm,' as he looked down at the Tutor's chest. 'Open his shirt.'

The Tutor tensed as two men restrained him while a third pulled open his doublet and shirt to reveal the tattoo on his chest.

Veleno's eyes grew bright with excitement. 'If you are not a demon hunter, then what is this?'

'It is the tattoo of a demon hunter, but I am no longer in the service of the emperor.'

'Very noble,' said Veleno, for he was no fan of the Emperor. 'And very foolish.' His face suddenly creased in thought and he raised a finger to his lips. 'Now that I come to think of it, I remember talk of a man who betrayed the demon hunters… Is that you?' he asked with enthusiasm. 'I thought you were dead!'

At this point, Abbess Shimitsu urged her horse forward.

'Please,' she said. 'These men are helping me on a mission of grave importance. I'm sure the grace of the Inja would bless your days if you would allow us to be on our way.'

'My dear Revered Mother,' said Veleno with a bow. 'I am sure you are right. But I am also sure that the tattoo of a demon hunter is worth a king's ransom, *if* one has the skills required to transplant it from one host to another. Is that not so, Lord Fate?'

Fate's expression was dark as Veleno turned towards him. However, before he could reply, the apprentice mage spoke up.

'I told you,' he said. 'I told you he was a demon hunter.'

With a weary sigh, Veleno turned towards the young man.

'What is your name, boy?'

'Torsten Gest, my Lord.'

'Gest,' said Veleno. 'As in, Magistrate Gest?'

'The same, my Lord. Only I'm to become a mage rather than studying law.'

Veleno looked as if he had just eaten something bitter. The morning had been going so well.

'You see, my Lord. I told you the truth. Is that not worth some sort of reward?'

'Indeed it is,' said Veleno and the young man gave a pitiful smile of relief. However, his reprieve was short-lived. 'You were the ring leader of the attack on the merchant. I had intended to hang you from the bridge if you survived the hulls. But you are right. This knowledge is useful. Therefore, if you survive the next leg of the river I will not kill you. I will leave you on the river bank. If you can crawl back home that's fine, but woe betide anyone who helps you.'

'No!' wailed the young man as he was dragged through the gap in the wall and down to the waiting barges. 'No, please!' he cried, but Veleno ignored him as he turned back to the Tutor.

'Now, about that tattoo... I know that removing it will kill you... But that's a price I'm willing to pay,' he added with an unsettling smile. Pursing his lips, he turned to the mage, Xanda. 'Do you have the necessary skills to remove the tattoo without destroying the magical protection it provides?'

Xanda's face twitched with annoyance and a new crack appeared in the smoky glass of his cheek. Wincing with pain, he took the handkerchief from his pocket and gently wiped away a trickle of blood. 'No,' he said. 'Unfortunately I do not.'

Veleno turned to Fate.

'But you do, don't you old friend?' The smile on his face no longer veiled the threat in his eyes, while the expression on Fate's face was grim.

The tattoo of a demon hunter offered the host a level of protection from magical attacks. It was possible to transfer the tattoo from one host to another, but the process required considerable skill. Fate had only ever heard of it being done once before.

'How much do you want?' said Fate. 'How much gold to leave the demon hunter and me alone?'

Veleno laughed as if the question was ridiculous. 'My dear Fate. I doubt you could pay so much even if you emptied your entire vault!'

'How much?' said Fate.

'You are not listening,' said Veleno as the smile fell from his lips. 'To bring our long-standing relationship to an end you can do one of two things. You can work for me, or you can cut the tattoo from the demon hunter's chest and transfer it to my own.'

'And how much if I choose to do neither?'

Veleno rolled his eyes as if Fate were being tiresome, but finally he threw up his hands and turned to his watching men. 'Well boys, how much do we think?'

'A brick or two,' said one man with a nervous laugh.

'Make it a sack, to be sure,' said another.

'But that is rather mean,' said Veleno as if this were a valid debate. 'A strong man can carry two sacks.'

'Maybe we should hand the demon hunter over to the emperor,' said Xanda.

'But the emperor is such a sourpuss,' said Veleno. 'Gloomy people don't deserve such treats.'

'What about his weight?' said another of his men. 'What about his weight in gold?'

A genuine smile returned to Veleno's face.

'No,' he said as he looked from the Tutor to Fate. 'What about both their weights?'

Xanda ground his jaw and a fresh crack appeared in his cheek. He hated Fate and he hated the idea of him being let off with a mere payment of gold.

'So be it,' said Veleno, rubbing his gloved hands with glee. 'I'll give you till the next full moon to decide. Service, tattoo or the weight of two fine gentlemen in gold. And now we are all happy,' he added. 'Our agreement has new conditions and you are free to help the Revered Mother, so long as you return by the next full moon.'

He clapped his hands as if it was decided.

'Now,' he said. 'It's down to the next Chapter Bridge to see how these next two rapscallions get on with the river.'

With that, the Lord of the City mounted his beautiful black stallion. He paused to polish one of the gold buttons on his doublet and turned his horse to go. But then he stopped. Xanda was still holding the scroll of names. In his other hand was a writhing tongue of flame.

'Now, Xanda,' said Veleno. 'Don't do anything rash!'

'You should just kill him,' said the disfigured mage.

'And I will,' said Veleno. 'But not until I'm certain that he is of no further use to me. Now put that flame away.'

'No,' said Xanda. 'It is time for him to pay,' and with that he touched the flame to the parchment.

The scroll burst into glowing fragments that suddenly transformed into a small flock of birds; a dozen tiny black starlings, wheeling about and whistling as they flew up over the bridge. Once they circled... twice... and on the third pass they flew off in all directions.

'Oh dear,' said Veleno in a wistful tone. 'I suppose that complicates things.' He gave a little sigh, shook his head, and then set off for the next bridge on the river. 'Till the next full moon,' he called back over his shoulder. 'If you survive that long,' he added with a laugh.

The Tutor watched as the tiny starlings disappeared from view while Fate merely returned to his horse.

'What are you going to do?' asked Abbess Shimitsu as she and Master Ando came over to join them.

'I'm going to try and figure out what is ailing the monks of Tan Jit Su,' said Fate as he mounted his horse.

'And what about the list?' asked the Tutor. 'Aren't you worried about the people who want to kill you?'

'No.'

'Why not?'

'Because the people on that list are already dead.'

'How do you know?' asked the Tutor.

'Because I killed them,' said Fate.

*

High above the city, a dozen tiny starlings flew towards different parts of the land. However, hardly had the birds covered half a mile before they began to disintegrate. One by one the birds broke apart leaving nothing more than a trail of ash in the air. ... five, six seven were gone... eight nine and ten. Ten of the twelve had been reduced to ash, but two of the birds remained intact. Fast as the wind, they flew on. Two tiny black starlings, bearing tidings of an opportunity that had finally come to pass...

Decimus Fate is vulnerable.

He can be found in the river city of Guile.

6
The Hidden Realm

Even though he appeared calm, the Tutor could see that Fate was unsettled by their encounter with Master Veleno. Maybe he was trying to think of a way out of his predicament, a predicament that now included the Tutor. In simple terms, Fate had three choices:

Serve a powerful crime lord.

Pay a powerful crime lord.

Or cut the tattoo from the Tutor's flesh and transfer it to the crime lord's chest.

As they followed the road towards the northwest gate, the Tutor found himself thinking about the payment Veleno demanded.

'The weight of two men in gold,' he mused. 'No one can raise that amount of gold.'

Fate pursed his lips.

'What?' said the Tutor. 'Are you telling me you could?'

'Perhaps,' said Fate with a shrug. 'If I sold some of my more valuable items.'

'You mean, there really is a vault! And you really *could* pay him?'

'I might consider it,' said Fate. 'If I could get into my vault.'

'What's the matter? Lost the key?' The Tutor spoke in jest, but a stern look from Fate put paid to any sense of amusement.

'The vault requires magic to open it.'

'And you no longer practice magic,' finished the Tutor.

'Correct.'

53

The Tutor rolled his eyes. 'And you can't make an exception?'

Fate shook his head.

'Not even to save your own life?'

'Not even then.'

The Tutor frowned. He could not imagine someone like Fate giving up so much power. He paused before asking his next question.

'What about the tattoo? Do you have the skills to transfer it to another host?'

'There's no guarantee of success but yes, I could perform the procedure.'

'And would you?'

Fate did not answer, but the expression in his dark brown eyes sent a shiver down the Tutor's spine. Feeling irritated and unnerved, the Tutor dropped back to ride with Abbess Shimitsu.

As they approached the city wall, they saw a group of children sitting beside the gate. The children were known as wayfinders, orphans who charged a small fee for leading strangers through the city. Clutching small loaves of bread, they were gathered round a steaming pot set upon a bed of glowing coals.

The Tutor was about to look away when he noticed a slightly older boy standing against the wall. Unlike the other children, this boy was looking up at Abbess Shimitsu. He was trying to hide it, but the Tutor could see him peering out from beneath a mass of thick dark hair. The Tutor was just wondering what the boy was thinking when Abbess Shimitsu called out a greeting.

'Good morning, Weasel,' she said in a pleasant tone.

Clearly embarrassed, the boy shifted and pulled a face at the other children who were now looking at him and grinning. Abbess Shimitsu drew up her horse, forcing him to answer.

'Morning,' said Weasel without raising his eyes.

'Are your brothers and sisters eating well this morning?'

'They aren't my family,' replied the boy.

'Oh, but they are,' said Abbess Shimitsu. 'Just as they are mine.'

'Come on, Weasel,' said a small girl with grubby blonde hair. 'This is even better than yesterday.'

The boy blushed and Abbess Shimitsu smiled.

'Farewell, my son,' she said, but Weasel simply ducked his head. Revealing his own loaf of bread, he went to join his companions around the steaming pot and the Tutor caught a waft of what smelled like rabbit stew.

'What was all that about?' he asked as they moved on through the gate.

'That young man led us to the Fool's Hope Inn when we arrived in the city,' said Abbess Shimitsu. 'His friends offered to lead us for a coin. Our friend Weasel said he would do it for a blessing.'

'Hah,' said the Tutor. 'I bet you still gave him a coin.'

Abbess Shimitsu raised an eyebrow at his cynical tone. 'In fact, I gave him two... on the condition that he promised to share the second coin with his friends.'

The Tutor shook his head. It was typical of the abbess to turn a simple transaction into a test of honesty.

'From the smell of that stew,' said the abbess. 'It would appear that the Weasel is a creature of honour.'

The Tutor and Master Ando exchanged a knowing glance, but Abbess Shimitsu looked entirely satisfied as they passed through the gate and set off along the forest road that would take them to the great escarpment and the monastery of Tan Jit Su.

For the first few miles the forest road was busy with people heading into the city, but as the morning wore on it grew increasingly quiet until they passed barely a soul. A few miles on and they passed through an area known as the Opal Fields where the forest floor was pockmarked with abandoned mining pits and dotted with conical mounds of excavated earth. It was a notoriously dangerous place and children from the city would sometimes dare each other to 'take a walk among the fields'. But the opals had dried up years ago and the mounds of earth were now covered with moss and low growing bilberries.

The weather remained fine and by midday they had covered about ten miles. They stopped in a riverside clearing to eat and water the horses, but they did not tarry long.

'We're doing well,' said the Tutor as they packed away the remaining food. 'If we continue like this we'll definitely reach the monastery tomorrow.'

'That's good,' said Abbess Shimitsu. 'It already feels as if we've been away too long.'

Moving back onto the road she found herself riding beside Fate.

'So tell me more about this sickness,' said Fate as the Tutor and Master Ando fell in behind them. 'What are the symptoms?'

On hearing this, the Tutor glanced at Abbess Shimitsu. She still looked pale and unwell, but she seemed a little stronger than she had when she arrived in Guile.

'The symptoms are fairly generic,' said the abbess in reply to Fate's question. 'Sickness, headaches, lack of energy…' Recalling the suffering of her fellow monks was difficult and she sighed before continuing. 'There are stomach cramps and aching joints, and some of the monks have complained of losing hair. It's like they are being slowly poisoned.'

'And you've tested the food and water?'

'Of course,' said Abbess Shimitsu.

'And there are no other physical signs? No rashes or discolouration of the skin? No suggestion of parasites or contagion?'

'None,' said Abbess Shimitsu.

'And has anyone died?'

'Not yet. Some of the older monks have come close and the others are growing weaker with each bout. I fear it is only a matter of time before we all succumb.'

The Tutor could hear the despondency in her voice and for the first time he thought it might be worth getting the help of a man like Fate if he really could help.

A little further on they crossed a shallow ford and then it was Fate and the Tutor who took the lead. They continued for another half hour when Master Ando urged his horse forward to speak with the Tutor.

'We're being followed,' said the lean-faced monk.

'I know,' said the Tutor.

'It's Veleno's men,' said Fate.

'Will they cause trouble?' asked Master Ando, but Fate shook his head.

'They're just keeping an eye on us.'

Master Ando dipped his head and dropped back to ride with Abbess Shimitsu. The Tutor did not look back, but Fate saw one hand drift to the hilt of his sword while the other adjusted the bandolier of throwing stars strapped across his chest.

'You do know those won't kill a man,' said Fate. 'Not unless you're incredibly lucky or the points are laced with poison.'

The Tutor gave him an irritated look. 'I don't use poison.'

'Poison can be useful,' said Fate, his hand resting on the black dragon-handled dagger on his belt. 'And what about that?' said Fate, nodding to the sword at the Tutor's side. 'That's not the Hadean blade of a demon hunter.'

The Tutor's expression darkened as he glanced down at his sword. 'The fighting I do now is against normal foes,' he said. 'I don't need a Hadean blade to defeat city thugs and wilderness brigands.'

'Did you sell it?' asked Fate.

'No,' said the Tutor. 'I did *not* sell it!'

'Well I hope you keep it somewhere safe,' said Fate. 'The blade of a demon hunter is worth almost as much as the tattoo on your chest.'

The Tutor gave him a disapproving look, but Fate merely smiled as they continued on their way.

As the light began to fade, Fate noticed a change in the Tutor's demeanour. For some reason he seemed suddenly quiet and subdued. The former demon hunter kept glancing to the right, towards a valley that led away to the north. Since leaving the city, they had past numerous side roads and branching valleys, but for some reason this particular valley was different.

Looking around, Fate could see no reason for this apparent reaction, but then he noticed a few unusual species among the normal forest flora. There were miniature columbine and a faint scattering of silver anemones. Veils of trailing white celandine hung from some of the trees and Fate now noticed that one of these

58

trees was a black oak, a tree that was considered sacred in the Hidden Realm of Faerie.

Frowning, Fate looked more closely at the mouth of the valley and, sure enough, he caught the faint silvery glow of enchantment. This valley was one of those rare places where the essence of the 'Hidden Realm' seeped through into the normal world of men. Fate was no stranger to the world of Faerie. Indeed the 'Fair Folk' were fascinated by him. But for some reason, this place made the Tutor distinctly uncomfortable.

'Are you all right?' asked Fate.

'I'm fine,' said the Tutor, but his head remained bowed.

'Do you know what this valley is called?' asked Fate. 'It seems to have a touch of...'

'I've no idea,' snapped the Tutor, and with that, he spurred his horse on.

Fate watched him go as Abbess Shimitsu drew up alongside him.

'Don't worry,' she said. 'We all know places that stir painful memories, do we not?'

Fate nodded slowly as they watched the Tutor fade into the gloom. 'Do *you* know the name of this valley?' he asked. Turning to look at the abbess, he was surprised to see that her eyes were filled with tears.

'It is called Tearmann,' she said and Fate recognised the language of Faerie.

'Sanctuary,' he breathed and Abbess Shimitsu nodded.

'It is sad,' she went on. 'That beauty and sorrow so often lie hand in hand.'

She gave a sigh and then, without further explanation she moved on. Fate stared up into the mysterious valley until Master Ando spoke beside him.

'Don't ask him about it again,' said the normally quiet monk. 'Not unless you want a punch in the face.' And then he too continued down the road leaving the sorcerer alone.

They made camp in a clearing beside the river where the rustle of leaves mingled with the flow and gurgle of the river. Overhead the branches of the trees seemed to shimmer in the firelight. Fate could hear the horses softly chomping at their nose bags and Master Ando was laid out in his bedroll, breathing heavily. He could not tell if Abbess Shimitsu was sleeping, but the Tutor was still awake. He was sitting on the far side of the fire pushing half burned sticks back into the growing bed of embers.

Fate was about to close his eyes when he heard something more than the wind in the trees. It was a sound he was familiar with, but one he had not expected to hear. Bright as spring water and soft as the hush of a barn owl's wing, it was the faint sound of Faerie voices.

'*Strange*,' he thought. '*It's almost a week until the next Penance Moon.*'

The music of their chatter grew suddenly louder and Fate looked over at the Tutor. Just passing close to a Faerie glen had caused him discomfort and Fate wondered how he might react to the actual presence of Faerie. With any luck, the demon hunter could not hear them. Humans were often deaf and blind to the denizens of the Hidden Realm.

The voices continued and Fate looked up into the trees. These were not the Moribundium that visited him on a Penance Moon; these were some form of sprite. Far smaller than a normal Faerie, the inquisitive creatures were staying hidden, but still Fate could see the faint shimmer that betrayed their presence. He winced at their boldness and considered sending them away. He may not have magic, but the human voice had a power of its own, if one knew how to use it. Then suddenly, from across the fire...

'Don't worry,' said the Tutor. 'They're causing no harm.'

'I'm sorry,' said Fate. 'I didn't expect them to follow me. Normally they would only visit me at certain times.'

The Tutor's dark face was unreadable, but his blue eyes shone in the firelight. 'They're not here for you,' he said. 'They're here for me.'

Fate stared at him and slowly he caught something of what the sprites were saying.

'Beidh sé ag teacht?'

'Ang Cuirfidh sé in iúl dúinn?'

'Will he come?' the gossamer whispers said. 'Will he let us share?'

Fate could only speculate on what the Faeries were referring to, but the look in the Tutor's eyes made it clear, that on this particular night, the people of Faerie would be disappointed.

*

Back in Guile, the lifeless figure of a young man lay on the west bank of the River Scéal. It was dark and the river looked flat and featureless as it flowed away into the night. The young figure wore the robes of an apprentice mage, but the robes were torn and wet. In the faint light of distant oil lamps, a rat came to investigate what appeared to be a free meal. The rat climbed onto the unmoving figure, but still it gave no signs of being alive. Only when the rat took its first bite of human flesh did the figure stir... a weak but frenzied attempt to dislodge the unwelcome guest followed by a pitiful moan of pain.

'Easy, there,' said a voice as another figure emerged from the darkness.

Dressed in the filthy robes of a pilgrim, the new figure crouched down and placed a hand on the young man's back.

'H..help me,' mumbled the apprentice mage, hardly able to lift his face from the mud.

'I will,' said the pilgrim. 'Even though the Lord of the City has forbidden it.'

Putting his grubby hands under the young man's shoulder he heaved him over eliciting a groan of agony as the apprentice mage rolled onto his back. Now the pilgrim could see that the young man's shoulder was dislocated. His left hip also appeared misshapen and the clean line of his right shin displayed the telltale 'notch' of a fracture.

The pilgrim put his hand on the young man's chest as he stared out over the dark expanse of the river.

'Give me your lost and abandoned souls and I will make them servants of the Divine,' he intoned as if he were reciting the lines of a prayer.

'Help me,' repeated the apprentice mage and the pilgrim looked down.

'I will, my son. I will.'

Placing a hand on the young man's cheek he looked across the bank where the rat was now cleaning itself just a few yards from the water's edge. Moving slowly, the pilgrim removed his tattered cloak before throwing it over the unsuspecting rat. The creature squealed as the pilgrim lunged forward, pinning it to the ground before gathering it up in a bundle. Returning to the young man, he gripped the writhing body in his thin and dirty hands. Then, with surprising strength, he gave it a savage twist.

The rat gave a muffled squeal and then went silent as bones gave way with a gristly crunching sound. Unfolding the cloak, the pilgrim removed the dead rat and held it over the young man's face before bringing the creature to his mouth. With rotting teeth he tore open the small black body and the young man spluttered as hot blood spilled onto his face.

Eyes closed, the pilgrim began to murmur.

'Rejected by heathens, and washed up on the banks of despair, you are reborn in the blood of the lowly to be a servant of the Divine.'

Casting the dead rat aside, the pilgrim now laid both hands on the young man's shoulder and began to pray. It is impossible to say what unholy gods might have heard his prayers, but somehow the pain of the apprentice mage's dislocated shoulder began to ease. Then darkness closed in around them as the pilgrim dragged the young man away into the night.

7
Coming Home to Roost

Fifteen miles west of Guile a tiny black starling arrived at the estate of Count Leopold Cévaro. Passing over the extensive grounds, the starling flew directly towards the grey stone mansion which sat at the heart of the estate. A light shone from a window in the northwest tower and it was to this window that the starling now flew.

The window was formed from panes of leaded glass, but the tiny bird seemed not to care as it flew straight at the diamond lattice. An observer might have expected a soft thud and a broken neck, certainly the small bird was not heavy enough to break a pane, but no. With a faint '*shnick*', the ethereal bird passed through the window unscathed.

Count Cévaro looked up from the sprawl of maps and land registries strewn upon the table at the centre of his study. He frowned as the small black bird fluttered round the room emitting a sharp, insistent trill. Annoyance clouded the count's dark eyes and he looked to the window then frowned again when he saw that it was not open. Furling a map, he stood up from his chair and focussed on the bird, determined to swipe it from the air and silence its grating cries. However, before he could take aim the small black bird swooped down to a writing desk in the corner of the room and began pecking at a scroll of parchment.

The writing desk contained all the correspondence pertaining to his brother's estate. That estate would now be part of his own, were it not for the meddling of a sorcerer named Fate, whose intervention had resulted in the estate being sold to pay off his brother's gambling debts instead of swelling Cévaro's coffers.

Fate had killed his brother. Cévaro was sure of it, even though the physicians had been unable to determine the cause of death. But Cévaro knew, just as his brother had known. He remembered the night his brother had come to him for help, half witless with fear.

'He's coming for me,' Lorenzo had said in this very room. 'Fate knows I signed it and he's coming for me.'

'What are you talking about?' said Cévaro. 'What did you sign?'

By way of an answer, his brother produced a scroll of parchment sealed with a glowing watermark depicting a circle of flames coiled around a set of scales. On the parchment was a list of names, which included the signature of his brother.

For those hereby named to be notified in the event of accident, injury, or any other circumstance that weakens, or makes vulnerable, the sorcerer known as Decimus Fate.

'Please, brother!' Lorenzo begged. 'You have more influence than me. You know people who could help.'

Cévaro thought his brother was overreacting. Surely no one would be foolish enough to kill a member of such a powerful family. But he was wrong and now his brother was dead. Following Lorenzo's death, Cévaro had summoned his personal mage, Lorden Sole.

'I want him dead,' the count had cursed, but Lorden Sole advised against it.

'It's too dangerous,' said the mage. 'Fate is too powerful.'

'But I have to do something!'

Lorden Sole thought for a moment before nodding slowly to himself. 'Do you still have the parchment?'

Cévaro crossed the room to remove it from a chest.

'We could replace your brother's name with your own,' said Sole. 'Fate would never know and if it works, you would be notified if he ever becomes vulnerable.'

And so they had erased Lorenzo's name and used Cévaro's own blood to write *his* name on the magical parchment. And now that parchment had begun to shine with the faint glow of magic.

Crossing to the writing desk, Cévaro picked up the scroll that had not been touched in almost four years. As he did so the mystical bird became still, sitting on the corner of the desk and watching intently as Cévaro slipped the black ribbon from around the scroll. Hardly had he unfurled the parchment when the bird took flight. It leapt off the writing desk and Cévaro flinched as the bird flew into the scroll and disappeared in a puff of black cinders. The cinders did not fall to the floor. Instead, they settled onto the parchment in the form of words.

'Decimus Fate is vulnerable,' the words read. *'He can be found in the river city of Guile.'*

*

The following day dawned cold and bright and, as the Tutor's party continued on its way to the monastery, another tiny starling was reaching its destination. All through the night the magical bird had flown to the port city of Dymhaven.

Weaving through the plumes of peat smoke, it made its way to a disused market square in a derelict corner of the city. There, on the weed-choked paving stones, stood a young woman, surrounded by four unsavoury looking men. Somewhere in her mid twenties, the woman was of medium height and slender build. She stood with her head bowed, looking up through an unruly fringe of dark blonde hair.

The freckles over her nose spoke of innocence, but there was nothing innocent about the expression in her hazel eyes. She was tense. Her limbs trembled slightly and the sword in her right hand looked inadequate compared to the heavy scimitars of the men who stood around her. They looked at her with amusement and hunger in their eyes, and little by little they edged their way closer.

'Now, now,' said one of the men. 'No need to be drawing that fancy poker of yours.' Judging by his expensive lamellar armour, this man was clearly the leader of the group and he looked at the young woman with an unpleasant gleam in his eye. 'We only want to use your body and leave you bleeding in the street.'

The woman said nothing, her eyes the only thing that moved as she looked at the three men she could see. She knew the fourth was behind her and her ears strained for any sound of him coming closer.

She was dressed like a man in a sand-coloured cloak with dark leather breeches and knee length boots. Her long hair was uncombed and tied back with a knotted leather cord.

'Ooh! Look at her scowl,' said the leader, grinning at his men who leered in turn. 'Happen she might be quite pretty if she didn't glower so.'

If the leader had expected the young woman to be intimidated, he was wrong.

'Which one of you is Dimitri Organza?' she asked in a surprisingly confident tone.

The three other men immediately turned to look at the leader and the woman smiled.

'How do you know that name?' he asked, but the young woman did not answer.

With a shrug she threw back her cloak to reveal a tailored shirt of fine scale mail. The small plates of metal covered her shoulders and torso like the scales of a dragon. Her right hand suddenly tightened on the hilt of her sword and the nervous shaking of her limbs disappeared.

'I have a message from Amon Farl of the Dockers' Guild,' she said and the leader's eyes took on a murderous glint. 'He says he knows what you took from the customs lockup, and your services are no longer required.'

'Why, that...' began the leader but the woman cut him off.

'Your contract is terminated, with immediate effect,' she said and the leader of the men bared his teeth in a snarl.

'Kill this bitch!' he barked and his men rushed forward with scimitars raised.

For a moment it seemed as if she was sure to be cut down, but then the woman moved. She dropped below one strike and swept her sword low, slicing the tendons of the first attacker's ankle. Avoiding a scything attack from the second man, she slashed his forearm and kicked him in the knee before thrusting the point of her sword into the third man's hip.

Even as the third attacker fell to one knee, the woman darted forward and parried a strike from the leader himself. He was clearly a practised fighter and he recovered quickly to launch a whirl of savage attacks, but the woman retreated calmly before choosing her moment. As the man's curved blade flashed towards her face, she spun round, avoiding the attack before stabbing her own sword into the man's unprotected armpit. His sword arm went limp and the heavy scimitar dropped to the flagstones with a clang.

The leader of the group staggered back, his left hand now trying to stem the bleeding from under his arm.

'Wait!' he gasped. 'Whatever Amon is paying you, I will double it.'

The woman gave a sneer of distaste and stabbed him deftly in the heart. Blood gurgled in his throat as the leader collapsed to his knees before falling flat on his face. Stepping away from his body the woman turned to watch the leader's companions dragging themselves away. There was no price on their heads and so she let them go.

Taking a green silk handkerchief from a pocket, she carefully wiped the blood from her sword before dropping the handkerchief on her latest mark. Then, with the signature grace of a swordmaster, she sheathed her sword and began to walk away only to be stopped by a tiny black starling that swooped out of nowhere to bar her way.

Frowning with annoyance, she swiped a hand at the bird, but it was too quick for her. It darted forward, hovering and flapping around a leather pouch attached to her belt. Becoming still, the woman watched as the mysterious bird came to rest on the hilt of a discarded scimitar. She did not know what the bird could be interested in, but as she opened the pouch she saw the faint glow of magic coming from a folded piece of parchment that she had not taken out for years.

The bird became agitated as she removed the parchment and unfolded it. Even though it was creased and crumpled she could still make out the arcane script and magical designs along with the list of names. She smoothed out the parchment, and as she did so the small

69

bird flew directly into it, disappearing in a scatter of black cinders that settled on the page and slowly coalesced into words.

'Decimus Fate is vulnerable,' the words read. '*He can be found in the river city of Guile.'*

The woman raised the parchment to stare at the name that had just appeared.

Decimus Fate… the man who had killed her father.

Looking down at the parchment, she could see where she had erased her father's name before replacing it with her own. Sienna Arturo Blade, daughter of Matthias Arturo Blade, the finest swordsman in all the Seven Vales. Her father had wanted this man dead. Now she would see it done.

The Monastery of Tan Jit Su

The monastery of Tan Jit Su was perched at the edge of a yellow sandstone cliff that rose more than a thousand feet above the trees in the valley below. Built from the same yellow stone, the outer wall of the monastery glowed a deep golden colour in the light of the setting sun.

It was late afternoon when the Tutor and his party arrived at the base of the great escarpment and now they had been climbing for almost an hour. The route up the cliff switched back and forth, sometimes cutting across the vertical face and sometimes delving into the cliff itself in a series of sloping tunnels. Their progress was steady, and they stopped to rest on a wide ledge some four hundred feet from the top of the cliff.

Moving to the edge of the path, the Tutor looked out over the forest. They were just two days from Guile and yet the crowded city, and characters like Master Veleno, seemed to belong to a different world. Movement at the base of the cliff caught his eye and the Tutor looked down into a clearing where he could just make out the vague shapes of three men with horses.

Maybe the influence of Guile's crime lord was not so far away after all. The Tutor gave a sigh then he tensed as Fate came to stand beside him.

'They're being surprisingly persistent,' said the sorcerer looking down at the men who had been following them. 'Veleno must really want that tattoo.'

The Tutor shook his head at the sorcerer's dark humour. 'Doesn't look like they're going to follow us up.'

'And why would they?' said Fate as he returned to his horse. 'This path is the only way up to the plateau, and beyond the monastery it's just endless miles of barren desert. They know we have to come back this way.'

Looking out over the forested valleys, the Tutor's mind was transported back to the night he first arrived at the monastery. Exhausted and severely injured, he remembered standing on a spot just like this swaying back and forth with the gusts of wind and grief. Then, the night had been dark and his heart felt as if it had been carved from his chest. Now, the sky was bright, but the pain in his chest felt almost as raw.

He closed his eyes and his hand drifted to the hilt of his sword.

'Alexander.'

The Tutor turned to see Abbess Shimitsu looking at him with an expression of concern in her eyes.

'Come away, my son.'

She extended her hand and it was only then that the Tutor realised just how close he was standing to the edge of the path. With a frown he moved away from the dizzying drop and took up the reins of his horse.

'First the Faerie valley, and now the climb,' said Abbess Shimitsu. 'I did not intend to reopen old wounds.'

'Come on,' said the Tutor without meeting her gaze. 'You look tired and we still have some way to go.'

Twilight descended and the sky was a deep shade of blue as they finally reached the top of the cliff and crossed the rocky ground towards the monastery. As they approached the outer walls a bell began to toll and several monks came out to meet them. They were clearly delighted to see Abbess Shimitsu and Master Ando, but the Tutor was immediately struck by how weak and unwell they appeared.

'Inja be praised for your safe return,' said an older female monk with silver white hair who the Tutor recognised as Sister Hīra, the monastery's most gifted healer.

'Thank you,' said Abbess Shimitsu. 'Now tell me quickly... how do our brothers and sisters fare?'

'Not well,' said Sister Hīra. 'Fully half are confined to their beds and Sister Myuko has fallen into a sleep from which she will not wake.'

Abbess Shimitsu's mouth tightened into a thin line. 'Have faith,' she said. 'See... we have brought people who might be able to help.'

The healer gave Fate an appraising look, but her gaze softened when she saw the Tutor.

'Welcome back, Aoimoku!' she said, using the Shīku word for 'blue eyes'.

'Come,' said Abbess Shimitsu. 'Take us to Sister Myuko and we shall see what can be done.'

Even as they entered the monastery, the Tutor could tell that things were bad. Normally there would be people milling about the low square buildings, monks carrying out chores, reading in the gardens or practicing martial arts in the central courtyard. This evening, however, there were only a few monks to be seen, and they were gathered on a raised stone area where an old toothless monk faced a young female monk across a wooden board covered with black and white stones.

The younger monks stood up to greet them, while the old man merely turned his face in their direction. His eyes were clouded with cataracts and yet it was almost as if he could see them. He greeted Abbess Shimitsu and Master Ando with a bow and smiled as he recognised the Tutor presence. When his face angled towards Fate, however, he frowned as if he could not quite make out what he was sensing.

'Has Master Ganjin been affected by the illness?' asked the Tutor. To his mind, the scrawny toothless monk appeared very much the same as ever.

'Not that we can tell,' said Sister Hīra. 'He and Nawashi appear largely unaffected.'

'Nawashi?' asked Fate as his eyes lingered on the old monk.

'Nawashi is one of the monastery's gardeners,' said Abbess Shimitsu. 'He is not comfortable around people, but he has a gift for tending plants. There he is,' she said, nodding towards the monks who had been watching the game. 'The young man with the broad shoulders and shaggy hair.'

'He's lost a lot of weight,' said the Tutor, remembering the well built young man from his time at the monastery.

'Yes,' said Sister Hīra. 'But he and Master Ganjin have not fallen ill like the rest of us.'

Up on the raised platform the young man lowered his eyes as they continued to look at him.

'Take us to the woman in the coma,' said Fate and Abbess Shimitsu winced at the use of such a serious word.

Covered by a white sheet and woollen blanket, Sister Myuko lay on a low bed in a simple whitewashed room. A small vase of flowers sat on a table and a brazier of scented coals filled the room with the healing scent of jasmine.

'How long has she been like this?' asked Fate as he crouched down to examine the unconscious monk.

'Almost four days,' said Sister Hīra.

'And there's been no change in her condition?'

'Only that she is growing weaker,' said Sister Hīra.

Standing beside the table, the Tutor watched as Fate examined Sister Myuko. He checked her pulse and breathing, and gently opened her eyes and mouth before probing various parts of her body with his fingers. The Tutor shifted awkwardly and lowered his eyes. He felt uneasy about the intimacy of Fate's examination.

'He's just looking for signs of infection,' said Abbess Shimitsu, laying a hand on the Tutor's arm.

Opening a box he had taken from his saddlebag, Fate took out a thin silver lancet and turned to Abbess Shimitsu as if he were asking her permission. The abbess gestured for him to continue and Fate pierced the end of Sister Myuko's thumb before squeezing a small amount of blood into a glass vial. Into this he added a few drops of clear liquid from a small bottle.

'What are you testing for?' asked Sister Hīra.

'Toxins,' said Fate. 'The blood will turn black if any contaminants are present.'

He shook the bottle, but the colour of the blood did not change. His tests continued and his face betrayed the fact that he was learning little. Finally, he adjusted the bracelet on his wrist until he isolated a charm in the form of a tiny wren. Letting the charm hang free, he extended his arm over Sister Myuko.

'And what's this for?' asked the Tutor. 'I thought you no longer performed magic.'

'I don't,' said Fate. 'The charms on this bracelet have magical effects of their own. I don't need magic to use them.' He held the charm close to Sister Myuko's chest. 'If this illness is caused by a curse the wren's tail will lift and we'll hear a sharp metallic chime.'

The room was silent as they waited for any sign. At one point the tiny bird seemed to tilt forward slightly, but then it settled back and Fate gave a low grunt of displeasure. He stood up from Sister Myuko's bed just as the young man called Nawashi entered the room with a plate of food. He stopped and bowed his head as everyone turned to look at him. His face was concealed behind a thick mop of dark hair and a crude wooden pendant hung from a leather cord around his neck.

'Food for Sister Hīra,' he mumbled, looking distinctly uncomfortable.

'Thank you, Nawashi,' said Abbess Shimitsu. 'Just leave it on the table.'

Nawashi bobbed his head and the Tutor stepped back so the young man could place the food on the table. As he turned to leave, Fate noticed the way he shied away from the Tutor and placed a hand on his pendant, tucking the wooden disk beneath the neck of his yellow robes.

'I hear you are one of the gardeners?' said Fate.

Nawashi stopped and looked to Abbess Shimitsu.

'It's all right,' said the abbess. 'This is Lord Fate from the city of Guile. He has come to help us.'

Nawashi gave a barely perceptible nod. 'Yes,' he said. 'I help Brother Henza and Sister Nahru in the gardens.'

'And you grow the food?'

Nawashi's head drooped a little lower.

'Abbess Shimitsu tells me you have a gift for growing things,' Fate continued and Nawashi blushed.

'Will you show me where you grow the food? In the morning, of course…'

For a moment, Nawashi glanced up at the sorcerer. He seemed pleased by the idea that someone might be interested in his skills and terrified that he might have done something wrong. Finally he gave another bob of the head then he rushed out of the room before any more questions could be asked.

'You still suspect the food?' said Master Ando with some annoyance. 'Abbess Shimitsu told you it has been tested.'

Fate quirked his head to one side. 'There are tests and tests,' he said as he walked over to the plate that Nawashi had brought. 'And all the monks eat the same food?'

'Of course,' said Abbess Shimitsu.

Returning to his box, Fate removed four more glass tubes and took pieces from each of the food items on the plate... bread, cheese, purple kiui fruit and some kind of fresh bean salad with herbs. He added a small amount of the clear liquid to each tube and frowned when nothing happened. Reaching out his arm he dangled the wren charm over the food but still there was no reaction. Finally he lifted the small round kiui fruit to his mouth.

'Are you sure that's wise?' said the Tutor.

'The monks have been eating this food for months,' said Fate. 'One bite is unlikely to do me any harm.' For all his confidence, even he seemed a little hesitant, but the moment he took a bite his expression changed to one of wonder.

'Nawashi is a very talented young man,' said Abbess Shimitsu with a smile. 'He grows the tastiest food you can imagine.'

Looking down at the purple fruit, Fate nodded distractedly. He had half expected to detect some kind of taint, but it really was the nicest kiui he had ever tasted. Almost without thinking, he popped the rest of the fruit in his mouth before turning back to Abbess Shimitsu.

'I will start by collecting samples from around the monastery,' he began in a tone of some authority. 'And then I will interview all the monks who are well enough to speak with me.'

'Do you have some idea of a cause?' asked Abbess Shimitsu.

'No,' said Fate. 'None at all.'

9
A Date With Destiny

Count Cévaro's study reverberated with the sound of his displeasure.

'What do you mean, you can't do it? Why, in the Vales, do I retain your services if you can't perform a simple task when I ask it?' Slamming his hand down on the table, Cévaro glared at the man standing opposite him.

The man's name was Lorden Sole, Count Cévaro's personal mage. Dressed in blue velvet robes, the man looked more than a little shaken. His features were well proportioned, his dark hair and beard carefully manicured. His appearance spoke of intelligence but his eyes were filled with fear.

'This is not just any man we're taking about,' Sole argued. 'This is Decimus Fate!'

'I know,' said Cévaro. 'He killed my brother! I know exactly who it is.' The count's dark eyes burned with fury and Sole's gaze wavered as the count held up a small strip of paper from a carrier pigeon that had just arrived from Guile. 'But Fate no longer has magic! My contacts in the city have confirmed it.'

'Even if that is true,' said Sole, 'Fate will have ways of protecting himself … ways of killing others.' He raised a cautionary finger. 'He has at least two vindicta tattoos on his body!'

'But they need magic to activate them,' said Cévaro. 'And if Fate no longer uses magic they are useless.'

'No,' insisted Sole. 'I do not have the power to attempt the life of Decimus Fate… but I know of two people who do.'

'Who?' said Cévaro as he leaned forward expectantly.

'They go by the names of Tilluvian and Divorian.'

'The *Kane* twins?' said Cévaro, and now it was *his* voice that held a note of fear. 'You know how to contact the Kane twins?'

Sole nodded and Cévaro sat back heavily in his chair.

'They will want payment,' Sole went on.

'Money is no problem,' said Cévaro with a dismissive wave.

'Money is of no interest to the Kane twins,' said Sole. 'They will want promises or people they can use in their dealings with the Daemonaria.'

'They're demonologists?'

'Among other things,' said Sole.

'And they use people?'

'Use them, or trade them,' said the mage, and he lowered his eyes at the very thought of how the Kane twins might use the people they were given.

Cévaro raised a hand to his mouth. His eyes shifted uncertainly, but then resolve hardened his gaze.

'How long would it take them to get here?'

'They might not accept the contr...'

'How long?'

'Several weeks by road and sea,' said Sole. 'But they could be here in a matter of days if they traverse the Daemonaria.'

'They can do that?' asked Cévaro in a tone of horrified awe. 'They can travel through the demon realm unscathed?'

Sole nodded and Cévaro felt a chill crawl up his spine. Sole noticed the reaction and wondered if his master would balk at such a dangerous collaboration, but Fate had damaged the fortunes of the Cévaro estate, and that was an injury that could not be tolerated.

'Do it,' said Cévaro and Sole felt his legs go weak. Tonight he would contact two sorcerers who cavorted with demons and drew their power from the capricious well of chaos; two sorcerers who had the power to kill Decimus Fate.

*

In the port city of Dymhaven, Sienna Blade watched from a second storey window as the port authority soldiers closed on her father's home. The building was a fortified townhouse with small windows and thick walls rising up from the modest grounds. Not an easy place to take by force, but Sienna knew this was not the time to defend it.

Even as she watched, four of the soldiers made for the front door while four more peeled off to cover the sides and rear of the building. Glancing further up the road, she saw a figure standing in the shadow of a doorway. There was just enough light from a nearby oil lamp to make out the royal blue of a haulage strap wrapped around the figure's waist. Only the dockers wore those haulage straps like belts.

'*Amon Farl!*' she cursed to herself. Leader of the Dockers' Guild.

In a bitter flash Sienna realised what had happened. Farl had used her to kill a rival and then given her name to the authorities. He had probably taken the items from the customs lockup for himself. She had no idea what had been taken, but it did not matter. Farl had betrayed her, and for that he would die, but not just now. Now she had other matters to attend to.

Walking over to a chest of drawers, she opened the top drawer and took out a green silk handkerchief and laid it on a writing desk where she used black ink and a small brush to write the name, 'Amon Farl'. She blotted the ink with a pad and wafted it in front of the fire before tucking it into a pocket in her leather breeches.

A series of loud booms echoed through the house as the soldiers began to hammer on the main door, and Sienna moved to a series of metal D rings hanging from cords that disappeared into a wooden panel on the wall. In a normal town house those cords might be connected to various bells in the servants' quarters, but not in her father's house. Reaching for the left-hand ring, she gave it a firm pull, and from down on the ground floor she heard a heavy 'thunk' as a gate of steel bars fell into place behind the main door.

The soldiers would not get through that in a hurry.

Moving quickly now, she went about the room gathering up jewellery, pouches of money and anything else that was of particular value. She placed all this in a chest in the corner of the room before filling a shoulder bag with some travel clothes and a few personal effects. Her sword and other weapons were already on her person, but she stopped by a glass fronted cabinet to take out a signet ring engraved with the image of a wasp. Finally she swept up a shortbow and a quiver full of arrows before heading through a narrow archway in the corner of the room where a set of narrow stairs led up to the roof. Rushing up the stairs she followed the curtain wall round to the north and looked out over the rooftops of the sleeping city.

About sixty yards away was the bell-tower of a derelict school. Putting down her bag, Sienna nocked an arrow from the quiver and took aim at the bell. Taking a deep breath she drew the bow back to full draw and loosed. The first arrow missed by half a yard and went skittering across the roof tiles. The second arrow hit squarely and the sound of the bell rang out. Sienna counted to ten before releasing her next arrow and once again the bell rang out, slowly getting fainter as the swing of the bell grew less.

Satisfied, Sienna returned to the second storey room and moved to the corner where she had left the chest. The walls of the room were covered in wood panels, and close to this corner was a large bookcase. Reaching under the wooden trim of the bookcase, Sienna slid back a small piece of veneer and pressed. In the corner, part of the wooden panelling opened up to reveal a narrow doorway. Sienna pushed the chest of valuables through the narrow opening and then, as the sound of hammering drifted up through the house, she slipped into one of the secret passages her father had built into the house. With a grunt, she closed the wood-panel door, which was made heavy by a slab of stone that would frustrate any efforts to find the cavity by listening for a hollow knock.

Taking a flint and steel from her belt, she struck a shower of sparks and used the light to direct more sparks onto the head of a torch, which instantly flared into life. As the port soldiers struggled to get into the house, Sienna worked her way down a tight spiral staircase and then along a tunnel that continued under the city for over a mile. Finally she came to a dead-end where the tunnel sloped down to a drainage sump. On the wall beside her, a wrought iron ladder led up to a heavy metal grill in the ceiling. Extinguishing her torch, she waited in the darkness.

Barely a minute passed before a glare of light appeared through the grill overhead. With one knuckle, Sienna rapped on the wrought iron ladder and a moment later there was an answering tap from above. With a grating sound, the grill hinged open and Sienna climbed the ladder into the dung laden air of a stable yard.

'Trouble at home,' said a deep voice as someone reached down to give her a hand.

'Just a few unwanted dinner guests,' said Sienna as she climbed out of the tunnel and the grill was replaced with a gritty clang.

'You couldn't have waited till morning?' said the man, somewhat grumpily.

The man asking the questions was broad shouldered and dressed in nothing more than a nightshirt and stable boots. His hair was a thick, unruly red and his beard was almost black, but his dark eyes shone with a grudging fondness. Shaking his head, he carried his lamp over to a dapple coated mare that whinnied softly at their approach.

'She's all ready for you,' said the man, adjusting the saddle bags he had just strapped in place. 'Maggie put some food and water together for you. Just some bread, fruit and a couple of pies to tide you over.'

'Thank you, Amos,' said Sienna, handing the man a number of silver coins.

Tying her own bag behind the saddle, she looked around as if she was looking for someone.

'Is Isaac not here?'

'He's gone into hiding.'

'Again?' said Sienna. 'What was it this time?'

'Fire-starting,' said Amos. 'He says it was self defence, but a building caught fire so the port authorities are after him.'

'That boy is terrible! said Sienna shaking her head. 'Tell him we'll sort it out when I get back.'

'I will,' said Amos before turning the conversation back to Sienna.

'So is this a job or an escape?'

'A bit of both.'

'Hoof'n'hock, girl! You're as bad as yer father.'

Sienna's gaze darkened at the mention of her father, but still she leaned over to kiss the stocky man on the cheek.

'Or maybe you've got a date,' said Amos as Sienna untied the mare's reins and led her out of the stable. 'Epona knows! You should have been saddled by now.'

Sienna arched an eyebrow as she swung up onto the horse's back.

'Don't tell me,' said Amos with a sigh of resignation. 'You've got a date with destiny.'

'Something like that,' said Sienna, and the smile in her eyes raised the hair on the stable owner's neck.

'Stay quick,' said Amos, laying a hand on the horse's cheek.

'Stay smart,' replied Sienna.

'Stay safe,' they said together, and with that she tapped her heels into the horse's side and set off into the dark streets of Dymhaven. It would take almost three days to reach the city of Guile. All she had to do then was find the man she was looking for, and kill him.

'*A date with destiny*,' she repeated to herself, and laughed.

10
The Talisman of Dreams

Standing with Abbess Shimitsu, the Tutor watched as Fate followed Nawashi around the fruit and vegetable gardens in the corner of the monastery. The sorcerer had spent a full day and two nights collecting samples and conducting numerous tests on everything from the sand that blew in from the desert, to the whitewash mixture the monks used to paint the walls of their homes.

'Found anything?' asked the Tutor as Fate concluded his tour of the gardens and made his way over to join them.

'Nothing,' said Fate with an air of frustration. 'I was convinced it must have something to do with the food, but I can't find a single trace of contamination. That young man grows some of the finest food I have ever seen.'

Together they looked at Nawashi who picked up a basket of cuttings before making his way towards a workbench covered in compost and small terracotta pots. After a nervous start, he had been happy to share his knowledge with someone as learned as Fate. He wore a faint smile of pride as he glanced towards the sorcerer. However, as his eyes passed over the Tutor, his gaze wavered and he raised a hand to something beneath the neck of his robes.

Fate frowned and was about to say something when Abbess Shimitsu spoke.

'The first monks are ready to speak with you,' she said, drawing their attention away from Nawashi.

'Good,' said Fate. 'Maybe now we'll find some answers.'

Abbess Shimitsu had decided that they would question the monks in a domed building known as the

Chamber of Echoes. Partially sunk into the ground, the circular room was designed to enhance the power of meditation and personal reflection. Descending into the room, the Tutor remembered spending many hours in the chamber, listening to the sound of his breathing and the womblike beat of his heart. He had been hoping to find relief in the absence of conscious thought, but he had found something more precious... a private place to grieve.

A table and chairs were set out in the middle of the room and one by one, the monks came into the chamber to speak with Fate. By midday he had interviewed all those who were strong enough to walk, and he was still no closer to figuring out what was afflicting the monastery.

Rising from his chair, Fate stretched the stiffness from his back before moving to the far side of the chamber where a number of religious relics lay in small recesses set into the wall.

'That's a soul cleanser,' said Abbess Shimitsu as the sorcerer leaned forward to examine a crystal that shone with a pure white light. 'It helps to calm the minds of those who suffer from mental afflictions.'

Fate pursed his lips, impressed. It was one thing to affect the mind in a specific way; far more difficult to smooth the disrupted pathways of mental illness.

'A water compass,' he said as his attention moved to a bronze device, at the centre of which sat an elongated crystal. The crystal was mounted on a fine silver gimbal that allowed it to swivel in any direction.

'Our ancestors used it to cross the Plains of Despair,' said Abbess Shimitsu as she moved to stand beside him. 'Alas, the crystal was drained of energy which made it impossible for us to return.'

Fate nodded. He was familiar with the Shīku story. How they were the only people ever to have crossed the great desert. It was amazing to think that this device had made such a feat possible.

'And what stood here?' he asked, pointing to an alcove where a small wooden stand stood empty. The stand looked like it was designed to hold a pendant or necklace.

'That went missing from the monastery some time ago,' said Abbess Shimitsu. 'It was an icon of fortune,' she went on. 'A good luck charm, if you will.'

'A real one?' said Fate with more than a touch of scepticism. 'Genuine good luck charms are rare, and powerful, especially when used over time.'

'Yes, it was real,' said Abbess Shimitsu. 'And we will struggle without the blessings it bestowed upon us.'

'Forgive me,' said Fate. 'I did not mean to doubt…' He stopped and frowned as something occurred to him.

'What is it?' asked the Tutor, but instead of answering, Fate turned to Abbess Shimitsu.

'Tell me,' he said. 'Which market town do you use for supplies?'

'Leeford, mostly,' said Abbess Shimitsu. 'Why?'

Fate nodded. 'And the road to Leeford takes you through the Cardini estate?'

'It does.'

'And does Nawashi ever go on these excursions?'

'Frequently,' replied Abbess Shimitsu. 'He's always on the lookout for new plants and seeds.' The abbess glanced at the Tutor, unsettled by this line of questioning.

Fate nodded as he turned to the Tutor. 'Nawashi seems nervous around you. Has he always been this way?'

'He's nervous by nature,' said the Tutor. 'But he was fine once we got to know each other.'

'And yet now he shies away and avoids your presence.'

'Yes... He *does* seem more uncomfortable than usual.'

Fate nodded as if things were beginning to make sense then he turned back to Abbess Shimitsu. 'I think we need another word with your young gardener?'

A few minutes passed before one of the monks ushered Nawashi into the chamber. He stood with his head bowed as Abbess Shimitsu tried to reassure him.

'Don't worry,' she said. 'Lord Fate just has a few more questions.'

'Yes, Hahoya,' mumbled Nawashi. He cast a sideways glance at the Tutor and his hand rose to the crude pendant around his neck as if he were seeking comfort from it, or trying to hide it.

Stepping back, Abbess Shimitsu invited Fate to come forward while the Tutor stood to one side.

'Abbess Shimitsu tells me you sometimes go to the market in Leeford,' said Fate and Nawashi gave a barely discernible nod.

'The growers help me,' he said. 'They give me special deals.'

'And has anyone ever offered *magical* help to improve the quality of the food you grow?'

The nervousness in Nawashi's gaze was suddenly replaced by a distinct shadow of guilt. 'No,' he said, but his gaze flicked towards Abbess Shimitsu.

'The truth, please, Nawashi,' said the abbess. 'The truth is always best.'

Nawashi's face flushed and he shifted awkwardly.

The abbess and the Tutor exchanged a look of concern as Fate changed the subject.

'Your pendant,' he said, taking a step towards Nawashi. 'Would you mind if I took a closer look?'

Instantly, Nawashi's hand closed around the crude wooden pendant and he took a step backwards, his expression suddenly hard, almost aggressive.

'Nawashi,' said Abbess Shimitsu gently. She had never seen the young man react like this before. 'May *I* please have a look at the pendant?'

If he had been uncomfortable before, now Nawashi positively squirmed. For a moment it seemed as if he might turn and flee, but Abbess Shimitsu's voice calmed him.

'It's all right,' she said. 'There is nothing to fear.'

The Tutor could feel the gentle touch of magic in her voice and slowly some of the tension went out of Nawashi's body.

'Did someone offer you a trade?' said Fate. 'One magical item for another?'

Still Nawashi hesitated, but then he let out the breath he had been holding.

'I didn't want to take the monastery's relic,' he said in a voice that was close to tears. 'But *he* said it was a useless ornament and he could give me something that would be far more useful.'

The abbess shot a look of concern towards the Tutor. 'Who, Nawashi? Who said these things?'

'The rich man in the forest,' mumbled Nawashi. 'The man in the big house.'

'You mean Lord Cardini?' said Abbess Shimitsu and Nawashi bobbed his head.

'He said I could bring it back if it didn't work.'

'Bring what back?' asked Abbess Shimitsu.

With great reluctance, Nawashi reached up to remove the wooden pendant from around his neck. His arm seemed to tremble with effort as he held it out towards the abbess and Fate arched an eyebrow in surprise as he laid the leather cord across her palm. Hardly had it touched her skin before the pendant began to change.

Abbess Shimitsu gasped, and the Tutor frowned as the simple wooden pendant transformed before their eyes. The dusty leather thong became a bold silver chain and the crude wooden disk became an ornate pendant of silver twisted around a smooth turquoise gem. The rare earthstone had a depth and a shimmer to it, but it also radiated a sense of malice and heat as if it offered a window into some dark infernal realm. Indeed, one could almost imagine a livid fire burning deep within its heart.

The abbess and the Tutor stared in amazement while Nawashi hung his head in shame. Everyone seemed lost for words until Abbess Shimitsu broke the silence.

'What is it?' she asked.

'It's an amplifier of intent,' said Fate. 'An enchanted item filled with a malignant spirit from the Daemonaria. In layman's terms, it would be known as a Talisman of Dreams.'

'But what does it do?' asked Abbess Shimitsu.

'The demon spirit makes the wearer more successful at whatever they are trying to achieve. In this case it improved the quality of Nawashi's food. But it did so at a cost.'

'The sickness,' said the Tutor and Fate nodded.

'They are clever,' he said. 'Cunning…' He spoke as if the talisman were a living thing. 'Nawashi's food has been tastier than ever, but even as the monks enjoyed the food, so the talisman absorbed a little of their life force.

Not enough to cause serious harm, just enough to give the impression of some mysterious illness.'

'What about Nawashi and Master Ganjin?' said Abbess Shimitsu. 'They also ate the food.'

'Master Ganjin lives in a permanent state of fast,' said Fate. 'And as for Nawashi, well... why affect the one who is using the talisman when there are others who can pay the price of using it?'

'So the monks became ill,' said the Tutor. 'But then they stopped eating the food and began to recover.'

'And as their appetite returned, so the cycle repeated itself,' said Fate. 'Over time they would have grown weaker and weaker until...'

'I'm sorry,' said Nawashi in a small and desolate voice.

'It is not your fault,' Fate told the young man. 'You were deceived. And few can resist the lure of such a talisman.'

Even as he spoke, his gaze shifted to Abbess Shimitsu who had not moved since taking the pendant from Nawashi.

'Perhaps you should put that down,' suggested Fate.

'Yes, you're right,' said the abbess but still she did not move.

'Abbess Shimitsu,' said the Tutor but the abbess did not appear to hear him.

'This could help us achieve so much,' she said, almost as if she were talking to herself. 'If we used it sparingly... Just think of the work we could do.'

'Nakita!' said the Tutor, the use of her first name finally cutting through the abbess's fascination with the talisman. Gently, the Tutor took the pendant from her and placed it quickly on the table. The tattoo on his chest shielded him from the allure of the pendant, but even he seemed unnerved by the demonic presence he sensed within it.

A veil of confusion seemed to lift from Abbess Shimitsu's eyes and she stared at the talisman in horror. 'Who would give such a thing to a child?' she asked, her eyes suddenly tearful as she looked at Nawashi.

'Someone who had learned the danger of using it,' said Fate.

'And someone who knew the monastery had something to replace it,' said the Tutor.

'Lord Cardini,' said Abbess Shimitsu. 'I remember him showing an interest in our relics when he visited last year. But I didn't know he was a magician.'

'An alchemist,' said Fate. 'A wealthy man trying to increase his wealth. A genuine good luck charm would increase the success rate of his experiments, and without the danger of using a Talisman of Dreams.'

For all her bronze coloured skin, Abbess Shimitsu's face was suddenly scarlet. The Tutor had never seen her so angry. 'I think we need to pay Lord Cardini a visit,' she said in an ominous tone.

'Yes,' said Fate. 'I think we do.'

'And you will come too, Nawashi.'

'Please, no,' Hahoya,' said Nawashi. 'I don't want to be near that thing. I do not have the strength to resist the promises it makes.'

Abbess Shimitsu frowned. She too had felt the compulsion to use the pendant for her own purposes.

'The boy is right,' said Fate. 'The talisman exerts a powerful force, and the quicker you return it, the better, but you cannot ask him to touch it again. The demon spirits bound to such items feed on our desires. The longer we resist, the stronger the temptation becomes. Lord Cardini was foolish to create such an item without putting in place the safeguards to limit the demon's power.'

'Then what should we do?' asked Abbess Shimitsu. 'For I will not expose my fellow monks to the lure of its temptation. In truth I do not even trust myself.'

'We shall return it as soon as possible,' said Fate. 'And in the meantime, I will watch over it.'

'Is that wise?' asked the Tutor. 'Surely the spirit in the talisman will try to tempt you?'

'Yes,' said Fate with a dark, unsettling smile. 'It will try.'

11
We Are Kane

The dining hall of Count Cévaro's mansion was illuminated by the low flames in the fireplace and the candles burning in each corner of the room. The centre of the room had been cleared and the servants had been given strict instructions to stay away. Tonight the entire building was free from watching eyes. Only one single serving woman remained in the house and she was now bound to an iron post standing upright in the centre of the room.

'How much longer?' asked Cévaro, as he stared at the terrified woman.

'I'm almost done,' said his personal mage, Lorden Sole.

The mage was kneeling on the floor, using a rod of silver graphite to complete the second of two arcane designs on the smooth flagstones. Completing the final circle he stood up to survey his work.

The young woman was tied to the metal post with her wrists chained to the floor so that her arms were extended out to her sides. Her mouth was bound with a silk gag and her eyes were wide with fear.

'Strange,' said Cévaro as he moved closer to look at the terrified woman. 'She's served in this house for five years and I never noticed this... peculiarity before.' He waved a finger at the woman's face.

'It is an unusual trait,' said Sole. 'It's an indication of latent magical power, which is why I chose her to open the portals.'

'One blue and one green,' said Cévaro, staring into the woman's eyes. 'And pretty too.' The woman flinched as he ran a finger down her cheek. 'Can't think why I haven't noticed her before.'

Not only were the woman's eyes two different colours but so too were her eyebrows and even the hair on her head. One side was a light honey blond, the other a deeper shade of red.

As his master studied the woman's face, Sole took two gemstones from a small lacquered box. One was a pale turquoise, the other an equally ethereal shade of blue. With great care he placed one stone in the centre of each design, directly beneath the fingers of the woman's outstretched hands.

'Are you sure this will work?' asked Cévaro.

'It should do, my Lord. I burned a sample of the woman's blood and sent the vapours through the ether so the Twins would have a trail to follow, and these stones are a perfect match for their eyes. That should be enough for the sorcerers to find us... if they can survive the torments of the Daemonaria.'

'Could you complete such a journey?'

Lorden Sole flushed and bowed his head. 'No, my Lord,' he said without raising his eyes. 'My powers are considered quite advanced for an estate mage, but I am not in the same league as the Kane twins.'

'Or Lord Fate?' added Cévaro with an unpleasant sneer.

'No, my Lord,' said Sole without raising his eyes.

Cévaro gave a contemptuous sniff and turned to look at a long-clock that stood opposite the fireplace. 'It's almost time... Are you ready to begin?'

'If you're sure we won't be disturbed.'

'We won't be disturbed,' said Cévaro. 'The servants have their instructions and the countess left for the Shīku monastery this morning.'

'You still allow her those religious visits?' asked Sole.

'I indulge her whims,' said Cévaro. 'She lends our estate an air of piety, and that can hide a multitude of sins. But come now… let us begin.'

Sole bowed his head and the bound woman gave a muffled cry as he drew a serpent bladed dagger from beneath his robes.

'Don't worry,' said Cévaro as he watched Sole approach the woman. 'We're not going to kill you.' The woman's eyes flicked from the count to the knife in Sole's hand. 'We just need a few drops of your blood.'

The woman cried out as Sole took hold of her left arm and made a small cut on the inside of her wrist before making a similar cut on her right arm. Standing back, he watched as a slow trickle of blood ran down her hands and dripped off her fingers.

The drops of blood spattered on the floor, falling around the blue and turquoise stones at the centre of the designs. Whenever a drop of blood hit a stone it was instantly absorbed and the stone flared as the magical designs on the floor began to glow. The process continued and the glowing designs began to pulse as if in time to the woman's heartbeat. Slowly the magical designs grew brighter until the air above them began to shimmer.

Count Cévaro watched in awe as portals to another dimension opened up before his eyes. Just a few paces away, Lorden Sole was beginning to wonder if he had done something wrong, but then the two stones flared brightly before bursting into clouds of shimmering dust. Rising up, the dust took on the form of ghostly figures as two robed figures appeared in the dimly lit room.

The ethereal spectres flanked the terrified woman, each standing in one of the arcane designs drawn upon the floor. Then the two figures reached out a hand to catch the blood still dripping from the woman's fingers. The scarlet fluid seeped into their veins and slowly their translucent bodies began to solidify until two robed sorcerers stood in the reception hall of Count Cévaro's mansion.

Lowering their hands, the two figures squeezed the last of the blood into their corporeal veins and stepped out of the arcane circles to examine their new surroundings.

Lorden Sole bowed at the waist as the Kane twins got their bearings, while Count Cévaro stared at the two men in horrified fascination. Tall and thin, the two sorcerers were almost entirely white. From their long white hair to their robes and boots, the two men looked as if they had been dusted with chalk. Even their skin was deathly pale, but it was marked by a host of scratches and cuts. Likewise, the sorcerers' robes were torn and discoloured with burns from their journey through the plane of the Daemonaria. Their lean faces were tense, jaws clenched as if from pain, and their breath came out in clouds of vapour that smelled of burnt stone and sulphur. But it was their eyes that held Count Cévaro entranced.

They were not normal eyes, more like orbs of opalescent stone. The eyes of one were a silvery turquoise, the other an ethereal shade of blue, almost exactly the same shades as the stones that Lorden Sole had placed within the circles. The gaze of the two sorcerers passed over Sole and came to rest on Cévaro who felt his scrotum contract with fear.

'Tilluvian,' said he of the turquoise eyes.

'Divorian,' said he of the blue.

'We are Kane,' they said together. 'We were told you have a job for us.'

'That's right,' said Cévaro, and for all his arrogance, he could not keep the nervousness out of his voice. 'There is someone I want you to kill.'

'Fate,' said Tilluvian.

'The man who slew the Demon of the Vale,' added Divorian.

'He is dangerous,' they said together.

'He was,' said Cévaro. 'But I am told on good authority that he no longer uses magic.'

'Lies,' pronounced Tilluvian.

'No one would surrender so much power.'

'But it's true,' said Cévaro. 'It was confirmed by Xanda Migrez, personal mage to Master Veleno of Guile.'

'Xanda Migrez,' said Divorian. 'This mage is known to us.'

'That's right,' said Cévaro. 'Xanda would not lie about such a thing. And he also told me about one of Fate's associates; a demon hunter with a tattoo that protects him from magical harm.'

'Demon hunters are under the protection of the emperor,' said Tilluvian.

'Not this one. This one is a deserter… a renegade.'

'A demon hunter tattoo is valuable,' said Divorian. 'But such a man is dangerous. We will take the tattoo, but we require additional payment for Fate.'

'I'm told you use *people* in your… work,' said Cévaro somewhat hesitantly. 'You could take one or two from the estate if you took them from remote communities like the miners or woodcutters.'

'No,' said Divorian.

'We have already chosen,' said Tilluvian and together they turned to face the woman tied to the post in the centre of the hall; the woman with different coloured eyes and different coloured hair.

'We will take her,' they said together.

'Just the one?' asked Cévaro.

'She is different.'

'She is unique.'

'The creatures of the demon realm hunger for such things.'

Cévaro shuddered. Even for one as ruthless as him, these pale sorcerers made his blood run cold. But what did he care what they did with this woman if it allowed him to avenge his brother's death?

'So be it,' he said at last.

'So be it,' said Divorian, and his brother continued.

'We will kill Fate, take the demon hunter, and use the woman in our dealings with the Daemonaria.'

'When?' said Cévaro. 'When will you kill Fate?'

'Soon,' said the twins. 'We will go soon.'

12
Finding Fate

It was midmorning in Guile and Sienna Blade was standing at the clerk's desk in the city's Hall of Records. Across the desk, an old man with a liver-spotted scalp was running his finger down a list of names in a large leather-bound book. The reception hall was largely empty except for a group of four guardsmen who looked bored and whispered to each other as they appraised the young woman standing at the desk.

Sienna ignored their lecherous attention as she waited for the clerk to complete his search of the city's most recent census. She was used to the looks, and the sniggers, and the crude comments that cowardly men muttered between themselves.

She remembered how such comments had bothered her when she first developed into womanhood. How she had blushed and bowed her head in embarrassment, angry with the men for making her feel so small, and even angrier with herself for allowing them to get away with it. She still found it irritating, but it bothered her less now that she could kill most of the men who behaved in such a way.

'Is it a girl or a boy,' she heard one of the guards say.

'Hard to say with that cloak'n'all.'

'If it's a boy, he needs a haircut.'

'An' if it's a girl she needs a good…'

'No,' announced the scribe from behind his desk. 'No record of a 'Fate' being resident in the city. Not common man or sorcerer.' He took the brass-rimmed spectacles from the bridge of his nose and laid a wavering hand on the desk. 'Of course, he could be here under another name, or never registered with the census. Many never do, you know. Ne'er-do-wells and slum dwellers. I'm sure this record covers barely half the population of the city. Of course we *could* look under...'

'That's fine,' said Sienna, cutting him off. 'No need to look any further.' Turning away from the desk she headed towards the exit.

The chances of Fate registering with an official census were highly unlikely, but her enquiries in the seedier parts of the city had drawn a blank. She was not disheartened. Even in a city as large as Guile, a man like Fate should not be too hard to find. Ruthless men like that tended to leave a trail, even if the trail was little more than gossip and rumour.

Moving through the large double doors she emerged from the Hall of Records and started towards the steps that led back down into the city streets.

'Leaving so soon?' said a voice behind her and looking back she saw that the four guards had followed her out of the building. 'Surely you're not going to leave without showing us what's under that cloak.'

Sienna's eyes darkened, but these were men of the city guard and killing them in broad daylight would not be a good idea. With an irritated sigh she turned away.

'Not so fast,' said one of the guards.

Reaching over, he grabbed her cloak then cried out as Sienna caught his hand and twisted his wrist in a way that forced him down to one knee. Two of the others rushed forward, but Sienna kicked one in the groin and spun round, cloak whirling, until the point of her sword came to rest at the second man's throat. And she still hadn't let go of the man on one knee who groaned at the intense pain that was shooting up his arm.

The fourth guard was just staring at Sienna in shock. Almost in a daze, he reached for his sword, but Sienna arched an eyebrow and his hand stalled.

'What's going on here?'

Sienna looked round to see three more soldiers striding towards her. Two were normal guardsmen, while the armour of the third man bore the marks of an officer: a gold lion's head embossed on his chest, and three studs on the collar of his leather hauberk. A captain.

'Well,' said the captain in the confident tone of authority. 'Is someone going to tell me what's going on here?'

Lowering her sword, Sienna let go of the guard's wrist and the man cradled his arm as he got to his feet.

'Captain Monetti, Sir,' said one of the guards. 'This woman was causing a disturbance. We were just trying to apprehend her when she attacked us.'

The captain seemed less than convinced as he turned to look at Sienna. Her cloak now hung open and they could all see the fine scale mail shirt she wore underneath. Straightening up, she sheathed her sword and from that gesture alone the captain could tell that she knew how to use it.

'So is that what happened?' he asked. 'Did you cause a disturbance?'

'Only in their pants,' said Sienna and Captain Monetti raised his eyebrows in surprise. 'I was just leaving the Hall of Records when these knob whackers tried to grab me.'

The captain's surprise rose to new heights, but his eyes twinkled with amusement.

'Knob whackers,' he said, as if testing out the words for himself. 'Can't say I've heard that term before, but I take your point.'

Turning away from Sienna he cast a stern eye over the four guards involved in the altercation. At twenty-eight, he was young for an officer. Reasonably tall, with broad shoulders and a medium build, he had the look of a fighting man. His hair and eyes were dark and his rugged face was pleasantly symmetrical but for a scar that ran down across his lips to the bottom of his jaw. He was not smiling, but Sienna could see the glint of a gold tooth when he talked.

'So,' he began in a no nonsense tone. 'Are you going to stick to this story of a disturbance, in which case I want a full written report? Or are you knob whackers going to apologise to this woman and volunteer for latrine duty at the barracks for the next three days?'

The men's shoulders slumped and they lowered their eyes, but one by one they muttered a few grudging words of contrition.

With a jerk of his head, Captain Monetti sent the men on their way before turning to Sienna. 'Please allow me to apologise on behalf of my men,' he said with a gracious bow.

If anything, this courteous response made Sienna more uncomfortable than the guards' lechery, but she dipped her head in acknowledgement.

'So what brought you to the Hall of Records,' the captain went on. 'Is there anything I can do to help?'

'I was looking for someone,' said Sienna. 'But it doesn't matter. There's no record of him in the census.'

'That's hardly surprising, but what's their name? The city guard covers all parts of the city. We might have heard of the person you're looking for.'

Sienna looked at him suspiciously. 'His name's Fate,' she said somewhat warily. 'Decimus Fate.'

'I'm not familiar with the name,' said Captain Monetti, raising a gloved hand to his chin. 'Is he a military man?'

'A sorcerer,' said Sienna.

The captain shrugged his shoulders as if this meant little to him then turned as one of his men stepped forward to speak with him.

'Marcus tells me he heard of a man called Fate a few days ago.' The captain turned back to the guard as if he had just remembered something. 'That business on the bridge?' he said. 'With Veleno and the ferrymen?'

The man called Marcus gave a nod. 'He was with two monks and a black mercenary that bides at the Fool's Hope.'

Captain Monetti pursed his lips as if this news were of some mild interest.

'There you have it,' he said, turning back to Sienna. 'Apparently this *Fate* has fallen out of favour with one of the more dangerous criminals of the city. If you're a friend of his, you might want to be careful.'

Sienna was careful to control her reaction. She did not want to betray her true intentions.

'The Fool's Hope…?' she said.

'It's an inn near the Norward Locks. There's a hired sword that stays there. A Southern Isles man. Goes by the name of The Tutor, I believe.'

Sienna looked at the captain as if she could not believe her good fortune.

'Would there be anything else?' he asked and Sienna found herself blushing.

She had been staring at the man, and now she came to think of it, Captain Monetti of the city guard was actually quite good looking.

'No,' she said, lowering her eyes. 'Nothing else. Thank you, captain.' With that she drew her cloak across her chest and turned to leave.

'Just be careful what you do with that sword,' the captain called out as she walked away. 'I'd hate for us to meet under more unpleasant circumstances.'

Captain Monetti knew enough about fighting to know a skilled swordsman, or a skilled swordswoman, when he saw one. His eyes narrowed in thought as Sienna walked away.

Sienna did not look back as she made her way down the steps and back into the streets of the city.

Fate was travelling in the company of a dark-skinned mercenary who stays at the Fool's Hope Inn, a man known as the Tutor.

Sienna smiled to herself. Not a bad start for being in the city barely a day. Not a bad start at all.

13
The Countess

Having found the source of the mystery illness, Abbess Shimitsu was eager to confront Lord Cardini and demand the return of the monastery's relic. It had been only a day since Fate had taken charge of the Talisman of Dreams, but already the monks were beginning to show signs of recovery, with the exception of Sister Myuko who showed no sign of emerging from her coma.

'Her life is in the balance,' said Sister Hīra as she and Abbess Shimitsu shared an evening meal with Fate and the Tutor. 'We can only hope that providence shines on her.'

'An icon of good fortune would certainly help,' said the Tutor.

'Yes, it would,' said Abbess Shimitsu. 'We will leave for the Cardini estate in the morning.'

'In the morning?' said Sister Hīra. 'Are you forgetting that Countess Cévaro is due to visit us tomorrow?'

Abbess Shimitsu's face creased with frustration. 'Yes,' she said. 'I *had* forgotten, but it cannot be helped. I will not put off a meeting with the alchemist. Besides, there is always the chance that we might meet the countess on the road.'

'I hope not,' muttered the Tutor and Abbess Shimitsu gave him a disapproving look.

'The countess has been a good friend to this monastery,' she said. 'Many people are helped by the donations she makes.'

The Tutor gave a dismissive snort. 'It'll take more than a purse of silver to make up for the sins of *her* estate.'

'It is her *husband's* estate,' said the abbess. 'And does the Inja not teach us that we should not be too quick to judge?'

The Tutor gave a sigh, but then he bowed his head in concession. Abbess Shimitsu's expression softened as she bade them goodnight and the Tutor turned to Fate. 'I assume you're familiar with Count Leopold Cévaro.'

'I knew his brother,' said Fate and the Tutor felt a familiar chill run down his back. Count Cévaro's brother was dead.

The following morning they set out for the home of Lord Cardini, the alchemist who Nawashi referred to as the rich man in the forest. Reaching the base of the escarpment, they continued along the forest road and the Tutor gave Fate a knowing look as Veleno's men began to follow them once more.

They headed south towards the market town of Leeford and, as luck would have it, they *did* meet Countess Cévaro on the road. Riding with one maid and an escort of five armed guards, the countess smiled as she urged her horse forward before dismounting to greet Abbess Shimitsu. The Tutor watched as the two women embraced like old friends. With her long brown hair, full mouth and prominent cheekbones, the countess was a striking woman, although it was often said that she lacked the beguiling beauty of her sister.

'She's certainly well protected,' said Fate as the countess's guards looked on with hostile eyes.

'Cévaro is a jealous man,' said the Tutor. 'He guards his property well.'

'You've had dealings with the Cévaro estate?'

'Only once,' said the Tutor. 'I was hired to protect a forest community that was being pressured to leave their homes. After giving Cévaro's thugs a beating, I told them that I would only discuss the matter with the count himself.'

'And did Cévaro agree to your terms?'

'No. The brave count sent his wife to do his dirty work. She seemed perfectly pleasant, but she insisted on speaking to the elders in private.' The Tutor's eyes darkened as he remembered the scene. 'When they emerged from the meeting, the elders were white with fear. They gathered up their people and fled the village the following day.'

Fate glanced at the Tutor as Abbess Shimitsu and the countess moved towards them.

'I will arrange another visit soon,' said the countess, her rich voice echoing slightly beneath the trees.

'Yes,' said Abbess Shimitsu as the two women mounted their horses. 'And next time, I will be there to greet you.'

As they moved closer, Abbess Shimitsu looked at the Tutor and the expression in her eyes could not have been clearer, '*behave!*'

'I remember you,' said the countess as she recognised the distinctive figure of the Tutor. 'You tried to help the people on the garnet river.'

'And I remember you,' said the Tutor. 'You succeeded where your husband failed.'

'I only tried to prevent…' began the countess, but the Tutor cut her off.

'Your husband tried to intimidate the people with clubs and swords,' the Tutor's voice was filled with contempt. 'You drove them out with a smile.'

The countess's face flushed with indignation, but then her expression hardened.

'And I remember that you were a demon hunter,' she said, her dark eyes burning with a touch of fire. 'I will not be lectured by a man who would murder innocents for imaginary crimes.'

The Tutor looked genuinely stung and for a moment it seemed as if the countess might take back her words, but then she raised her chin and urged her horse forward.

'Inja be with you, sister,' she said, speaking to Abbess Shimitsu.

'And with you,' said Abbess Shimitsu. Her face was filled with genuine warmth but as the countess and her bodyguard moved on, she turned to the Tutor and her smile took on a note of sadness. 'Do not take her words to heart,' she told him. 'Creatures in pain will often lash out when threatened.'

The Tutor heard her words, but they did little to drown out the screams that echoed in his mind. The words of the countess had opened a door to the past, a door that he would rather have kept closed. With an effort of will he closed door and the screaming was replaced by silence, but the silence offered little in the way of peace.

14
Of Golems and Gold Handprints

The encounter with the countess left the Tutor feeling unsettled and his dreams were filled with images of the past as they camped for the night in the forest. By morning, he was still distracted and it took some effort to bring his mind back to the task in hand. They were on their way to confront Lord Cardini, an alchemist who had endangered the lives of innocent people for the sake of his own wealth and power; a man who had ensnared a demon spirit and bound it in the form of a silver pendant.

Still riding beside Fate, the Tutor glanced across at the leather satchel tied behind the sorcerer's saddle. In it was a lead box about the size of a thick book. Fate had suggested using such a box when the seductive aura of the pendant began to leak out from the Chamber of Echoes.

'The longer the pendant is ignored, the stronger the temptation to use it will become,' Fate had told them. 'The dense metal of the box will help to contain its effects.'

Abbess Shimitsu had provided a small lead box used to hold the ink and pens of a Shīku calligraphy set. She and the Tutor remained outside the chamber until Fate had closed the lid and secured the hasp with a bamboo peg.

'Will that make it safe?' asked the Tutor.

'Contact with human flesh is the best way to conceal the demon spirit's presence,' said Fate. 'But the box should contain it for now.'

'I certainly can't sense its presence anymore,' said Abbess Shimitsu as they looked down at the metal box. 'I don't know how to thank you.'

'Don't thank me yet,' said Fate. 'I can't imagine that Lord Cardini will be pleased to see the talisman and he might refuse to return the monastery's relic.'

'That would not be wise,' said the Tutor, but Abbess Shimitsu put a hand on his arm.

'We shall help Lord Cardini see the error of his ways,' she said in a placating tone. 'I'm sure he will see reason once we explain the harm his actions have done.'

Abbess Shimitsu seemed convinced, but Fate and the Tutor exchanged a knowing look. They both knew too many men like Lord Cardini to share her optimism.

Raising his eyes from the leather satchel, the Tutor stole a sideways glance at Fate. The sorcerer had not asked for payment and the Tutor could not help thinking that Fate would find some way of turning things to his advantage.

'You still don't trust me,' said Fate with the hint of a smile.

'No, I don't,' said the Tutor. 'Should I?'

'Probably not,' said Fate, and the Tutor was unnerved by the conviction in his voice.

They rode on in silence until they heard the whinny of a horse from some distance behind them. Veleno's men had been following them since they came down from the plateau.

Turning in the saddle, the Tutor could see the three men on horseback. 'They're not even trying to hide it anymore.'

'Well, not since Abbess Shimitsu invited them to join us for an evening meal,' said Fate.

The Tutor gave a despairing shake of his head as he turned back to the road. 'So how do you know Cardini?' he asked.

'People who use magic tend to know of others who practice the Arts.'

'And I suppose you know more than most.'

Fate gave a modest tilt of the head. 'Yes,' he said. 'I probably do, although I have only met Cardini once.'

'Is he powerful?'

'He's a talented alchemist, from what I've heard,' said Fate. 'But only a mage of very poor judgement would create an object like the talisman, never mind passing it on to an innocent community.' He stopped as he saw the Tutor looking at him. 'What?'

'Nothing,' said the Tutor. 'I'm just surprised that Decimus Fate would balk at using a few nameless monks.'

Fate's eyes narrowed. 'I despise those who prey upon the weak. They have no self respect. Far more satisfying to take down the arrogant and powerful.'

'And was that your speciality?'

'I took on contracts that furthered my own ends,' said Fate. 'If that meant dealing with someone powerful, then so be it.'

'And now?' said the Tutor. 'It must be quite demeaning for a man of such ability to take on the problems of common folk.'

'Not at all,' said Fate. 'There are many good people who need help with problems of a magical nature.'

'You sound like a man who's trying to make up for the wrongs he has done.'

'I can never make up for the things I have done,' said Fate, and the Tutor almost felt as if he should apologise. However, before he could speak, Master Ando called out.

'We're here.'

Looking up, the Tutor saw a large pair of wrought iron gates opening onto a driveway that led away into the forest. They followed the driveway for about half a mile to a large mansion house built from pale grey stone. The central block of the house was topped with crenulated walls, while the pitched roofs to either side were faced with dark timber and whitewashed daub. It was a substantial building, but the Tutor gave a grunt of contempt.

'You're not impressed,' said Fate as they dismounted in the open space before the house.

'The plaster work's crumbling, the ivy's getting into the masonry, and those battlements are fake.'

Fate seemed amused by the Tutor's indignation, while Abbess Shimitsu wore an expression of fierce determination. With Master Ando at her side, she made directly for the main door which was flanked by two stone phoenix set on plinths carved to look like flames.

'Wait!' said the Tutor as he felt a prickle of energy from the tattoo on his chest.

Master Ando and the abbess paused as the Tutor moved forward to examine the statues.

'They're definitely imbued with protection magic,' said the Tutor. 'But I think it's safe to approach the door.'

'You *think* it's safe!' said Master Ando. His expression suggested that he would have preferred a little more certainty, but still he stepped forward and reached for a large door knocker that was formed in the likeness of a pestle and mortar.

Standing beside his horse, Fate removed the leather satchel containing the lead box. He slipped the strap over his shoulder and turned to the house as Master Ando's knocks reverberated through the mansion's internal halls.

A good few seconds passed before the door opened to reveal a tall and slender manservant. In his black silk breeches and green velvet doublet, the man was handsomely dressed, but his skin was pale and his black hair was combed flat against his narrow scalp.

Abbess Shimitsu began to speak, but the manservant cut her off.

'Lord Cardini offers his apologies, but he will not be entertaining visitors today.'

Abbess Shimitsu raised her chin and took a breath.

'We are not *visitors*,' she said in a measured tone. 'Please tell your master that Abbess Shimitsu of the Tan Jit Su Monastery is here on a matter of some importance.'

'I'm afraid Lord Cardini is working,' said the manservant. 'He is not to be disturbed.'

'And when will he be finished? For we are quite prepared to wait.'

'Why, it might be several days. Lord Cardini's work demands prolonged spells of concentration.'

The Tutor tensed as he saw the anger rising in Abbess Shimitsu. However, before she could say anything more, Fate stepped forward.

'Please tell Lord Cardini that a fellow magician would like to speak with him,' he said.

'Apologies, sir. But my lord simply does not have the time.'

'He will find the time for me.'

'Oh?' said the man with a patronising little laugh. 'And which magician shall I say is calling?'

'Decimus Fate.' said Fate, and it was clear from the manservant's stricken face that he knew the name. 'I would be grateful if your master could spare a few minutes to speak with me.'

For a moment the manservant said nothing as he wrestled with indecision.

'Shall I take it that he refuses to see me?' asked Fate and the manservant's eyes shifted nervously.

'No, my Lord,' he said at last. 'I'm quite sure the master could find the time to speak to the great Decimus Fate.' He attempted a smile and failed. 'P... please,' he continued, as he opened the door to let them in.

The door gave onto a large reception hall with a number of smaller doors and archways leading off to different parts of the house. The room might once have been impressive, but the air was filled with the musty smell of mildew and the panelled walls were devoid of any decoration. The only thing of note was the statue of an armoured warrior, standing like a sentinel beside a heavy oak door. The statue was fashioned from some kind of dark metal, and the Tutor watched as Fate walked towards it. The sorcerer was just reaching out to touch the door beside the statue when the manservant's shrill voice stopped him.

'Might I enquire as to the reason for your visit,' he said in an anxious tone.

'I'm afraid I can only discuss that with Lord Cardini himself,' said Abbess Shimitsu.

The manservant insisted on more clarification, and as they debated the matter the Tutor moved to stand with Fate.

'You know what that is?' murmured Fate.

'I'd say it was an eight-foot statue cast in pewter,' replied the Tutor. 'But I'm guessing you think it's something more.'

'Look at the breastplate and the brow of the helm,' said Fate and sure enough, the Tutor could just make out the faint engraving of magical script.

'A security golem?' said the Tutor and Fate nodded. 'Expensive and dangerous,' the Tutor continued. 'You'd need magical weapons to damage a golem like that.'

116

'Or the Hadean Blade of a demon hunter,' said Fate, and the Tutor gave a grunt of annoyance.

'Well this is not a Hadean blade,' he hissed, placing his hand on the hilt of his sword. 'So just make sure you don't activate that thing!'

'But you *could* defeat such an opponent... if you had your demon hunter's blade?'

Despite his annoyance, the Tutor looked again at the large metal figure. The statue's head was angled down and the eye slits in the visor of its helm were dark and empty. Its gauntleted hands were holding the handle of an upright sword. Standing almost eight feet tall, it was an imposing figure and the Tutor could imagine how terrifying it would be if it ever came to life.

'Well? Could you defeat it?' insisted Fate, but the Tutor just turned away as if he was above answering such hypothetical questions. 'I thought so,' said Fate with a self-satisfied smile.

Across the hall, Cardini's manservant had finally conceded that he had no option but to summon his master without knowing the reason why.

'If you would care to wait in the drawing room, I will inform the master of your arrival.'

'Thank you,' said Abbess Shimitsu as the man ushered them into an adjacent room that had also seen better days. The upholstered furniture was faded and the dusty tables and sideboards were positively bare. There were none of the gaudy ornaments or decorative objects that one would normally expect to see.

'So much for the rich man in the forest,' said the Tutor and Fate also seemed surprised by the shabbiness of the house.

Wearing his customary frown of thought, Fate gazed around the room as if he were trying to make sense of

117

something. Suddenly he walked to one side of the room where a pewter tankard sat on a semicircular table.

The Tutor ambled over as Fate bent down to examine the heavy tankard.

'What is it?' he asked.

'A handprint,' said Fate, indicating the impression of a hand gripping the tankard's handle. In contrast to the rest of the dull metal, the handprint shone with the lustre of gold. However, before they could look any closer, the door opened and a tall man with red hair and a manicured beard entered the room. The buttons on his crimson doublet were clearly made from gold, as were the buckles on his polished shoes. His black velvet breeches spoke of quality, while his handsome brow shimmered with a sheen of nervous sweat.

With an air of panic the man swept his gaze around the room until his eyes came to rest on the tall figure in the charcoal grey robes.

'Lord Fate!' said Cardini, his voice breaking with barely suppressed fear.

'He thinks you're here to kill him,' muttered the Tutor.

'He might be right,' replied Fate as Lord Cardini crossed the room to greet him.

'What an unexpected pleasure.' Lord Cardini extended his hand, but the expression in Fate's eyes made him think better of it. With a nervous laugh he clasped his hands together, and as he did so, the Tutor noticed that the tips of the fingers on his right hand were missing. Yes... the ends of his fingers were clearly gone and the scar tissue that remained had a definite glint of gold.

Still clasping his hands, Lord Cardini swept a glance over Abbess Shimitsu and Master Ando, and flinched at the expression in the Tutor's hard blue eyes. 'Now,' he said. 'What can I do for the illustrious Decimus Fate?'

Fate did not answer at first. He simply held Cardini in his dark gaze. And smiled.

*

Back on the driveway of the Cardini estate, three of Master Veleno's men considered their options as they stared at the dilapidated mansion and the four horses tied up outside.

'We should go and find out what's going on,' said one of the men.

'We can't go bursting in on Cardini,' said one of his companions. 'Not now he's working for Veleno.'

'But Fate might be trying to screw up the boss's deal,' said the third man.

'Or he might be making a deal for himself.'

'Maybe we should go in and drag the sorcerer out. The boss said he wouldn't kill him till the next full moon, but we could still rough him up a bit.'

'Are you mad! Even Xanda's afraid of that grey robed bastard.'

'But the boss said he no longer uses magic.'

'Yeah, right... Well after you then... You go and get your ass fried or turned into a slug. I'll find you a nice piece of lettuce when you come crawling out.'

'And that dark-skinned devil is dangerous,' said the other man. 'They say he was a demon hunter. And you heard what he did to those ferryman lads.'

'Well we can't just sit here twiddlin' our thumbs.'

'Let's just wait till they come out.'

'And if they mess up Veleno's gold supply?'

'He'll kill'em for sure.'

'We should let him know that the sorcerer's here.'

'Yeah, we should.'

'I'll go.'

'No way, tosser. I'm the fastest. I'll go.'

'Well, all right, but be quick. I'm sick of sleeping out here in the forest.'

'And tell Veleno that if he wants them dead, we'll need more men. Lots of 'em.'

And with that, one of the men set off on the road to Guile.

15
Contrato Indissolibus

Lord Cardini feigned sympathy as Abbess Shimitsu described how the alchemist's talisman had made the monks sick. She also explained that they needed the relic of fortune in order for them to survive on the edge of the great desert.

'And besides,' she concluded, 'the relic was not Nawashi's to trade in the first place.'

But Lord Cardini was standing his ground.

'I am sorry,' he said for what must have been the fourth time. 'Under normal circumstances I would be happy to negate the bargain and return the monastery's relic. However… this particular bargain was bound by magical rules. It can only be undone if both parties are 'happy' to return the items. I'm afraid the relic is now an essential part of my work. I could agree to return it, but I would not be happy, and so the contract cannot be annulled.'

Abbess Shimitsu just stared at the alchemist, but the Tutor had heard enough. There were other ways to make this pompous magician see sense. Flexing his fists he started forward, but he had barely taken a step when Fate spoke up.

'Do you mind if I ask the nature of the contract that was made?' he asked.

'Contrato Indissolibus,' said Cardini, giving the Tutor a wary glance.

The corners of Fate's mouth turned down and he nodded in understanding. Adjusting the leather satchel that hung from his shoulder, he began to undo the buckles.

'Lord Cardini is quite right,' he said. 'Such a contract can only be annulled if both parties are happy to do so.' Opening the satchel he brought out the lead calligraphy box and placed it on a table in the centre of the room.

Lord Cardini's eyes widened in shock as realisation dawned.

'You brought it with you!?'

Fate shrugged.

'We were under the impression that this matter could be resolved with a simple exchange,' said Fate. 'But a contrato indissolibus is binding. I'm afraid we brought the talisman for nothing.'

'This is nonsense!' said the Tutor. 'There must be a way to force him to cancel the agreement.'

Abbess Shimitsu and Master Ando clearly agreed but Fate sighed.

'I'm afraid not,' he said. 'Not unless you are willing to kill Lord Cardini,' he added with a little laugh. 'But I think such extreme measures are beyond the peace-loving monks of Tan Jit Su. Are they not?'

He looked at Abbess Shimitsu whose eyes were shining with anger.

'Indeed they are,' she said as Fate picked up the lead box and placed it back in the satchel.

'I think the best thing to do is to take this back to the monastery and keep it safe.'

121

Crossing the floor, he handed the satchel to Master Ando.

'Is that really all you can do?' asked Abbess Shimitsu.

'I am sorry,' said Fate. 'Magical contracts are not easily broken.'

'Then we have made this trip for nothing.'

'It would appear so,' said Fate and Lord Cardini let out an audible breath of relief.

'We'll see about that!' said the Tutor and once again he started forward.

'No!' said Abbess Shimitsu. 'The Talisman of Dreams has caused enough harm as it is. I will not allow it to be the cause of violence.'

The Tutor was clearly furious, but Abbess Shimitsu raised a placating hand as she turned to face Lord Cardini.

'Thank you for taking the time to see us, but we will not give up on the relic,' she said. 'We shall return each month to see if we can change your mind.'

'I'm afraid there is little chance of that,' said Lord Cardini in the voice of one who had clearly been let off the hook.

'Even so,' said Abbess Shimitsu. 'We shall return in one month's time.'

'As you wish,' said Cardini, although it was clear that without the presence of Decimus Fate, they would never get past the front door.

'Farewell, Lord Cardini,' said Abbess Shimitsu.

'Farewell, Revered Mother.'

With that, Abbess Shimitsu gave Master Ando a nod and together they started for the door.

'Alexander,' said Abbess Shimitsu when the Tutor made no move to follow them.

The Tutor was clearly furious, but he had no choice but to accept that there was nothing else to be done, for now. With a final look in Cardini's direction, he turned to Fate.

'Are you coming?'

'I thought I might stay a while, if that is all right with Lord Cardini.' Fate turned to look at the alchemist. 'The quality of his work is widely admired and I would be very interested to learn more.'

Lord Cardini looked suddenly conflicted. He found Fate's presence deeply unsettling, but he was also flattered by the sorcerer's praise. 'But of course,' he found himself saying.

'Then that's settled,' said Fate turning back to Abbess Shimitsu and the Tutor. 'I am sorry that things could not be fully resolved, but at least your fellow monks should recover in time.'

'You'd do that,' said the Tutor. 'You'd exchange magical tips with this man, after what he did to the monks?'

'No one died,' said Fate and Cardini smiled as if he could not have said it better himself.

The Tutor shook his head in disgust. 'I knew it,' he said. 'You find yourself in need of gold and then you cosy up to someone who has the skills to produce gold.' He shook his head. 'I knew you'd find some way to turn this to your advantage.'

'I don't know *what* you mean,' said Fate.

'Of course you don't,' said the Tutor, and with a final glare he turned away from the two magic users and followed Abbess Shimitsu and Master Ando out of the room.

Fate looked mildly amused, while Lord Cardini appeared surprised that the great Decimus Fate would be so interested in his work.

Out in the reception hall, Lord Cardini's manservant escorted the monks and the Tutor out of the house. There was a dismissive 'boom' as he closed the front door behind them.

'I knew he'd betray us,' said the Tutor as they approached the horses.

Abbess Shimitsu was too angry and upset to reply. Instead she turned to Master Ando who was now strapping the satchel containing the lead box to the back of his own saddle.

'When we get back to the monastery I want you to dig a deep hole and bury that thing,' she said. 'We will dig it up in a month's time when we return.'

Mounting their horses they started back along the driveway, but as they drew close to the road they found two of Veleno's men blocking the path and the Tutor's dark mood grew a shade darker.

'What are you doing here?' asked one of the men. 'What do you want with Lord Cardini?'

'That's no business of yours,' said the Tutor. 'Now get out of the way before I do something you'll regret.'

The two men looked suitably intimidated, but still they held their ground.

'We can't let you pass until you tell us what you're doing here,' insisted the man.

'Where's the sorcerer?' asked the second man. 'Where's the one called Fate?'

The Tutor frowned but before he could answer, the second man continued.

'If he's done something to the alchemist, there'll be hell to pay.'

'How do you know Cardini's an alchemist?' said the Tutor.

'We all know,' said the first man. 'He's making gold for the boss.'

The Tutor gave a sigh. So this was where Veleno was getting his gold. Things had suddenly become a good deal more complicated.

'I'm warning you... if Fate's done something to Cardini.'

'Relax,' said the Tutor. 'Cardini's fine. Fate's with him now. They're talking 'magic' like the best of friends.'

'I told you!' snapped the first man. 'That grey robed bastard is gonna make a deal of his own.'

'Veleno'll kill him for sure.'

'Let him,' said the Tutor.

'Aye,' said the man. 'But he'll kill you too.'

The Tutor gave another heavy sigh. Just a few days ago he was living a quiet life as a hired sword. Now he was caught up in a tangled web of power and greed.

'We'll be seeing you, demon hunter,' said one of the men as they moved off along the main road through the forest.

'Yes,' said the other. 'We'll be keeping an eye on you.'

The two men disappeared around a bend in the road, but the Tutor knew they would not have gone far.

'You must come back to the monastery with us,' said Abbess Shimitsu. 'Guile is too dangerous for you just now.'

'No,' said the Tutor. 'I will not hide away, and I will not bring more trouble to your door.'

Abbess Shimitsu gave him a sad smile that was filled with warmth. 'So once again we say goodbye.'

The Tutor returned her smile as he looked into her deep brown eyes.

'Here,' said the abbess, twisting in the saddle. 'Take the horses back to Madam Carletta. Master Ando and I can walk from here.' However, before she could even dismount there came the sound of a horse approaching from the direction of Cardini's house.

It was Fate.

16
The Snare of Temptation

Fate had kept his feelings hidden as he watched the monks and the Tutor leave the room. He got no pleasure from deceiving them, but he did not want them tarnished by what he was about to do. Staring at the door, he shook his head and gave a patronising little laugh.

'Ordinary people have no idea of the commitment that real magic requires. Don't you agree?' He turned to Lord Cardini who seemed to be in a state of some confusion.

'I do,' he said at last. 'Indeed I do.'

'So tell me,' said Fate. 'The last time we met, you had some interesting ideas on how to overcome Larondo's Uncertainty Principal with regard to transmutation. Have you made any progress in this respect?'

'Yes I have,' said Cardini. He was clearly pleased that Fate remembered a lecture he had given several years ago. He was also wary of sharing his secrets. Indecision played across his face and then the words came out in a rush.

'The uncertainty principle cannot be overcome, but I have found a way to limit its effects.' He smiled as his own cleverness. 'I have designed a device that amplifies the alchemical resonance, a magical flux to prime the base material, and an incantation to initiate the chrysopoeian cascade.'

Fate raised his eyebrows as if he were impressed. Fighting hard to conceal his true intentions, he adopted an expression of wonder.

'The incantation and the flux are clever,' he said. 'But a device to amplify the resonance... that is surely a work of genius.'

Lord Cardini positively swelled with pride.

'I would be very interested to see such a device.'

Lord Cardini's expression became guarded, but he could not resist the urge to share his accomplishments. 'I've heard that Decimus Fate is a man of his word,' he began. 'I would be willing to show you... if you promise to keep my innovations a secret.'

'But of course.'

Still Cardini seemed uncertain then... 'Follow me,' he said, and with that he led Fate back into the reception hall where his manservant was hovering beside the door. 'You're dismissed,' said Cardini. 'I am taking Lord Fate below, and we are *not* to be disturbed.'

'Yes, my Lord,' said the manservant as he disappeared down a passageway leading off from the hall.

Lord Cardini now walked up to the heavy oak door beside which stood the large metal statue of an armoured warrior. Producing a key from a pocket, he unlocked the door. However, as he went to open it Fate heard an ominous grating of metal and the slits in the statue's helmet glowed as its head turned towards them.

This small motion was distinctly intimidating, but the light faded from the statue's eyes as Cardini reached out to place his hand on the pommel of the massive sword. Deactivating one security measure, he now opened the door to reveal a wall of glazed green tiles set in a radiating pattern that created the illusion of looking down a tunnel.

'A phase door,' said Fate and Lord Cardini gave a conceited smile as he stood before the magical door. 'That must have cost you a tidy sum.'

'The better part of my estate,' said Lord Cardini. 'But it's worth it, to keep my work secure.'

With that he closed his eyes and took a moment to compose himself before reaching out to touch a number of bricks in the door. The complex sequence of bricks was impossible to follow, unless one had the carefully trained mind of a man like Decimus Fate. The sequence was completed in just a few seconds and yet Fate was fairly confident that he had it fixed in his mind.

'That is a bewildering entrance code,' he remarked. 'What if you were to make a mistake?'

'Incineration,' said the alchemist as the pattern of tiles fell away to form the walls of a descending passage.

'And where is the workshop, actually?' asked Fate as they walked down the sloping passage.

'Now that *would* be telling,' said the alchemist with a smug smile.

Fate had to admit that he was impressed. You could break through a phase door with a sledgehammer, but that would not lead you to the alchemist's workshop. The workshop itself could be miles away. Only by picking out the right sequence of tiles would the phase door lead to the 'correct' location.

Reaching the end of the passage, they came to a wooden door that opened with a simple latch. The very fact that it was not locked was evidence of the confidence Cardini had in his security measures.

Before entering, the alchemist paused for a moment as if savouring the moment, then he pushed the door open and Fate raised an eyebrow in surprise. Constructed from pale stone, the room was surprisingly large with a high vaulted ceiling. The room was lit by phosphorescent lamps and filled with alchemical paraphernalia. There were numerous designs of mortar and pestle, weighing scales and crucibles along with jars and pots filled with all manner of exotic substances. There were racks of glass tubes, intricate arrangements of lenses and mirrors, and entire frameworks of interconnected pipes and flasks. However, it was the device at the centre of the room that captured Fate's attention.

Constructed from brass and silver, the device consisted of a series of interwoven hoops with various crystals set into the metal at very specific locations. At the top of the device a glowing sphere filled the room with a shimmering light that pulsed like a heartbeat.

Sitting at the very centre of the device, was a disk of solid gold; what alchemists referred to as a progenitor. However, unlike all the similar devices that Fate had seen, this disk was not in contact with any other part of the structure. It was hovering between a series of intricate coils that thrummed with magical force.

The whole thing was covered in obscure writing and Lord Cardini watched as Fate moved closer to examine the magical script.

'I adapted the spells,' he admitted. 'But the isolation coils are all my own.'

'Isolating the sample means that you would need to touch it.'

'Yes,' agreed Cardini. 'But it also amplifies the effect.'

'Impressive,' said Fate as he turned his attention to the rest of the room. He surveyed the crowded work surfaces until he spotted a gold pendant engraved with Shīku script.

'I assume this is the pendant that Abbess Shimitsu was hoping to retrieve.'

'Yes,' said Cardini with a sigh. 'It is now an essential part of the process.'

'So it really does work.'

'Oh yes,' said Cardini. 'The effect is subtle, but the success rate of my experiments has more than doubled.'

Fate gave a nod of appreciation. Crossing the room, he stopped beside the table containing a series of metal objects including a candlestick. The candlestick appeared to be solid gold, but there was a series of raised shapes on the stem; four down one side with one on the opposing side. He was just raising it to take a closer look when Cardini stepped forward to take it from him.

'Forgive me,' said the alchemist. 'It has been a pleasure to entertain you, but I really must be getting back to my work.'

The alchemist laid the candlestick down and covered it with a polishing cloth. However, as he withdrew his hand, Fate looked at the missing tips of his fingers and the faint golden hue of the injured flesh. He also noted that the strange shapes on the stem of the candlestick would correspond to the fingers of someone holding it.

Lord Cardini gestured towards the door, but Fate did not move.

'When did you first realise the danger in using the Talisman of Dreams?'

Lord Cardini swallowed hard as Fate raised his dark eyes to look at him. He knew there was no point in lying.

'I'd read about the dangers, but I thought I would be able to control the demon spirit if I used it sparingly.'

'And that's why you chose not to include any spells of restraint.'

'It would have reduced the talisman's effectiveness.'

Fate nodded and pulled back the polishing cloth from the candlestick. 'Did it hurt when you tore your fingers from the gold?' he asked and Cardini's face went slack at the memory of that terrible night.

'I couldn't stop the reaction,' he began. 'If I'd waited any longer the transmutation would have taken my hand.'

'And that's when you decided to get rid of the talisman; to trade it for the monastery's relic.'

'I'd seen the icon of fortune during a previous visit,' said Cardini. 'I knew it could improve my chances of success.'

'And what of the harm to the monks?'

'I knew the effects would be reduced when spread over so many individuals.'

'But you also knew that it would be fatal in the end.'

Cardini curled his lip. 'The monks don't appreciate the powers they have,' he said in a tone of contempt. 'The icon of fortune was wasted on them.'

The two men turned to look at the Shīku pendant lying on the bench.

'And what if I were to take it now?' said Fate and Cardini gave a nervous laugh.

'As I told the abbess… It would do you no good. The nature of the contract would render it useless.'

'And there's no way I can convince you to rescind it?'

Cardini laughed as if the idea was absurd. 'None,' he said with conviction.

Fate pursed his lips. 'I was afraid you would say that.' He reached under the neck of his charcoal grey robes and Cardini watched in horrified silence as Fate removed the Talisman of Dreams from around his neck. His arms trembled with effort as if he were fighting against an invisible force, but finally he held it at arm's length, as one might hold a poisonous snake.

'I thought it was in the lead box!' cried Cardini.

'The box reassured the monks,' said Fate. 'But contact with human skin is the best way to conceal the demon's presence.'

'You had it on your person!' said Cardini. 'You had it on your person and yet you were able to resist!' He looked at Fate as if such a thing was unthinkable. 'How long?' he added. 'How long has the temptation of the demon spirit been denied?'

'Three days,' said Fate and the alchemist could only gape in disbelief.

'What are you going to do?' he breathed.

Fate did not answer at first. He looked across to where the monastery's relic lay on the workbench. He wished he could take it now, but the magical contract would render it useless.

'I think you need some time to reflect on your actions,' said Fate. He moved slowly towards the door and Cardini watched as he hung the talisman on the handle. Even for Fate, letting go of the demonic talisman was incredibly difficult and he gritted his teeth with effort as he withdrew his hand.

'You can't do this!' said Cardini. He looked at Fate imploringly but there was no trace of mercy in the sorcerer's gold-flecked eyes.

'You were a fool,' said Fate. 'You should have known better than to consort with demons.'

'I'm sorry,' cried Cardini. 'I will return the monastery's relic.'

'The contract cannot be annulled,' said Fate as he opened the door. 'Not under duress and only if you are happy. Is that not what you told the abbess?'

Wide eyed with fear, Cardini moved to follow him but then he stopped. He was torn between the fear of approaching the talisman and an overwhelming desire to use it. Now that it was no longer in contact with Fate's flesh, the force of temptation radiating from it was terrifying.

Fate flexed the stiffness from his hand as he passed through the doorway and began to ascend the tunnel.

'Fate!' screamed Cardini as the door to his workshop hung open. 'You can't leave me here with that thing! At least take it off the door so I can get past.'

Cardini's pleading voice was shrill with fear, but Fate was deaf to it. The alchemist had brought this upon himself. The power of the talisman had been building for days and Fate knew that the alchemist would never be able to resist its malign presence. He might hold out for a few hours but eventually his willpower would crumble and he would don the talisman once more.

Stepping back through the phase door, Fate turned to look down the passage. Any attempt to re-enter the passage would cause the phase door to close. He knew the door would open if Cardini approached it from the other side, but he also knew the sorcerer would never leave his workshop again.

'Fate! Please!' wailed Cardini. 'I'll do anything you want. Please, just help me hide this thing away!'

Fate took a step forward and the bricks seemed to break away from the three dimensional passage to form the pattern of the two dimensional door. They came together with a tinkling of ceramic chimes, and the last sound to be heard from beyond the magical barrier was a despairing...

'FAAATE!'

Silence descended and the gold seams in the eyes of Decimus Fate glowed.

17
The Sword of a Demon Hunter

Still sitting on their horses, the Tutor and the two monks watched as Fate pulled up his horse beside them. 'I thought you were staying to talk shop with your new friend.'

'I'm afraid Lord Cardini was not as interesting as I thought he might be,' said Fate.

The Tutor's brows loured with suspicion but Abbess Shimitsu just looked at Fate with her dark brown eyes. 'Did you hurt him?' she asked.

'No,' said Fate. 'I gave him something to think about.'

'But you didn't hurt him.'

'No,' repeated Fate, surprised by their sudden concern. 'Why?'

'He's working for Veleno,' said the Tutor.

'Ah,' said Fate and his face creased as if with guilt.

'So you *did* hurt him.'

'No, I didn't,' said Fate, being careful to reveal nothing of the predicament in which he had left Cardini.

'Veleno'll kill us for sure if we interfere with his pet alchemist.'

'We'll be fine,' said Fate as if he was performing some mental calculations. 'All we need is for you to go back to Guile and get your demon hunter's sword.'

'What?'

'Your Hadean blade,' said Fate. 'We will need it to get past the security golem.'

The Tutor gave a heavy sigh.

'What's the matter?' said Fate. 'You do still have the sword… You told me yourself that you didn't sell it.'

'I threw it from the cliff,' said the Tutor and Fate raised his eyebrows in surprise. 'The night I first arrived at the monastery... I threw the sword from the cliff.'

Fate just stared at him.

'It's gone,' said the Tutor. 'The sword is gone.'

Fate squeezed his eyes shut as his clever plan was brought to an abrupt end. He put a hand to his forehead and was just trying to think of another solution when Master Ando spoke up.

'That's not entirely true,' said the normally quiet monk.

'What's not entirely true?' asked Fate.

'The Tutor's sword,' said Abbess Shimitsu. 'Nawashi found it while he was searching for mushrooms in the forest.'

'I wrapped it in oiled cloth and tucked it beneath my cot,' said Master Ando. 'Your sword isn't gone... it's back at the monastery.'

The Tutor stared at Master Ando before turning to look at Abbess Shimitsu.

'You never mentioned it, and so neither did we,' said the abbess. 'But we didn't know who might come looking for you, and so we kept it safe in case you ever needed it.'

The Tutor felt his heart quicken as he stared at Abbess Shimitsu. That sword had saved his life more times than he could count. It had slain numerous demons, or sent their ravening spirits back to the pits of hell. And yet it had not helped him to save his family and, somehow worse than this, it was a blade that had known murder.

'A sword is just a sword,' said Abbess Shimitsu as if she could read his thoughts. 'It can be used for good or for evil.' She paused. 'Perhaps a sword that is used for good could make up for the mistakes of the past.'

136

The Tutor seemed unconvinced, but finally he turned to Fate.

'Would it help us to retrieve the monastery's relic?'

'Yes.'

'And would it help to get Veleno off our backs?'

'I hope so,' said Fate and the Tutor gave a heavy sigh.

'All right,' he said. 'Let's go and get the sword.'

'No,' said Fate. 'We need to stay here in case anyone tries to find Cardini.'

'What do you mean, *find him*?' asked the Tutor.

'Cardini is currently on the other side of a magical door,' said Fate. 'If someone were to damage that door, we might never find Cardini or the monastery's relic again.'

The Tutor rolled his eyes.

'I'll get it for you,' said Master Ando. 'If we take the horses, I can be back by midday tomorrow.' He looked to Abbess Shimitsu who bowed her head in consent.

'Then that's settled,' said Fate. 'We'll wait for you here, beside the road.'

The sorcerer sounded entirely satisfied while the Tutor still seemed unsure.

'Is that all right with you, Alexander?' asked Abbess Shimitsu and finally the Tutor gave a nod.

'You must learn to forgive yourself,' said Abbess Shimitsu as she moved her horse closer to the Tutor. 'A soul cannot reach its potential if it's bound to the earth with feet of clay.' She waited for the Tutor to look at her. 'Don't be a stranger,' she said. 'It would bring us great happiness if you would visit us from time to time.'

'I will.'

'And if you don't,' said the abbess with a smile, 'then we shall visit you at the Fool's Hope Inn.'

Finally the Tutor smiled.

'Master Ando will bring back the horses when he returns with your sword. And please convey our thanks to Madam Carletta once more.'

She raised her hand to touch the Tutor's arm, before turning to Fate.

'And my thanks to you, Lord Fate. I dread to think what would have happened if you had not unmasked the demon spirit that plagued us.'

'It was my pleasure to be of service,' said Fate with a gracious bow.

'We will be sure to keep the talisman safe until we can convince Lord Cardini to reverse the bargain he made with Nawashi.'

'That would be wise,' said Fate, and not even Abbess Shimitsu could detect the deception in his eyes.

'Until we meet again,' said Abbess Shimitsu as she gave the Tutor a final smile.

'I'll be back as quick as I can,' said Master Ando as the two monks set off along the forest road.

'All right,' said the Tutor as the monks disappeared round a bend in the road. 'What are you up to?'

'Just trying to kill two birds with one stone,' said Fate.

'You're taking a big risk in messing with Veleno's gold supply. You know he loves gold more than anything else in the world.'

'We just need to defeat that security golem and get back to Guile before Veleno gets impatient. I don't want his men giving my housekeeper any more trouble.'

The Tutor gave Fate a withering look. If the last few days were anything to go by, the sorcerer's housekeeper was probably used to dealing with trouble.

18
Raven Mother

Weasel was sitting in his normal spot when a wayfinder arrived from the West Gate to warn him about some dangerous individuals who had just entered the city.

'Pale sorcerers,' said the girl. 'Two of 'em. Like twins... Long white hair and skin like chalk. They asked Freya about the location of a house then hurt her to find out what she knew about the man who lived there.'

Weasel frowned. It was not uncommon for a customer to seek information, but he had never heard of a wayfinder being interrogated like this. 'What was the place they were asking about?' he asked.

'Blackfell House,' said the girl. 'It's a big place in the First Quarter with a fence of black railings.'

Weasel knew the house in question. He also knew of the man who lived there, the so called 'Sage'. He had seen the man just a few days ago, riding out of the city with a dark-skinned mercenary and the two Shīku monks. People said the Sage helped people who were in trouble and now it seemed that trouble was coming to call on him.

Weasel thought for a minute... Anyone living in a house like that obviously had money to spare and they might be willing to pay for information about two dangerous sorcerers who were looking for them.

With a nod of thanks, Weasel slipped a silver thimble into the girl's hand.

'Thanks, Weasel,' she said. 'And take care. Them pale twins ain't messin' about.'

Closing his eyes, Weasel pictured the quickest route through the city. Then he set off at a run for the dark stone building known as Blackfell House.

*

Motina felt their presence before she saw them. Moving to the window she looked down to see two robed figures standing at the main gate.

'*Visitors?*' she asked an absent Fate. '*You didn't tell me you were expecting visitors.*'

The warning call of a raven drew her gaze to a handsome black bird sitting outside on the window ledge.

'Don't worry,' she told the bird. 'The fence will keep them out if they intend any harm. And if they want the master's help, they will just have to call back.'

Turning from the window she made her way through the house. However, as she approached the front door she heard more raven calls coming from the garden. The housekeeper felt a shudder of apprehension. There was something about these visitors that put the birds on edge.

Suddenly wary, she turned to a sideboard lying against the wall. On it was a slender box of finely grained laburnum wood. Motina paused. The birds were right; there was definitely something unsettling about these two pale visitors. Maybe it would be better to arm herself before she went out to speak with them.

Pausing for a moment she reached out towards the box then stopped.

'*No,*' she thought. If these visitors intended any harm, she would simply keep the gate closed and deny them entry.

Feeling strangely anxious she slid back the bolts, opened the front door then stopped. The visitors were no longer standing on the outside of the perimeter fence. They were on the driveway, just ten feet from where she stood.

'*How did they get past the fence?*'

Motina's thin body tensed as she looked into the eyes of the sorcerers, first turquoise then blue. '*Twins*,' she thought and some dark chord chimed in her memory.

'Can I help you, gentlemen?'

'Where is Fate?' said he of the blue eyes.

'The master is not at home.'

'We know that,' said he of the turquoise. 'We want to know where he is.'

'And the demon hunter who travels with him. The one they call the Tutor.'

'Tell us where they are.'

For a moment, Motina just looked at them.

'How did you get past the gate?' she asked.

The sorcerers' pale faces suddenly hardened and Motina knew she was in terrible danger. Turning in the open doorway, she started towards the laburnum box on the sideboard, but it was too late, and the small witch was yanked off her feet as something sharp and burning wrapped around her ankle. Her cheek slammed into the floorboards as she fell and then she gave a cry as she was dragged out of the house and onto the gravel of the driveway.

Twisting round, Motina saw the thongs of an incandescent whip wrapped around her ankle. The strands of magical force glowed an icy blue, the exact same colour as the eyes of the sorcerer holding the whip. With a wrench of his arm the sorcerer dragged the witch further away from the house, further from the only weapon that could help her.

'Where is Fate?' said the sorcerer holding the whip as Motina looked up into his pale blue eyes. The man's figure loomed over her, the bare branches of one of the driveway trees fanning out behind him like dark lightning against the sky.

'I've told you, he's not here,' gasped Motina as her ankle burned with a cold fire.

'So tell us where he is,' said the other sorcerer. He too held a magical whip while his other hand gripped the handle of a serpentine sword, the blade of which seemed to be forged from some kind of crystal.

'Go to The Pit!' spat Motina and then she cried out in pain as the strands of magical force cut into her flesh.

These sorcerers were powerful and Motina began to panic, but then she heard the familiar croak of a raven. Looking up she saw one of the black birds sitting on the branch of a nearby tree.

'Greitai, vaikas,' said Motina, speaking to the bird in her native tongue. 'Mano lazdelė. greitai jį įgykite.'

Motina gasped as the sorcerer silenced her with a twitch of his whip, but the raven gave a croak and flew towards the house.

*

Hidden behind the low wall of the perimeter fence, Weasel watched as the black bird flew in through the open doorway of the house. It was almost as if the small scrawny woman had spoken to it.

Arriving just a few seconds ago, Weasel had seen the sorcerers attack the woman with the magical whip and his heart was beating quickly. Was that what they had done to the wayfinder from the West Gate?

His thoughts were broken as the small woman cried out in pain, but then he saw the black bird emerge from the house with something in its talons. It looked like some kind of rod. He saw the woman reach out a hand towards the bird, but then the other sorcerer lashed out with his whip and the bird was struck from the sky. Black feathers flying, it tumbled in Weasel's direction and the slender rod went spinning through the air. The rod landed just a dozen paces from Weasel on the other side of the fence.

It was a wand.

Weasel cursed as he saw the wand land close to him because it meant that he had to do something. For a split second he considered slinking away, but then he heard the woman give another cry of pain and before he knew what he was doing, he was vaulting the fence.

Sailing over the spiked railings, he felt a moment of resistance and his body tingled with energy as if he had passed through a curtain of invisible force. Weasel remembered stories of how some rich people protected their homes with magical barriers and he tensed in anticipation of pain, but for some reason the invisible barrier allowed him through. With no time to wonder why, he dropped into the garden and rushed forward to grab the wand before darting to the corner of the house.

*

Motina cried out as the raven was hit by the whip. The impact dashed the bird to one side and her wand went flying from its grasp. She was lost.

Turning back to her captor, she began to summon her power, but she was not a feral mage. She could not unleash bolts of force by will alone. Her strength lay in understanding nature and using the materials of the natural world to help or harm. Without her wand she was all but defenceless. The only thing left to her was the spoken power of a curse.

Still caught by the blue-eyed sorcerer, she began to speak the words, but then the other twin gave a flick of his whip and strands of burning energy wrapped around her face, trapping the words behind a gag of pain.

'We will let you speak when you are willing to tell us where Fate and the demon hunter have gone.'

'And when they will return…'

Motina began to struggle but there was no way she could escape the cords that bound her. Jonas might have come to her aid, but the stable-hand had gone to collect food and wine from the market. There was no one else to help her.

Frantically she looked around for anyone who might be able to help her. Unfortunately the streets were empty, but then she noticed a grubby youth crouched behind the near corner of the house. His eyes were wide with fear as he glanced at the pale sorcerers, and then he held up her wand.

*

Terrified of being discovered, Weasel stared at the captive woman, willing her to look at him. Finally her terrified eyes settled on his and he held up the wand. The glowing thongs of a second whip were now wrapped around the woman's face. She could not speak, but her dark eyes were filled with urgency. Staring at him, she gave a quick nod and Weasel threw the wand towards her.

*

Motina watched as the rod of polished wood landed on the driveway, just beside her captor's feet. The sorcerer with the blue eyes looked down at the wand just as Motina's bony fingers closed around it. With a snarl he prepared to defend himself, but Motina did not point the wand at him. Instead she pointed it at the tree behind him. Focussing as much energy as she could muster, she plunged the wand into the grass at the side of the driveway.

With a hiss the two sorcerers pulled Motina away and she lost her grip on the wand as more ropes of energy emerged from their whips to bind her arms and legs. The pain was incredible and Motina gave a muffled cry as her flesh was branded with burning welts.

'Where is Fate?' asked he of the turquoise eyes.

'We will not ask again,' said he of the blue.

From the corner of the building, Weasel watched as the scrawny woman began to writhe in pain. Then, from behind the blue-eyed sorcerer, there came a rending sound, like a tree being torn from the earth by a storm. Even as he watched, Weasel saw one of the leafless trees coming to life. Standing on gnarled roots, the tree reared up over the two pale sorcerers. Its bare branches flailed as if in a strong wind and then it struck.

The sorcerer with the turquoise eyes dodged backwards and the strands of his whip slipped free of Motina's body. However, the sorcerer with the blue eyes was not so lucky. Even as he withdrew his own whip, a twisted branch struck him hard across the chest and he was thrown to the ground. The tree rose up to strike again, but the downed sorcerer had just enough time to lash out with his whip. The magical strands flared brightly as they cut through the attacking branches.

The tree emitted a deep groaning sound before attacking once more, but now the twins were forewarned. The sorcerer flexed his whip and raised his crystal bladed sword. Meanwhile the blue-eyed twin on the floor cried out as the animated tree stamped down with a clump of roots. The sorcerer's left leg was broken and he barely managed to roll to one side as the tree slammed its branches into the loose stones of the driveway.

Still trembling from the lash of the whips, Motina crawled away from the fight. Retrieving her wand, she tried to summon more power, but her limbs twitched with aftershocks of pain and she could not focus her mind. In something of a daze, she watched the sorcerers do battle with the tree.

The sorcerer on the ground was clearly injured, but his twin was not. As Motina watched, he reached into a dark rift that had appeared in the air. The edges of the rift shone with a fiery light as he drew forth a handful of glowing shale. Then, as the tree turned towards him he threw the shale into the tree's branches where it ignited in a mass of tiny flames.

With a howl of pain, the tree reared back and as it did so, the sorcerer lunged forward, plunging his crystalline sword into the tree's trunk. A high-pitched shriek echoed off the walls of the house as the tree shivered from root to claw-like twig. Then it began to split apart and disintegrate. The knobbly trunk cracked and crumbled until the whole tree burst apart in a cloud of fluttering ash.

The blue-eyed twin on the ground clutched at his chest as he tried to get up, while his brother turned to face Motina, his face set in a pale and murderous mask.

Still unable to stand, Motina managed to crawl towards the next tree along the driveway. Looking up at the turquoise sorcerer, she could see the realisation in his face as she held her wand, poised like a dagger beneath the branches of another leafless tree.

For a moment the sorcerer looked at her, but then he sheathed his sword and crossed the driveway to help his brother. They had underestimated the defences of Blackfell House, but Motina knew they would not make the same mistake again. Feeling like she might pass out, she watched as the turquoise sorcerer made a slashing gesture with two fingers of his right hand. The air before him seemed to shimmer as a rift was opened up in the fabric of reality.

Motina heard the unnerving sound of guttural snarls, high pitched wailing and the heart-rending cries of creatures in pain. With the turquoise sorcerer supporting his brother, the pale twins stepped into the rift, which closed behind them with a ringing 'shhhnick!' Silence descended, and all that remained of the rift was the lingering smell of burnt stone and sulphur.

The twins were gone.

'Are you all right?'

Motina started as the voice spoke out beside her. Looking round, she saw it was the youth who had been hiding at the corner of the house, the one who had thrown her wand.

'I'll be fine,' she murmured, although she felt anything but fine.

Slowly the youth helped her into a more comfortable position.

'The bird?' she asked, but the youth shook his head.

Motina's face creased with grief, but then her expression grew more resolute. Opening her eyes, she gave a strange trilling whistle which was followed by a series of croaking bird calls as perhaps a dozen ravens settled in the nearby trees.

'Go,' said the witch. 'Find the master. Warn him of the danger that came to call. Tell him to be careful.'

Fascinated, and more than a little unnerved, Weasel watched as the birds flew away to the north and west. As the birds disappeared he turned back to the woman. 'Can you stand?' he asked and Motina gave a weary nod.

Slowly the youth helped her to her feet and together they made their way back to the house. As they approached the front door the youth looked up at the warning carved into the lintel.

Thinking of the dark tree that had just torn itself from the ground, he paused.

'You can read then,' said Motina with a note of surprise. 'It's all right,' she continued. 'You've nothing to fear while you're with me.'

'I always wondered why no one ever tries to rob this place.'

'What's your name, boy?' asked Motina.

'Weasel,' said Weasel, and Motina smiled.

'Of course it is,' she said, and together they passed into the reception hall of Blackfell House.

*

But Weasel was not the only person to watch the scene in the garden unfold. Outside the fence, on the far side of the property, Sienna Blade had watched the two pale sorcerers approach the gate and stop as if they sensed danger. Rather than try to open the gate, she had seen them disappear into a writhing shadow only to reappear on the gravel driveway just a few yards from the house. And the rest had served as a warning...

Don't try to take Fate at home!

She was annoyed that someone else might be looking to kill Fate, and she hated the fact that the hunchbacked witch had tried to protect him. However, she could not deny that the witch and the street urchin had acted bravely, a fact that only served to annoy her even more.

No. She could not afford to challenge Fate in his lair, and she would need to be careful of the dark-skinned mercenary who travelled with him. The one they called the Tutor. She now knew that they had left the city together, and that they should be returning sometime soon. And so she would pay some wayfinders to watch the roads leading into the city.

When Fate returned to the city, Sienna would be waiting.

19
The Price of Healing

As Motina's ravens began their search for Fate, the Kane twins were arriving back at the Cévaro estate. Injured, frustrated and furious, the two sorcerers staggered as they emerged from the glowing rift in the centre of the mansion's dining hall.

'What happened?' cried Cévaro as he saw the condition of the twins. Divorian was injured, and both the sorcerers had clearly suffered during their passage through the demon realm.

'We were attacked,' said Tilluvian as he lowered his brother to the floor before turning round to close the rift.

'By Fate?' exclaimed Cévaro.

'No,' said Tilluvian. 'By his... vassals.' He could not bring himself to say housekeeper.

'So Fate is still alive?'

Tilluvian ignored the count's question as he helped his brother up from the floor.

'Does he know you came from here?' said Cévaro. 'That I sent you?' The fear in the count's voice was nauseating, and the expression in Tilluvian's turquoise eyes was filled with contempt.

'He knows only that *we* came after him,' said the sorcerer. 'Now, where is the woman you gave to us?'

'She's upstairs,' said Cévaro. 'We locked her in a room in case you needed her again.'

'Take us to her.'

Together they helped Divorian up the stairs. Supported between Sole and Tilluvian, the injured sorcerer hissed and groaned as his broken leg left a trail of blood on the floor and Cévaro was relieved when they finally reached the room where the woman with different coloured eyes was being held.

Tied to the bed, the woman struggled as the door to the room opened. She tried to call out, but her mouth was gagged and her eyes were filled with fear as the Kane twins appeared in the doorway. They helped Divorian across the room and the woman shrank back against the wall as they set the blue-eyed twin down on the bed.

'You have power,' said Tilluvian, turning his cold eyes on Lorden Sole. 'I am weary from protecting us both in the Daemonaria. You will replenish me so that I can tend to my brother's leg.'

Before Sole could object, Tilluvian grabbed his wrist and he instantly felt a great sapping of his strength as the magical energy was drawn out of his body. He was on the verge of passing out when Tilluvian finally let go. Struggling to remain upright, Sole stumbled to the side of the room and slumped against the wall.

Standing in the centre of the room, Cévaro watched in silence as Tilluvian drew a deep breath and opened his eyes. The cuts and scratches on his skin began to fade and the sorcerer no longer looked so utterly tired. He rolled his shoulders and flexed his fingers, then gestured for his brother to lie down on the bed.

Divorian let out a snarl of pain as Tilluvian removed his boot and cut away the leg of the pale trousers he wore beneath his tunic. Cévaro felt his stomach lurch as he saw a jagged shard of bone emerging from the bloody flesh of the twin's shin.

'Courage, brother,' said Tilluvian in a whisper. 'The pain will soon be gone.'

Divorian gritted his teeth as his brother turned to the woman cowering against the wall. She tried to wriggle further away, but Tilluvian reached out and grabbed her left ankle. The sorcerer's touch drove her into a panic, but Tilluvian sent a surge of energy into her body. Her back arched with a savage convulsion and then she was still.

Pulling her down the bed, Tilluvian now arranged her healthy leg until it matched the position of Divorian's. The unfortunate woman was about to pay the price for healing his brother.

Shifting round on the bed, he reached out to place his left hand on his brother's broken leg before placing his right hand on the undamaged leg of the woman. She groaned through the haze of her stupor. And then the sorcerer closed his eyes.

Cévaro was no stranger to inflicting pain on people and yet he winced as the woman began to scream. Her scream rose in pitch until they heard the sickening sound of bone breaking, at which point she lost consciousness and slumped back on the bed.

Finally, Tilluvian removed his hands. Both were bloody, but now his brother's leg was straight and whole, while the woman's leg was torn and broken. Wiping his hands on the blankets of the bed, the turquoise sorcerer rose to his feet.

'Make sure that leg is properly set,' he told Cevaro. 'Her value will be diminished if her form is misshapen.'

'And what about you?' Cévaro breathed as Tilluvian moved to a wash basin in the corner of the room. 'Have you given up on Fate?'

Tilluvian fixed the count with his cold turquoise eyes, but it was his brother who spoke.

'We are Kane,' said Divorian.

'We do not give up,' said Tilluvian.

'We will take a few days to recover our strength.'

'We shall watch for Fate and the one they call the Tutor.'

'And then.'
'When the time is right.
'We shall kill them both,' they said together.

20
The Golem and the Raven's Call

As dawn broke over the forest a dozen ravens continued their search for the man in the charcoal grey robes. There was no sign of him on the road to the monastery, so the birds cast further afield, searching the smaller ways that wound beneath the trees. Some doubled back to make sure they had not missed him. Others went north, and some went south towards the market town of Leeford.

*

Fate and the Tutor chose a point on the road where they could look out for Master Ando while keeping an eye on the driveway to Cardini's mansion. Fate was adamant that no one should try to approach the house.

'Not until we're ready to go in together,' he told the Tutor. 'And only when we have that sword of yours.'

The morning passed slowly and it was midday when Master Ando finally appeared.

'He's here,' said Fate as the monk's golden yellow robes came into view.

Rising from their makeshift camp, the Tutor walked into the open as Master Ando rode towards them with Abbess Shimitsu's horse trailing behind him on a length of rope. Getting down from his horse, the monk offered Fate a shallow bow before clasping the Tutor's hand. Returning to his horse, he drew out a long narrow object wrapped in orange cloth.

'Sister Hanju made a new scabbard,' said Master Ando as he pulled back the cloth to reveal the hilt of a sword. He held the weapon out, but still the Tutor hesitated. 'A sword is just a sword,' said the monk, repeating Abbess Shimitsu's words from the day before.

154

Finally, the Tutor raised his hands to take the sword and the rest of the cloth fell away.

The Tutor's eyes moved over the weapon as if he were remembering all the challenges they had faced together. Slowly he drew the blade and the layered steel shimmered in the dim forest light. A little shorter than a typical longsword, the blade had a single edge and a graceful curve that continued through the handle to the steel pommel that enclosed the heart-stone. It was the heart-stone that gave the blade its unique properties.

Fate glanced at the frosted gem as the Tutor held the sword out in front of him. Many people could activate a heart-stone if their emotions became strong enough, but only a few could channel that energy into the blade of a sword. It did not require magic in the conventional sense. The power of a heart-stone came from something deeper, more primeval.

As if to demonstrate, the Tutor gripped the long handle of the sword with two hands, and Master Ando gave a gasp of surprise as the heart-stone flared with a hint of fire.

'A Hadean blade,' breathed the monk as the energy flowed along the patterns in the folded steel of the blade. 'A weapon to cut through the infernal hide of demons.'

'Or the enchanted armour of a security golem,' said Fate. 'What?' he added in a tone of innocence when Master Ando and the Tutor turned to look at him.

With a final sigh of acceptance, the Tutor removed the ordinary sword that hung from his belt and replaced it with the sword of a demon hunter. Feet together and hands at his sides, he bowed to Master Ando.

'Thank you.'

'May its blade follow the way of truth,' replied the monk as he returned the Tutor's bow.

Master Ando joined them for a midday meal and the Tutor was pleased to hear that the monks at the monastery were continuing to recover. However, it was clear that Fate had plans that did not include Master Ando and so he did not stay long before setting off for the monastery once more.

'All right,' said the Tutor as the monk disappeared from view. 'Just exactly what do you have in mind?'

Fate did not answer, but the expression on his face offered little in the way of reassurance. A few minutes later they stood on the gravel driveway outside Cardini's mansion with two of Veleno's men barring their way.

'No, we're not gonna step aside,' said one of the men with a nervous glance in the Tutor's direction.

'You do know you can't stop us,' said Fate.

'Veleno'll kill us if we let you mess with his alchemist.'

'It's too late to worry about that,' said Fate. 'Now just step aside before someone gets hurt.'

The two men exchanged a nervous look.

'All right,' said the older of the two. 'But if you go in, we're coming with you.'

'I don't think that would be a good idea,' said Fate.

'We don't care what you think,' said the younger man. 'We're coming with you so we can make sure the alchemist is all right.'

Fate breathed a heavy sigh. 'Then you must do exactly as I say.'

'You ain't the boss,' said the older man. 'You don't tell us what to do.'

'Well, don't say I didn't warn you.'

As Fate walked towards the house, a raven was passing overhead. It was just one of a dozen birds searching the forest for the man in the charcoal grey robes, but one was enough. Flying high over the trees, the raven finally spotted Fate just as the sorcerer approached the front door of a large house. Down the bird flew, but it was too late. The man disappeared through the door and all the bird could do was croak and caw from the outside.

*

Fate was so focussed on the challenge ahead that he did not notice the muffled croak of a raven coming from outside the house. He walked to the centre of the reception hall as Cardini's manservant hovered in a state of some anxiety.

'Where is the master?' he asked. 'Why is the door closed? What have you done to him?'

'You should leave,' said Fate, ignoring the man's questions. 'Go to a far corner of the house, and hide.'

'I'm not going anywhere...' said the manservant, but he stopped mid sentence as Fate approached the door to Cardini's workshop. 'You shouldn't get too close,' he said, looking at the enormous warrior statue standing beside the door. 'Not without the master present.'

'Go,' said Fate, and the man gave the statue a frightened look before hurrying from the room.

'What's going on?' said one of Veleno's men. 'Where's the alchemist? Why's that guy so jumpy?'

'This is your last chance to leave,' said Fate as he stood before the security golem.

'We ain't going nowhere,' said the other man.

'Then move to a corner of the room and remain still,' said Fate. 'Don't move, don't run. And whatever you do, do not draw your swords.'

The men glanced at each other nervously. They were still reluctant to follow the sorcerer's orders, but slowly they moved to the side of the hall as the Tutor came to stand beside Fate.

157

'How quickly will it react?' he asked, gazing at the eight foot statue with an appraising eye.

'That depends on the skill of the animator,' said Fate. 'But judging from the quality, I would say very quickly.'

'And how is it activated?'

'It reacted when Cardini opened the door.'

The two men looked at the ordinary door that concealed the phase door. It was hanging partially open.

'I could open it and then move aside,' said Fate.

'No,' said the Tutor. 'You should stay back out of the way.'

Fate backed away as the Tutor took a stance before the statue. Still he hesitated. 'You really think this will help us with Veleno.'

'I think so,' said Fate.

'And you're sure this is the only way to retrieve the monastery's relic?'

'The only way I can think of,' said Fate and the Tutor gave a sigh.

Moving to one corner of the hall, Fate watched as the Tutor readied himself.

Security golems were imbued with rudimentary instructions, but they were all designed to react to violence.

Moving into position, the Tutor angled his body and braced his legs, hoping to dispatch the golem with a single decisive blow. However, it was a long time since he had used his sword and he wondered if he still had the ability to charge the blade with enough energy to damage such a heavily armoured opponent.

His greatest source of inspiration had always been his wife and daughter, but now that inspiration was eclipsed by grief. Burying his feelings, the demon hunter gripped his Hadean blade, and the heart-stone crystal began to glow.

As the Tutor prepared to attack, no one noticed the black raven flapping at the arch of small windows above the front door.

Staring at the metal statue, the Tutor chose a point on the golem's neck, a gap between its helmet and the armour on its shoulder. He tensed his muscles, drew a breath and struck. And as he did so the huge metal statue sprang to life. With surprising speed, the golem lurched to one side as the Tutor's sword cut a deep gouge in its shoulder. An angry light bloomed inside the metal statue, glowing between the gaps in its armour, and shining out from the eye slits in the golem's helm.

The reception hall was suddenly filled with the sound of grinding metal as the golem drew up its sword and swung it in a sweeping arc that could easily have cut the Tutor in half. Arching away, the Tutor allowed the massive blade to pass just inches from his stomach before delivering a second blow to the golem's upper arm. He tried for another attack, but was forced to duck as the golem's blade switched back towards him. Suddenly he was on the defensive and he backed away quickly, parrying a series of lethal blows as the golem drove him back towards one wall.

The Tutor dived to one side as the golem cleaved a great gash in the wood-panelled wall. Getting quickly to his feet, he regained his balance as the golem turned towards him. However, as the golem turned to follow him it noticed one of Veleno's men who was cowering in fear against the wall.

'Don't move!' cried Fate, but it was too late.

In a desperate panic the man reached for his sword and the golem's eyes flared with heat. The man barely had time to draw his own sword before the golem's blade stabbed him in the stomach. He gave an agonised cry and slumped to the floor as the golem raised its sword to kill him. However, before the metal warrior could strike, the Tutor attacked it from behind.

The Tutor's blade glowed with faint seams of light as he struck the golem at the base of its neck. Once again the blade bit deeply and a spurt of hot mercurial fluid splashed onto the marble floor, but the Tutor's sword snagged in the enchanted metal of the golem's armour. As the huge statue turned around, the Hadean blade was wrenched from the Tutor's grasp and sent skidding across the floor. He dived after it as the golem attacked, its heavy blade cutting through the air just inches from the Tutor's head.

The Tutor scrambled for his sword, but it was clear that he was not going to make it. For all its size, the golem was surprisingly fast and now it loomed over the Tutor, sword poised for the kill.

As he saw what was going to happen, Fate snatched one of the dragon handled daggers from his belt and hurled it at the golem. The blade of the dagger was imbued with magic, but it was not the kind of magic that could harm a security golem. Even so, the point of the dagger lodged itself in the statue's back and the Tutor was saved as it whirled to meet this new threat.

Locking its burning gaze on Fate, the golem surged towards him. However, unlike Veleno's man, Fate did not flinch. He flattened himself against the wall, held his breath and watched as the metal warrior charged forward, leaning down until its hot helm was just a hand's width from the sorcerer's face. The point of the golem's massive sword hovered just below his ribs, and then it stopped.

Fate's unnatural stillness seemed to confuse the golem. For just a second the two entities faced each other... the feral mage and the soulless security golem. Even the light of its burning gaze seemed to be reflected in the gold streaks in Fate's dark eyes. And then the golem staggered as the Tutor hacked his sword into the back of the statue's right leg.

Instantly it swung about, only this time the Tutor was ready and he dodged its sweeping attack before landing another blow to the top of the golem's left thigh. The golem staggered as more silvery fluid fell hissing to the floor, but the statue was still dangerous. The Tutor was forced to parry and dodge a series of vicious attacks, but Fate could see a new confidence in his movements. It was as if his body had needed time to remember exactly what it was capable of. His movements were assured, his blue eyes focused and his blade was a blur as the veined metal began to glow.

In the pommel of the Tutor's sword, the heart-stone was no longer a frosted gem; it burned and shone with an inner power. It was not as bright as it once had been, and yet it was enough.

As the golem prepared for another brutal attack, the Tutor struck it three times in rapid succession... first a deep cut across the front of its helm... followed by a rapid slice to its exposed middle, and finally a savage blow to the back of its neck.

Helm... belly... neck...

Faster than you could say the words, and the massive metal golem collapsed to the floor in a heap of metal. The alchemical glyphs on its armour faded as the heat of its inner fire died, and the Tutor stepped back as dark mercurial fluid formed a shallow pool around the golem's lifeless form.

161

'Hawk's teeth and fuckleberries!' cursed Veleno's uninjured man from where he was standing at the side of the hall. He had feared the worst when his companion was struck down by the golem, but now he peeled himself away from the wall as the injured man cried out in pain.

'I told you to stay still,' said Fate as he crossed the room to examine the man's injuries.

'I thought it was going to kill me,' hissed the man through gritted teeth.

'It was,' said Fate. 'But it might have overlooked you, if you had remained perfectly still.'

'Hard to stay still when you're shitting your pants,' said the injured man's companion.

Fate ignored the crude remark as he took a small vial from a pouch on his belt. The injured man cried out as the sorcerer poured a purple liquid onto the wound which fizzed and steamed with an acrid smell.

'He'll live,' said Fate as the healing potion cleaned and cauterised the wound. 'The golem's sword went deep, but I don't think it punctured anything vital. He was lucky.'

'Lucky?' said the injured man's companion. 'He don't look too lucky to me.'

'What now?' asked the Tutor.

'Now we see if I can remember the correct sequence to access Cardini's workshop.'

'And if you can't?'

'Then I will be burned alive,' said Fate as he crossed the hall and opened the wooden door to reveal the tiled pattern of the phase door.

'Bugger this for a game of dice!' said Veleno's man as he hauled his injured companion to his feet. 'We're waiting outside.'

Still shaking with fear, he helped his companion up from the floor. And still no one noticed the black bird flapping at the window above the door. However, as Veleno's men opened the door the bird flew in, hitting the men in the face as it tried to pass them in the doorway.

'Curse these bloody magic users!' cried the uninjured man. 'Ain't nothing natural about fighting statues and freaky birds that attack you for no reason.'

Ignoring Veleno's men, the Tutor moved towards the bird, raising his arms as he tried to herd it out through the open doorway.

'Wait!' said Fate as the bird came to rest on a table at the side of the room. Perched on the polished table, the bird hunched forward. It looked directly at Fate and opened its beak to give a series of harsh insistent calls.

'Something's wrong,' said Fate as he stared at the agitated bird.

'Oh, so now you can talk to birds?' said the Tutor.

'I don't need to talk to them to know that something's wrong,' snapped Fate as he stepped away from the phase door.

'What's wrong?' said the Tutor. 'I thought we were going to find Cardini.'

'Cardini can wait,' said Fate. 'I have to go back to Guile. Something's happened to Motina.'

'Your housekeeper!' exclaimed the Tutor. 'Why would a squawking bird mean that something has happened to your housekeeper?'

'Because she sent it to find me,' said Fate and the Tutor could only follow him as Fate strode from the house to the horses waiting outside.

'How do you know that bird came from your housekeeper?' asked the Tutor as Fate adjusted his horse's reins and stepped up into the saddle.

'Motina has an affinity with ravens and crows,' said Fate. 'They understand her and she understands them. And this is not the first time she's used them to send me a message.'

'So you think she's in danger?'

'I'm not sure. But something serious has happened.'

'Do you think it's Veleno's men?' asked the Tutor as he too mounted his horse.

'I don't think so,' said Fate, shaking his head. 'Veleno said he wouldn't do anything until the next full moon. He's a ruthless bastard, but he's also a man of his word.'

As they turned their horses to leave, Veleno's man stood up from his injured companion who was lying on the steps of the mansion.

'Where the hell are you going?' he asked. 'This man needs help and Veleno won't be happy if you've done something to his alchemist.'

'Your friend will be fine if you can get him back to the city,' said Fate. 'And you can tell Veleno, he'll have his payment by the next full moon.'

'Are you sure about that?' asked the Tutor as they set off down the driveway.

'Yes,' said Fate with a sideways glance that made the Tutor distinctly uncomfortable. 'One way or another, Veleno will get what he wants.'

An awkward silence settled between them as they set off on the road back to Guile.

The Tutor knew Fate was hiding something and he could not help wondering if it had something to do with the tattoo on his chest. In awkward silence they hurried along the forest road with no idea of what might be waiting in Guile.

It was late in the evening as they finally approached the city. As they drew closer, the Tutor noticed two wayfinders sitting in a tree beside the road. As soon as he and Fate came into view, they dropped down from the tree before sprinting away into the city. The Tutor frowned as he watched them go.

It was almost as if the children had been waiting for them.

21
Abigail

The temple of Abnoba was the perfect place to sit and wait for someone returning to the city. The dome of the temple was formed from interlacing stems and leaves of copper. It was designed, not to keep the elements out, but to let nature in. And rising above the dome was the Tower of the Dawn, a high graceful tower where the Scions of Abnoba marked every sunrise with the haunting sound of pipes. The tower offered an expansive view of the city and that was why Sienna had chosen it as a place to wait for Fate's return.

The Scions of Abnoba were a naive bunch of nature lovers. Sienna wondered how such people managed to survive in the world at all. The temple was never locked and the Scions had no idea that she was using their tower as a lookout; much less that she was using it as a lookout for murder.

Wrapped in her cloak, Sienna lay in the shelter of the tower's wall listening to the soft murmur of chanting and the everyday sounds of people in the streets below. She was waiting to hear from the wayfinders she had paid to watch the roads leading into the city. All day she had been waiting for news of Fate and the Tutor returning to Guile. Now it was getting dark and she had begun to doze when she heard the rapid patter of footsteps in the street. This was followed by a series of insistent hisses and the clatter of small stones hitting the stone walls of the tower.

Leaping to her feet, Sienna leaned out over the wall of the tower to see two grubby children staring up at her from the street.

'He's here,' said the eldest of the children, a girl with matted blonde hair. 'Westside gate. Ten minutes ago.'

Knowing she had no time to lose, Sienna flew down the spiral staircase of the tower. Emerging into the body of the temple, she strode quickly towards the exit then stopped as one of the Scions walked towards her. The red-haired woman was carrying a wooden bowl of freshly cut flowers from the temple's garden.

'Can I help you, sister?' she asked as Sienna put out a hand to stop her.

She had been thinking about how she might gain the initiative if she was required to fight the Tutor, and a bowl of flowers might just do the trick.

'Those are beautiful,' said Sienna.

'Yes, they are,' said the woman with a dreamy smile. 'They're healing flowers for our sisters in the infirmary.'

'Those will do nicely,' said Sienna, and before the red-haired woman could take a breath, she swept the bowl from her hands and hurried on her way.

Cradling the bowl of flowers, Sienna shouldered the door of the temple and emerged onto the street and fumbled in her money pouch for the coins she had promised the wayfinders.

'That's more'n you said,' exclaimed the blonde-haired girl. 'But you ain't getting no change.' With self-satisfied smiles the two wayfinders ran off and Sienna took a moment to get her bearings.

'*Westside gate to Blackfell House*,' she said to herself. And in her mind she pictured the route from the Westside gate to Fate's house in the first quarter. She had scouted several routes through the city to determine the paths that Fate was most likely to take. One of the routes was closed for bridge repairs so...

'*Second bridge over the Norward Canal*,' she decided.

That's where she would take him.

Trying not to spill the bowl of flowers, Sienna began to run. As she hurried through the dark streets she was surprised by the rapid beating of her heart. Normally, a job like this would barely quicken her breath, but this was personal, and this was Fate, and people said that the man travelling with him used to be a demon hunter. That was more than enough to set a flutter of anxiety in her chest.

Sienna reached the bridge quickly. Hugging the wall of a building, she looked down the length of the bridge in the direction of the Westside gate. It was now dark and the only person using the bridge was a tinker leading a mule laden with a noisy collection of pots and pans. He hummed to himself as he moved through the dim light cast by the oil lamps that lined the darkened streets.

Cursing his presence, Sienna kept her eyes on the far side of the bridge as the tinker disappeared from view. The rhythmic clank of metal slowly faded and then she saw them... two men on horseback leading two riderless horses. One of the riders was tall and lithe and dressed in black. The other was dressed in the charcoal grey robes of a sorcerer.

The rapid beating of Sienna's heart grew even faster. For a moment she felt lightheaded, but then she clenched her jaw and calmed her breathing. This was the man who had killed her father, a cowardly sorcerer who killed with magic. But people said he no longer used magic and Sienna would see how *great* he was without it.

The dark-skinned demon hunter was different. He was a very definite threat and she would need to neutralise him first. Glancing down at the flowers, she decided that the distraction she had planned might not work for a man on horseback. She would need something more.

Sienna paused for a moment then, pushing up the sleeve of her shirt, she drew her knife and made a small nick on her wrist. As Fate and the demon hunter reached the bridge, she put the cut to her mouth and sucked. With a mouthful of coppery blood she gripped her bowl of flowers, drew in her cloak and started across the bridge.

*

Fate and the Tutor drew their horses to one side as a tinker passed them on the narrow road. The tinker touched a finger to his brow in a gesture of thanks and the clanking sound of his pans receded as they approached the bridge over the Norward Canal. Fate had barely said a word on their way back to the city but the Tutor could sense his increasing tension as they got closer to Blackfell House.

It was dark and the streets were empty as they rode onto the bridge. The only person visible was a woman walking towards them, dressed in a cloak and carrying what looked like a bowl of bright flowers. The woman walked with her head bowed and the Tutor paid her little heed. However, just as she was about to walk past them, the woman stumbled on the cobbles and fell into the path of the Tutor's horse. The horse reared and the woman gave a cry as she collided with its forelegs. Bright flowers were scattered as the woman dropped her bowl onto the road.

Fate and the Tutor looked down at the woman who was now bent at the waist and spitting blood from her mouth. One of the horse's legs must have caught her in the face.

'Are you all right?' asked the Tutor as he calmed his horse and slipped down from the saddle.

'My flowers,' mumbled the woman, pointing at the wooden bowl.

The Tutor reached down to retrieve the bowl, and as he straightened up he saw a flash of movement as the pommel of a sword slammed into his temple. As he pitched forward the woman kicked him in the face. The kick threw him onto his back and his skull gave a dull 'clock' as it struck the cobblestones.

In the space of three seconds the Tutor was out cold, and Sienna turned to Fate.

The Tutor's horse whinnied at the violence, but Fate seemed unconcerned. With an expression of sad resignation he looked down at the young woman with the freckles and the dark blonde hair.

'Hello Abigail,' he said and the young woman's eyes flashed with anger.

Lunging forward she grabbed Fate's robes and dragged him from the saddle.

'The name is Sienna,' she growled as Fate tumbled to the ground.

'As you wish,' said the sorcerer, raising himself up on one knee. 'You've grow...' he began then he gave a gasp as Sienna's sword tip whipped across his face.

'Don't speak,' she snapped as Fate raised a hand to the gash that had appeared in his right cheek. 'Never give a sorcerer the chance to speak. One of the few things my father taught me.'

'Your father was a...' This time Fate's words were cut off by a slash to his shoulder. Clenching his teeth against the pain, he pressed his hand to the wound and looked up into the eyes of the woman who had come to kill him.

'I don't want to hear your poisoned words,' said Sienna.

'Then what do you want?'

'I want you to die,' said Sienna. 'And I want you to know who it was that killed you.'

'So be it,' said Fate and Sienna was disappointed by the lack of fear in his eyes. He offered no excuse, no entreaty. He did not even try to defend himself. It was as if he were resigned to death. His lack of reaction gave her a moment's pause, but Sienna was undeterred. Gripping her sword she swung at Fate's neck and her blade would have cut deep had the Tutor not charged her from the side.

Still woozy from the blows to his head, the Tutor staggered to his feet just in time to see the young woman about to strike. With no time to draw his own sword he simply lurched forward, knocking the woman off her feet.

Taken by surprise, Sienna rolled away from the attack, avoiding the Tutor's hands as he tried to grapple for her sword. Coming back to her feet she swung at the Tutor's middle, slicing through his black leather doublet. If this man was determined to come between her and Fate, then he too would have to die. However, the Tutor had recovered just enough to arch back out of the sword's path and he escaped with nothing more than a shallow cut to his stomach. Pure instinct kept him alive as his head began to clear.

Sienna swung at him once more before turning back to dispatch Fate. The sorcerer had not moved and once again he would have died, but this time Sienna's attack was deflected by the Tutor's blade.

With a cry of frustration, Sienna whirled about to attack the Tutor in earnest. The speed of her blade was so fast it left arcs of blurred steel in the gloom. She pressed forward, determined to overwhelm the demon hunter with the sheer number of attacks, but the Tutor had regained his composure and he met her attacks with a skill she had never encountered before.

A hint of desperation crept into Sienna's movements as she realised she was outmatched. Parrying a blow, she lunged for the Tutor's ribs then staggered as he blocked the attack before striking her in the face with the back of his hand. Spinning round, she feigned a low attack before aiming for his neck, but the Tutor spotted the feint and once again his blade met hers.

Suddenly she was on the defensive and her eyes grew wide as the demon hunter's attacks rose to a new level of aggression. She saw an opening and went to exploit it, only to feel the Tutor's blade slide across her forearm. She defended against a complex attack, and thought she had weathered the storm until she felt a dull stabbing sensation, just below the hem of her scale mail shirt.

Looking down, Sienna watched as the Tutor withdrew the tip of his sword from a point near her right hip. Stumbling back, she touched the wound, her hand trembling as it came away red with blood. Edging backwards, she shot a glance at Fate who was now getting to his feet, and for just a second their eyes met.

Fear and fury surged through Sienna's mind as she knew her chance was gone. She could not beat the man they called the Tutor, but she was not finished yet. Flailing her sword, she forced the demon hunter back, then she turned away, took a few limping strides and threw herself over the low wall at the side of the bridge.

Sienna clamped her mouth shut as the dark water of the canal closed around her. The sudden cold snatched at her breath and her lower stomach throbbed with a sickening ache, but still she forced herself to swim. Gripping her sword, and fighting the urge to breathe, she swam beneath the surface, trying to ignore the slimy things that brushed against her face in the darkness. Her lungs were bursting and her throat convulsed as something sharp snagged against her left thigh. Bubbles of air burst from her mouth as she was forced to surface.

Thirty yards from the bridge, Sienna's dark blonde hair was lost in the shadowed canyon of the canal. Sucking in air, she swam for the bank, slapping at the water as a rat swam past just inches from her face. The startled creature gave a squeal of alarm as it disappeared in a swirl of oily water. Gripping the stone blocks of the canal side, Sienna turned to look back at the bridge.

In the gloom she could just make out the two figures, coming together and checking their injuries before leading their horses across the bridge. As they reached the far side, she saw them get back into the saddle before disappearing into the night-time streets of Guile.

Sienna smothered a cry of rage as tears of frustration pricked her eyes. For three years she had dreamed of killing Fate and now she had squandered the chance. She pulled herself along the bank until she reached a gap in the stone wall where a series of shallow steps led down to the water. Wincing from the pain in her stomach and thigh, she hauled herself out of the canal, crawled up the steps and laid on the bank like the victim of a shipwreck.

She had a cut on her arm, a stab wound in the belly and blood ran down her thigh where something had caught her leg in the water. She could struggle back to the inn where she had stabled her horse, but she was not at all sure that the greasy-haired landlord would help her. No, she needed someone who would take in a wounded stranger; someone naïve enough to help her without asking too many questions.

Fortunately, Sienna knew just the place. Stifling a groan, she struggled to her feet and stumbled in the direction of the Temple of Abnoba.

22
Wreathed in Smoke

'What happened?' asked Motina as Fate slid from his horse on the driveway of Blackfell House.

'We were attacked,' said the Tutor.

'By whom?' asked the housekeeper as she went to examine Fate's injuries.

'I'm fine,' said Fate, waving her away. 'It's the demon hunter you should be checking. I'm fairly sure he's got a concussion.'

'Who attacked you?' persisted Motina. 'Was it magic users?'

Fate shook his head. 'It was Abigail Blade.'

'What! Arturo's daughter?'

'Yes,' said Fate. 'It would appear that she's all grown up and ready to kill me.'

'Well, she'll have to wait in line,' said Motina. 'Mind you, she always was a feisty one. I remember the time she…'

'Magic users,' interrupted Fate as Jonas appeared to take care of the horses.

'What?' said Motina.

'Magic users,' said Fate. 'You asked if it was magic users.' He turned suddenly; his eye drawn to the avenue of trees along the driveway. 'And what happened to the tree?'

The look in Motina's eyes brought a frown to Fate's face. His hawkish features became even more intense, and for the first time he noticed the welts on his housekeeper's cheeks, as if someone had wrapped hot wire around her face. Gently, he reached out a hand to lift Motina's chin.

'We were also attacked,' said the small hunchbacked witch. 'Well, I was attacked.'

'By whom?' asked Fate, echoing the question she had just asked him.

Motina looked up at the man she had served for the last ten years.

'The Kane twins,' she said and the gold flecks in Fate's eyes glittered like threats in a darkened room.

Sitting in the kitchen of Blackfell house, the Tutor watched as Motina tended to the cut on Fate's cheek. She had already stitched up Fate's arm and applied a dressing to the shallow cut on the Tutor's stomach. Now she used silk thread and spots of pine resin glue to hold the edges of this smaller wound together.

'So, who are the Kane twins?' asked the Tutor as Motina applied the last few strands of silk.

'They're sorcerers,' said Fate. 'Brothers from the mountain realm of Tundraal.'

'Are they feral mages?'

Fate gave a snort of contempt.

'Keep still!' said Motina in a tone of some annoyance. 'There,' she said as she stepped back to appraise her work. 'That should be sufficient, so long as you don't smile too much.'

Fate raised an eyebrow at his housekeeper's attempt at humour. Reaching up a hand, he gently probed his cheek. 'No,' he said in answer to the Tutor's question. 'The Kane twins are *not* feral mages. They use ancient magic to access the demon world.'

'Then they are fools,' said the Tutor.

'I think it's closer to insanity than foolishness,' said Fate. 'But whatever the case, they are powerful.'

'Then their souls will be forfeit,' said the Tutor. 'No one draws power from the demon realm without paying a price.'

Fate shook his head. 'The twins don't risk their own souls. They trade only those they have taken.'

'You know they'll be back,' said Motina as she tidied away the dressings and medicinal herbs.

'I know,' said Fate.

'And you're in no position to fight them.'

Fate did not reply but his dark eyes reflected the light of the open fire.

'I take it they were on the list,' said the Tutor.

'What list?' asked Motina.

'From a long time ago,' said Fate. 'Somehow Veleno managed to get hold of a copy.'

'And what was on this list?' asked Motina. 'Groceries to buy from the market?'

Fate gave a bitter laugh and took a sip of his tea.

'It was a list of people who wanted to kill him,' said the Tutor and Motina rolled her eyes.

'Not another one,' she said with a sigh of exasperation.

'There are others!' said the Tutor.

'Not anymore,' said Fate. 'And I thought this one was dealt with.'

'Well apparently not!' said Motina. 'At least this explains the surge in people wanting you dead.'

'But the Kane twins weren't on the list,' said Fate.

'Was Abigail?' asked Motina.

'No,' said Fate. 'But her father was. It's possible she replaced his signature with her own.'

At this, the Tutor looked up sharply. He remembered how Fate had explained why he was not worried about the people on the list. '*Because I killed them,*' the sorcerer had said. At least that explained why the young woman wanted him dead. Fate had killed her father.

'So, what about the Kane twins?' asked Motina.

'I don't know,' said Fate. 'Someone else must have exchanged their name and hired the twins to do the job. I can't see it being a coincidence.'

'But the twins also asked about you,' said Motina, turning to look at the Tutor.

The Tutor frowned while Fate narrowed his eyes. 'Then it must be someone local,' said Fate. 'Someone who heard that we were travelling together.'

'So what will you do?' asked Motina.

'I will make enquiries,' said Fate. 'I will try to find out who sent the Kane twins and how to get in touch with Abigail, I mean, *Sienna* Blade.'

'I think I know someone who could help,' said Motina.

'Oh?' said Fate.

'Yes,' said the witch. 'His name is Weasel.'

Twenty minutes later, Fate was still sitting in the kitchen, staring into the embers of the fire. Across the table, the Tutor was slumped forward, head resting on his arms, fast asleep. Maybe it was the concussion, or maybe it was the healing herbs that Motina had put in his tea.

'I've made up one of the beds in the guest wing,' said Motina as she returned to the kitchen. 'Should I wake him?'

'No,' said Fate. 'Let him rest.'

'So what are you going to do about the twins?'

'I don't know,' said Fate. 'But they won't attack me here. Not after what happened on the driveway.'

'Maybe not, but you can't stay in here forever. And you can't defeat them without magic.'

177

'Veleno could stop them,' said Fate and Motina arched an eyebrow. 'If I gave him the demon hunter's tattoo, Veleno would stop them for sure.'

The expression in Fate's eyes grew darker than ever. Looking back into the fire he continued to play with the charms on his wrist, his fingers coming to rest on the dagger wreathed in smoke.

'You know that charm's only good for one kill.'

'I know.'

'And there are two Kane twins.'

'I know.'

'Ah,' said Motina. Her face creased with regret, but she had decided long ago that she would never judge the man who had saved her life. Her gaze moved to the dark-skinned figure sleeping at the kitchen table. 'A shame,' she said. 'I really quite liked him.'

Following her gaze, Fate also looked at the Tutor.

'Well,' said Motina, eager to change the subject. 'I've also warmed *your* bed and put a tonic on your bedside table if you need it.'

'I'll be sleeping downstairs tonight,' said Fate and Motina put a hand to her mouth.

'Tonight's a penance moon?' she said in a guilty tone. 'With all that's happened, I clean forgot!'

'Don't worry,' said Fate.

'Nonsense,' said Motina. 'It won't take me a minute to set the fire in the basement. I just wish there was more I could do.'

'You do enough,' said Fate. 'This is the bargain I struck; the price I chose to pay. And I pay it gladly.'

'Well, let's just hope they don't stay too long,' said Motina glancing around the room as if there might be hidden figures hiding in the shadows.

'Goodnight, Motina,' said Fate.

'Good night, master.'

As Motina went to prepare the room in the basement, Fate went upstairs to his study. Moving to his desk he opened a drawer and rummaged to the bottom where he found a letter. Holding it to the light of a candle, he read the words on the faded parchment. How strange, he thought... how the past and the present are so intimately entwined.

With a wistful sigh he folded the letter and tucked it into a pocket in his robes. Then he drew a breath and went down to the basement to face the trials of another Penance Moon.

*

The Tutor woke with a start, and for a moment he was confused as to where he was. The fire in the hearth was little more than a ruddy glow, but there was a candle in the centre of the kitchen table with a glass of water and two pears on a plate.

'*Blackfell House*,' thought the Tutor as the day's events came back to him. Stretching the stiffness from his back, he reached for the glass of water and winced from a sudden pain in his head. Reaching up a hand he could feel the lumps and bruises that he had acquired during the fight with the young woman on the bridge. With a sigh he lifted the glass and took a slow drink of water.

As he put down the glass he heard a peculiar sound like a muffled moan coming from somewhere in the house. Slowly the Tutor got to his feet and walked to the door of the kitchen. The sound was a little louder.

Passing down a short corridor he emerged in a hallway with several doors and passages leading from it. He paused... Yes, there it was again. The sound was coming from a door in the far wall.

It was the middle of the night and yet it was not completely dark as the light from a gibbous moon shone in through a number of windows. Glancing around the room, the Tutor moved slowly towards the door. He paused as he listened to the sounds coming from the other side. They were the sounds of someone in distress. Carefully he opened the door and the sounds grew louder… mutterings and hissing and moaning.

Beyond the door, a set of stone steps led down to some kind of basement room. For a moment he wondered if it was wise to be sneaking around the house of Decimus Fate, but he did not feel any sense of danger from the tattoo on his chest and so he passed through the door and began to descend the stairs without making a sound. As he went lower he saw a large room warmed by the light from a fireplace set into one wall.

It was like the inner sanctum of some private collector. Expensive tables stood around the room bearing all manner of ornament and curiosity. Exquisite glassware and silver sculptures sat beside obscure scientific instruments. On a polished wooden sideboard sat an enormous tusk, gleaming black and fully ten feet long. Weapons, masks and shields lined the walls, while a display of stuffed birds in one corner of the room seemed as if it might suddenly spring to life.

Set into the wall opposite the fire was an enormous door forged from metal and embossed with serpents, fire and armoured warriors wearing eyeless helms.

'*Ha!*' thought the Tutor. '*So there really is a vault.*'

The enormous door looked impregnable and he could only imagine what kind of treasures and secrets might lie beyond. Close to the fire, on the opposite side of the room, were two comfortable armchairs. One of the chairs was empty, and in the other was Decimus Fate, lost in restless slumber and surrounded by a dozen shadowy figures; small humanoids with round bellies and large bulbous noses, grey-skinned and yet gleaming with the faint light of Faerie.

'*Imps*' thought the Tutor. '*Some kind of imp or gremlin.*'

Less than a foot tall, the imps were gathered round Fate, watching a series of images that seemed to float in the air like a vision of someone's dreams. So absorbed were they that they did not notice the Tutor's presence, and so he was able to watch as the images in the air changed from one scene to another. There was no sound but it did not take long for the Tutor to realise that he was witnessing scenes of death.

The Tutor felt a knot in his stomach as he realised that these were scenes from Fate's life, scenes where he had killed people, or at least been present at the moment of someone's death. There was a sudden flare of light and Fate moaned in his sleep as the man in one image was suddenly consumed by magical fire. The man's face contorted and his mouth stretched wide as he let out a soundless scream. Fate gave a groan as if he found the image painful, but the imps just gathered more closely as the man collapsed to the floor, his limbs convulsing as he died.

The scene faded and the imps moved to another image that was now growing brighter. The Tutor frowned at this unseemly voyeurism, but then he started as a voice sounded from the corner of the room.

'They call them the Moribundium,'

The Tutor turned to see Motina sitting in a chair, watching as Fate was forced to relive the sins of his life.

'They're an obscure race of Faerie, fascinated by the passing of human life.'

181

The hunchbacked witch did not look at the Tutor. She simply stared at the scenes hovering around Fate and the expression in her raven black eyes was sad.

'It causes him pain,' said the Tutor and Motina nodded. 'So why doesn't he send them away?'

'It's part of a deal he made with a Faerie queen,' said Motina. 'Once a month he allows them to come and feed on the memories of death... the deaths he has witnessed, and the deaths he has caused.'

'And what does he get in return?'

'I don't know,' said Motina as the vision of a woman appeared in the air, screaming in silence as her body dissolved like a statue made of sand.

The Tutor felt sick. The memory of his own wrongdoings was a source of torment in his mind. He could not imagine reliving them for the 'entertainment' of some morbid imps.

'And you also come to watch,' he snapped, immediately regretting the cynical tone in his voice.

'I sit with my master because he suffers, and I do not think he should suffer alone.'

'But he has done terrible things,' said the Tutor. 'Maybe it's right that he should suffer.'

'Maybe it is,' said Motina. 'But are we in any position to judge?'

The Tutor lowered his eyes as the images in the air began to fade. Fate's breathing was growing calmer and the glowing figures of the Moribundium were growing fainter as they slipped through the veil and returned to the Faerie realm.

'There's a room for you upstairs, if you would like it,' said Motina.

'Thank you, but no,' said the Tutor. 'I think I'll sleep better at the inn.'

'It would be safer here.'

'Would it?' said the Tutor. 'It seems that danger follows Fate like a shadow.'

Motina gave a half smile but she did not disagree.

'Thank you for your help,' said the Tutor.

'And you for yours.'

The Tutor gave a shallow bow as his gaze returned to Fate. 'Do you think he will work for Veleno?'

'Never?'

'Then he'll need to find another way to pay him off.'

'Yes, he will,' said the Housekeeper, and there was no way to read the expression in her small black eyes.

'Goodnight, Motina,' said the Tutor.

'Goodnight, demon hunter,' said the witch.

Motina remained in her chair as she heard the front door of the house close. Finally she rose to her feet, picked up a soft woollen blanket and crossed the room to lay it across Fate's lap.

'Has he gone?'

Motina paused at the sound of her master's voice. 'Yes,' she said. 'I think he prefers the comforts of the Fool's Hope Inn.'

Fate gave a wry laugh and drew the blanket up to his waist. 'At least I know where to find him,' he said as he closed his eyes for a more restful sleep.

Motina looked at her master as Fate's breathing grew slow and deep. The tension had gone from his face, but she noticed the hands now lying in his lap. Even asleep, his fingers sought out a particular charm from the bracelet on his wrist. It was the tiny charm of a dagger wreathed in smoke.

23
Weasel

The city wall of Guile was riddled with tunnels. However, in these days of relative peace, the tunnels went unused and the stonework had fallen into disrepair. Some sections were still used as storage areas while others had been taken over by poor communities who had nowhere else to go.

Close to the northwest gate, one section of crumbling tunnels had been claimed by a group of wayfinders. The entrance to their 'home' was a gaping hole surrounded by a tumble of stone blocks. Ten feet above this entrance was a smaller hole leading to a chamber that could only be reached by scaling the wall, and it was from here that Weasel liked to sit and watch the world go by.

It was the following morning and Weasel was dozing when he became aware of a commotion outside. Voices became raised and then he heard the sound of someone crying out in pain. Being careful to remain hidden, he edged forward until he could see what was happening.

On the ground below, one of his fellow wayfinders was writhing in pain with the strands of a glowing whip wrapped around his neck. And standing over the boy was a pale sorcerer dressed in chalky white robes. Weasel's heart quickened as he recognised one of the sorcerers that had attacked Motina at Blackfell House.

'This was not a request,' said the sorcerer as the rest of the wayfinders looked on in fear. 'You will do as I say or I will kill you all.'

'Yes!' cried the boy as the strands of the whip burned brighter. 'We'll do it.'

'What?' asked the sorcerer. 'What will you do?'

'We'll watch the dark-skinned mercenary and the man they call Fate. We'll watch where they go and where they stay.'

'But the Sage is clever,' said one of the wayfinder girls. 'What if he sees us watching?'

'It does not matter,' said the sorcerer. 'Fate and the demon hunter are going to die. So you will watch their every move until we come for them in two days' time. Do you understand?'

'YES!' screamed the boy, but the sorcerer did not withdraw his whip until the rest of the wayfinders had also given their consent. Standing in a horrified circle they nodded their heads.

Finally the sorcerer released the boy. He looked at the children with his pale turquoise eyes before turning away and walking straight towards the wall. However, before he reached the wall he made a sweeping gesture with his hand and the air split apart as a glowing rift opened up in front of him. Weasel caught the smell of hot metal and burning flesh as the sorcerer disappeared. The fiery portal closed behind him but it did not disappear completely. It remained as a small tear in the fabric of reality; a wavering rift of fire, and from the rift, the sorcerer's voice now emerged.

'Speak into this when you have news,' the disembodied voice said. 'But do not touch it. On pain of your immortal soul. Do not touch it.'

Heart beating rapidly, Weasel climbed down from his hiding place to stand with his fellow wayfinders. They were shaken and frightened but this was not the first time their lives had been threatened by someone with power.

'What should we do, Weasel?' said a girl of about thirteen.

'We could just leave,' said a slightly younger boy. 'Move to the other side of the city.'

'No,' said Weasel. 'This is our spot.'

'Then what?'

Weasel paused in thought.

'You will do exactly as the pale sorcerer says,' he said at last. 'You'll watch the mercenary and the master of Blackfell House, and you will tell the sorcerers what they want to hear.'

'And what about you?'

'Me?' said Weasel, his eyes shifting in thought. 'I'm going to see a witch.'

*

Fate's study was not particularly impressive and yet Weasel had never been in such a grand room before. And he had certainly never met anyone as intimidating as the man in the charcoal grey robes. He tried not to squirm as the man looked at him with a dark unsettling gaze.

'You came to the aid of my housekeeper,' said Fate. 'Why?'

Weasel shot a quick glance at Motina who was standing at Fate's shoulder.

'I don't like bullies,' said Weasel and Fate gave a wry snort of amusement.

'Bullies?' he repeated, his gaze turning slightly towards Motina. 'I've never heard the Kane twins described as bullies.'

Weasel raised his chin.

'Don't worry,' said Fate. 'I did not mean to mock you. Indeed, I would like to thank you.'

For some reason praise always made Weasel feel uncomfortable and he lowered his eyes as Fate continued.

'And now you come to warn us that these 'bullies' are going to return.'

Weasel nodded.

'And what do you expect in return for this information?'

'I've heard that you help people,' Weasel began. 'I thought that if I helped you, then maybe you might help me one day, if I ever got into trouble.'

Fate tilted his head as if this was reasonable.

'And the sorcerer you saw just now… he mentioned the Tutor?'

Weasel looked confused.

'The mercenary with the dark skin and blue eyes,' said Fate.

'Yes,' said Weasel. 'He definitely mentioned him.' Weasel paused. 'Is he really a demon hunter?'

'He was,' said Fate. He put a hand to his lips as he leaned forward on the desk. 'And you say these sorcerers will be back in two days' time?'

Weasel nodded.

'We should warn him,' said Motina. 'He won't be safe at the Fool's Hope. We should bring him here.'

Fate dipped his head in agreement as Weasel spoke again.

'Is it true that Master Veleno also wants to kill you?'

Fate arched an eyebrow.

'Ha,' said Weasel with a despairing shake of his head. 'Not exactly short of enemies, are you?'

Fate gave him a sideways look as he stood up from his chair. Moving to a table at the side of the room he opened a lacquered wooden box and removed a small pouch of coins. Coming back to his desk he handed it to Weasel.

'I thought copper might be easier to spend.'

Weasel's eyes grew wide as he felt the weight of the leather pouch.

'And yes, if you ever find yourself in trouble then I will do what I can to help. If I survive the next few days, that is.'

Weasel had earned himself a favour, but he was distracted by the pouch of money as Fate spoke to Motina.

'Go to the Fool's Hope,' he told his housekeeper. 'Tell the Tutor what we have learned and tell him I might be able to protect him from the Kane twins if he comes here.'

'He might not listen,' said Motina. 'I still don't think he trusts you.'

'Maybe he shouldn't,' said Fate. 'I'm not even sure I trust myself.'

'Then why should he come,' said Motina. 'He knows Veleno *and* the Kane twins want his tattoo. And he knows you have the skill to remove it from his chest. Think of it from his point of view. The Kane twins or Master Veleno... what's the difference?'

'The difference,' said Fate, 'is that Veleno would simply kill him to get the tattoo, while the Kane twins will take the tattoo and then sell his soul to the demons of hell.'

Motina's face blanched. 'I will go and speak to him at once.' She looked up to find Weasel staring at her.

'Demons?' he said, wondering what he had got himself involved in. 'And hell... No one said anything about hell.'

24
Veleno

Looking out from the window of his study, Fate sipped a glass of brandy as Motina returned from another fruitless trip to the Fool's Hope Inn.

'He won't come,' she told Fate. 'He says he would rather face these threats on his own terms.'

'I take it he counts me as one of those threats.'

Motina winced because it was true.

'You told him I have a plan for dealing with Veleno?'

'Several times.'

'And he knows the twins will be here tomorrow?'

'He does.'

'Then he's a fool.' Knocking back his drink, Fate strode out of the room and swept up his long-coat from the back of a chair. 'I'll go and speak to him myself.'

'There's no point going now,' said Motina, trailing in his wake. 'He's off to see someone about a job. He won't be back till this evening.'

'Do you know where he went?' asked Fate, but Motina shook her head.

Fate gave a sigh of frustration as he continued on his way.

'Then I'll sit in the Fool's Hope and wait for him.'

With that, he proceeded down the stairs, through the hall and out of the front door. He was just shrugging on his long-coat when he stopped. Master Veleno was standing on the drive with four of his blue-shirted guards.

'And here was I just about to knock,' said the self-styled Lord of the City. 'Now you've gone and spoiled the surprise.'

Fate looked from Veleno to the gate in his perimeter fence where a retinue of five mages were waiting. Four

189

were members of Veleno's 'arcane shield', the fifth was his personal mage, Xanda. The distinctive black glove on his left arm made him an easy figure to recognise. Fate saw the light glinting off the smoky glass from which the left side of his face was formed. And even from here he could feel the hatred in Xanda's eyes.

Eyes narrowed, Fate turned back to Veleno. 'How did you get past the gate?'

'Ah, yes,' said Veleno. 'Xanda was a little concerned about that. He tells me that the fence is dangerous for anyone who wishes you harm.'

'And you're trying to tell me that you don't.' Fate's tone was thick with scepticism, but Veleno just laughed.

'Well, no, my dear chap. I don't mean you any harm. Well, not until the next full moon. And only then if you refuse to do as we have agreed.' He smiled a dangerous smile and turned to look at the gate. 'You know, that gate won't keep me out if you fail to satisfy the conditions of our agreement. Xanda assures me that my mages have enough strength to tear your fence down, if it ever came to that.'

Veleno removed his fine leather gloves and slapped them lightly into the palm of his left hand.

'You do remember the terms of our agreement?' he asked. 'Only I've heard rumours that someone else has shown an interest in you and the demon hunter.' He paused... 'Of course, I could protect you from such threats, but only if you agree to work for me, or make the payment that was promised.'

Fate's frown deepened. He did not like the idea of being under this man's protection, but Veleno was one of the few people in the city who was capable of stopping the Kane twins.

'Should I be worried?' asked Veleno. 'Should I be asking for payment now?'

'Tomorrow,' said Fate. 'I can settle our agreement tomorrow.'

Veleno raised his eyebrows as if he were pleasantly surprised.

'But I need to wait for the Tutor.'

'Ah, yes,' said Veleno. 'Our friend the demon hunter. He seems remarkably indifferent to the threats on his life.'

'He is burdened by guilt and grief,' said Fate. 'Such things can give one a fateful perspective on life.'

'Guilt and grief,' said Veleno with a quizzical smile. 'Two afflictions that I do not suffer from.'

'So I can count on your protection tomorrow?' asked Fate.

'You can,' said Veleno somewhat warily. '*If* you deliver one of the things we agreed upon. I'll be peeved if you don't, and you know how unpleasant things become when I'm peeved.'

'Don't worry. You'll get what you want.'

'Splendid!' said Veleno. 'In that case I will leave you to meet with the demon hunter.' Placing a hand on his chest he gave a wistful sigh. 'Ah... just imagine having a tattoo that guards against magic. So much harder for your enemies to kill you.'

He gave a little shiver of anticipation then, with a shallow bow he turned and walked away. However, he had barely taken a step when he stopped, turning to look at the ruptured earth and the gap on Fate's driveway.

'Is it me...? He asked with mock surprise. 'Or are you missing a tree?'

Fate raised an eyebrow as Veleno's laughter echoed off the walls of Blackfell House. He waited until the Lord of the City had disappeared up the main street before setting off on his way to the Fool's Hope Inn.

25
Reckless & Free

Countess Cévaro had intended to stay for a week at the Shīku monastery. She enjoyed the peace and tranquillity and the long conversations with Abbess Shimitsu. However, with the abbess being absent, there had been little point in a prolonged retreat and so she just stayed overnight before leaving in the early hours of the morning. Normally she came away from the monastery feeling calm and rested, but on this occasion she felt unsettled.

Meeting the Tutor on the road had been brief and yet the countess was still troubled by the demon hunter's words…

'You drove them out with a smile.'

Is that what she had done? She had tried to save the river people from harm, but maybe she was nothing more than a smiling extension of her husband's will? These thoughts kept tumbling over in her mind and she gave a sigh. Weary from hours of riding, she offered a word of thanks as her maid held open the rear door of the Cévaro mansion.

'Where is everyone?' said the maid as she took the countess's travelling cloak.

'I don't know,' said the countess, unsettled by the unnatural quietness of the house.

She had dismissed her bodyguard at the boundary wall of the estate, acknowledging their service with a purse of silver. By now the guards would be drinking in the local town and it was only mid afternoon.

Standing in the main reception hall, the countess was wondering why it was so quiet when her maid spoke.

'Shall I draw you a bath, my Lady?' asked her maid, but the countess held up a hand. There were voices coming from the dining hall... men's voices.

Wearing a frown of concern she gestured for her maid to be quiet before moving carefully towards the dining hall. The voices became louder as they approached the door which hung slightly ajar.

'And you're sure the house will be empty?' said a hissing voice that the countess did not recognise.

'Yes,' said the voice of her husband. 'The countess won't be back for several days and I've told the servants to keep clear of the house.'

'There will be blood,' said a second cold voice.

'And screaming,' said the first.

'You're going to do it here?' exclaimed the count, and the countess edged forward until she could see who was speaking.

The centre of the dining hall had been cleared, and standing in the open space were four men. There was her husband with his personal mage, Lorden Sole. The other two were clearly sorcerers and both had the chalky paleness of ghosts.

'I thought you would take the demon hunter with you,' said the count. 'I didn't think you'd kill him here.'

'He is staying at the Fool's Hope Inn.'

'We cannot carry out the procedure there.'

'We will need peace and quiet to cut the tattoo from his chest.'

The countess's blood ran cold. They were talking about a demon hunter, and the only demon hunter in these parts was the Tutor.

'And what about Fate?' asked the count. 'He will be expecting you to attack.'

'We are counting on it,' said one of the sorcerers.

'In two day's time he will be prepared for us,' said the other.

'So we shall kill him tonight,' they said together.

Trying to control her breathing, the countess moved back from the doorway. There was no doubt about it... these two sorcerers planned on killing Lord Fate and the Tutor. To her shame, she had often turned a blind eye to her husband's cruelty, but here was a chance to do something good. Opening her eyes, she turned to her maid.

'Go to the stables,' she whispered as they moved quietly through the house. 'Saddle up Volatore and then go to the kitchen and wait for me there.'

'My lady?' queried the maid, her face filled with concern.

'Don't worry,' said the countess. 'I'll try to be back by morning.'

'What!' said the maid as she realised what the countess was planning. 'There's no way you can reach Guile tonight, never mind getting back before morning.'

'Nonsense,' said the countess. 'This is Volatore we're talking about.'

The maid gave her a disapproving look, but the countess's mind was set. With a shove she propelled her maid towards the stables before making her way to the kitchen. Feeling like an intruder in her own home, she quickly wrapped some bread, cheese and fruit in a cloth. She took a bottle of elderflower water from the pantry before leaving the house via the servants' entrance and crossing to the quadrangle of the stables.

Her heart was hammering in her chest as she crossed the open space and she kept glancing back towards the house. Never in her life had she done anything so bold and yet it felt good. It reminded her of the girl she had been before her family's estate had fallen on hard times and she had been forced to marry Cévaro. She tried to calm her breathing as she saw her maid leading a beautiful black stallion out of the stalls.

Tucking the bundle of food into a bag behind the saddle, she slipped her foot into the stirrup and swung onto the horse's back. Volatore could sense the tension in her body and she put a hand on his neck to calm him.

The maid looked at her mistress as if she barely recognised her. Indeed, the countess barely recognised herself. She had forgotten many things since becoming the wife of Count Cévaro, but one thing she did remember was how to ride.

She did not go by the gravel driveway. Rather she guided Volatore through the trees until they reached the boundary wall where the gate met the road to Guile and then she gave the stallion his head. Autumn leaves flicked past her face as she raced along the forest road, and for the first time in five years she felt wild and reckless and free.

26
He's Back

The main room of the Fool's Hope Inn was filled with the low murmur of conversation and a faint haze of pipe smoke. The air carried the familiar smells of sawdust, beer and roasting meat from the kitchens. Fate breathed it in as he glanced round the large room, the roof of which was supported by a series of thick oak pillars.

Fate had chosen a table that gave him a view of the main entrance. The inn was fairly busy and yet the tables beside him were empty. Over the last four hours the inn's patrons had grown used to his presence, but still they remained wary of the man in the charcoal grey robes.

When he first arrived, there had been a distinct ripple of disquiet, but Fate ignored the looks and the whispers and the muttered comments about the Sage of Blackfell House. He heard the words, 'Veleno' and 'the Tutor' and some confused murmurs about an attack on his housekeeper. And more than once he heard a reference spoken in lower tones.

'Used to be famous,' so the whispers said.

'They say he killed the *Demon of the Vale.*'

'He didn't?'

'That's what I heard.'

Fate let the gossip wash over him. They were speaking about a man who no longer existed. Eventually, the gossip subsided and he actually started to enjoy the sensation of being in a public place. Afternoon gave way to evening and still there was no sign of the Tutor so Fate ordered a plate of food and a pitcher of light ale. There was no point in going hungry as he waited for the Tutor to return.

*

At the East Gate of Guile, a girl sat with a group of wayfinders beside the gate leading into the city. The girl had been there all day and was beginning to doze when the boy she was sitting with gave her a nudge. Looking up, she saw that a man had appeared on the road leading up towards the gate. It was an hour after sunset but there were oil lamps beside the road and they could clearly see that the man was tall and dark-skinned, and dressed in black leather.

'Is that him?' asked the boy and the girl gave a nod.

Jumping to her feet, she snatched up a stick with a white rag tied to the end and ran to a point on the road where she could see a good distance into the city. She put two fingers in her mouth and gave a surprisingly loud whistle before waving the stick high above her head. Two hundred yards down the road another drowsy wayfinder was roused from his perch in the bell tower of a city council building. He saw the girl, recognised the signal, and immediately struck the bell with a thick stave of wood.

People on the streets looked up in surprise. The bell was not normally rung at this time of the day, but the ringing of the bell was not intended for them and within a minute the message was conveyed from one side of the city to the other.

The demon hunter has returned…

On the west side of the city Weasel watched as a frightened wayfinder approached a small fiery rift that seemed to twist and writhe in the air. The ethereal crack was hot and smelled of burnt stone and unmentionable filth, but still the wayfinder leaned in close as if it were the confessional grille of a temple.

'He's back.'

*

Count Cévaro and Lorden Sole watched as the Kane twins emerged from two shimmering rifts that seemed to hover above the stone floor of his dining hall. Both of the pale sorcerers were covered in cinders and their clothes smoked as if they had just emerged from a forest fire, but neither of them appeared harmed.

'How many did you get?' asked Tilluvian, the sorcerer with the turquoise eyes.

'Three,' said Divorian, his blue-eyed twin.

'Good,' said Tilluvian. 'I have two. That should be more than enough to prevent any interference, but we should let them cool before we use them.'

Walking to the dining table, the twins carefully placed a number of glowing orbs into a silver bowl before moving to pour themselves a glass of water from a decanter that had also been laid out on the table.

The room darkened as the two rifts closed but the orbs in the silver bowl gave off a faint orange glow. Unable to contain his curiosity, Lorden Sole walked over to see what the sorcerers had found in the hellish realm of the Daemonaria. Cévaro was still unnerved by the very presence of the twins, but he was also curious to see what they had found.

About the size of hens' eggs, the fiery orbs looked like some kind of exotic gem.

'Look!' said Sole. 'They're changing.'

Cévaro looked more closely and sure enough, he could see the fiery glow fading, and as it did so he could see the dark shape of a creature moving inside each of the orbs, twisting and slashing as if they were trying to get out.

'What are they?' asked Sole and for a moment the twins just stared at him.

'Demons,' said Divorian.

'Lesser demons from the plains of fire and steel.'

'Scholars call them lacerabi.'

'Those that rend,' they said together.

'Y... you brought demons into my home!' stammered Cévaro, taking a horrified step away from the table.

The twins ignored the count's shock as they moved to retrieve the small orbs that had now cooled to an orange shade of silver. They slipped the orbs into leather pouches on their belts and were about to speak when a small rift opened in the air and a disembodied voice spoke two words.

'*He's back.*'

Cévaro stared at the small rift as the twins moved closer to it.

'And Fate?' asked Tilluvian.

'*He's in the Fool's Hope,*' said the disembodied voice of the wayfinder. '*It looks like he's waiting for the demon hunter.*'

'Perfect.'

'Keep watching them.'

'We will be there tomorrow,' they said together.

*

Back in Guile, Weasel watched as the small rift disappeared in a plume of foul smelling smoke. The wayfinders looked nervous and there was a palpable sense of fear in the air.

'Is that it?' asked a boy of about ten.

'Of course it ain't,' said a slightly older girl. 'They told us to keep watching.'

'But the fiery crack has closed,' persisted the boy. 'How can we talk to them if the speaking crack is gone?'

The wayfinders had no answer, but the young boy had a point. There was something strange going on and

Weasel did not trust the pale sorcerers. Rising from his seat on a nearby wall, he brushed the sandy grit from his trousers and started towards the city.

'Where are you going?' asked the young boy.

'Something's not right,' said Weasel. 'I'm going to talk to the Sage's housekeeper.'

'But what if the sorcerers find out you've been blabbin'?'

'That's just it,' said Weasel. 'It's like they want us to blab.' And with that he set off for Blackfell House.

The wayfinders stared after him except for one girl, with matted blonde hair, who started walking in another direction.

'And where are you going?' asked the boy.

'Weasel's got a nose for this kind of thing,' said the girl. 'So I'm going to see the lady with the sword and the scale mail shirt.'

'She's hurt. She can't do nothin.'

'Maybe not,' said the girl as a young boy moved to join her. 'But she might pay to know that someone else is after the Sage.'

The other wayfinders shifted uneasily as the two children disappeared into the night. They had not asked for this trouble and they had no idea how to get out of it. They were still hovering uncertainly when the sound of an approaching horse surged up the road towards them. There was the clatter and skid of horse shoes on cobblestones and they looked up to see a dark haired noblewoman reigning in a beautiful black stallion that panted and heaved from having been ridden hard.

The woman herself was red-faced, breathless and spattered with mud, but her dark eyes flashed as she stared down at the children.

'The Fool's Hope Inn,' she gasped. 'Who can take me to the Fool's Hope Inn?'

The children looked at each other until the woman held up a silver coin.

'This to the one who can take me there,' she said and finally the children were shaken out of their stupor.

'I can take you,' said a ten year old boy, holding up his hand. 'Just follow me.'

'Too slow,' said the woman. 'You will ride with me.'

Reaching down, she grabbed the boy's outstretched hand and hauled him up onto her horse's back. Even before he was settled in the saddle, she tapped her heels and the stallion sped off into the city leaving the rest of the wayfinders staring in its wake.

27
A Difficult Choice

The Tutor was tired by the time he reached the Fool's Hope. The prospectors who wanted to hire him were camped further from the city than he realised, but it had been worth going. The men had made a significant find, but they wanted some protection before returning to the secret location in the mountains. The job could last some time and the Tutor would be glad of an excuse to leave the city for a few weeks.

Looking forward to a hot meal and a drink, he approached the inn where the Guillotto sisters were standing in their customary positions on either side of the doorway. Nodding to the two women, the Tutor was about pass through the door when Gizelda spoke.

'You've another visitor,' she said.

'Looks like a sorcerer,' added her younger sister, Megan. 'Tall guy with dark hair and weird eyes.'

The Tutor gave a sigh. He paused for a moment before opening the door and making his way to the bar. Looking around the large room, it was not difficult to spot Fate. The tables near him were empty as if people were wary of sitting too close. For a moment the Tutor stared at the hawkish man in the charcoal grey robes, and Fate stared back. There was a half smile on the sorcerer's lips and the Tutor shook his head and turned away as Madam Carletta placed a tankard of ale on the bar.

'He's been here for hours,' said the landlady of the Fool's Hope. 'I told him you might be late, but he just said he'd wait.'

The Tutor took a sip of his beer as a huge man leaned in close to speak to him. It was Viktor, Madam Carletta's doorman. The title was not entirely accurate as Viktor rarely manned the doors of the inn. However, he was very adept at throwing unruly patrons out of said doors, and so the title suited him well enough.

'Want me to throw him out?' asked the enormous man.

The Tutor gave a sniff of amusement. The image of Fate being thrown into the street was strangely appealing, but then he shook his head. 'No,' he said. 'I don't think he'll be staying much longer.'

Viktor seemed disappointed but Madam Carletta just smiled. 'Do you want to eat in the lounge?'

'No,' said the Tutor. 'I'll eat here.'

'I'll let you know when it's ready.'

'Thanks,' said the Tutor, then he picked up his tankard and made his way over to Fate.

*

Sienna was lying in the healing rooms in the Temple of Abnoba when the wayfinder girl found her.

'Where's Fate now?' she asked as she tried to sit up.

'Last I heard he was in the Fool's Hope,' said the girl. 'We think he's waiting for the demon hunter.'

'And the pale sorcerers?' said Sienna. 'Where are they?'

'I don't know,' said the girl. 'They say they're going to attack tomorrow, but Weasel thinks they're lying.'

'Weasel?'

'A wayfinder from the northwest gate. He's smart. He knows when things ain't right.'

'So these sorcerers might attack at any time.'

'I don't know,' said the girl. 'Maybe.'

That was good enough for Sienna and she winced as she eased her legs over the side of the bed.

'Mistress!' said the Abnoba Scion who had been caring for her. 'You must rest or you'll tear the stitches.'

Sienna waved the young woman away. 'Boots!' she gasped. 'Where are my boots?'

The Scion hovered anxiously, but the wayfinder girl spotted Sienna's clothes on a nearby shelf and darted across the room to get them.

'If Fate's going to die, I want to be there to see it.'

Sienna gritted her teeth as she pulled on her breeches. The stab wound from the Tutor's sword had caught her in the belly just to one side near the joint of her hip, and it throbbed now as if someone was twisting a hot knife in her flesh. Wiping sweat from her face she drew off her linen shift and pulled on her clothes, but she could not manage her boots and so the wayfinder girl helped her. Finally she fastened her sword belt around her waist.

Shaking off a wave of dizziness she handed the wayfinder a coin before making her way out of the temple. She ignored the Scion's concern for her safety as she set off for the Fool's Hope Inn. She might not be strong enough to kill Fate herself, but watching him die would be almost as good.

*

Standing in the kitchen of Blackfell House, Motina poured Weasel a glass of sweet wine as she listened to his account of the 'speaking rift' and the latest news of the Kane twins.

'So what exactly is troubling you?' asked Motina.

'It just seems weird,' said Weasel. 'It's like they want Lord Fate to know they're coming.'

Motina's face grew troubled. If the master was at home then she was confident they could hold off the Kane twins. However, if they were to catch him out in the open, there was no way he could defeat them. She paused for a moment before her face set with determination.

205

'Come with me,' she told Weasel as she left the kitchen and picked up her cloak from the hall.

'Where are we going?' asked Weasel, but Motina did not answer. There was little she could do against sorcerers like the Kane twins, but there was one person who might be able to help.

'This isn't the way to the Fool's Hope,' said Weasel as the small witch hobbled in the opposite direction.

'We're not going to the Fool's Hope,' said Motina. 'We're going to see Veleno.'

*

Fate watched as the Tutor moved through the inn towards him.

'Did you get the job?' he asked as the Tutor sat down at his table.

'I did,' said the Tutor. 'Should be good for a few weeks' work.'

'Not if you die tomorrow,' said Fate.

The Tutor stared at Fate as he took a drink of his ale.

'The sorcerers that attacked Motina,' said Fate. 'They're coming back tomorrow.'

The Tutor put down his tankard and wiped his mouth as Fate continued.

'I can protect you, but only if you come back to Blackfell House.'

'Are you sure you don't have another reason for getting me back in that house,' said the Tutor. 'A reason that might have something to do with paying Veleno.'

'I fully intend to pay Veleno,' said Fate. 'And once we pay him then he can protect us both from the Kane twins.'

The Tutor pursed his lips and gave a slow nod.

'I appreciate your concern,' he said. 'But as I told your housekeeper, I prefer to take my chances on my own. Besides, I'll be out of the city tomorrow.'

Fate just looked at him, while under the table he was toying with the dagger charm on his wrist.

'And you're sure I can't change your mind.'

'I'm sure,' said the Tutor. 'But I appreciate the offer, and I appreciate you helping Abbess Shimitsu.' He gave a little laugh. 'I was almost convinced you were a changed man.'

'I suppose that's progress of a sort,' said Fate, but even now the smile on his face concealed the thoughts in his mind.

At that moment there came a whistle from the bar.

'Looks like your food is ready,' said Fate.

'Can I get you something?' asked the Tutor as he stood up from the table.

'I've already eaten,' said Fate. 'But I'll join you for one last drink if you like.'

'Fair enough,' said the Tutor.

Fate filled his tankard with ale from the jug on the table. Then, as the Tutor went to get his food from the bar, the sorcerer looked down at the charm he had just removed from the bracelet on his wrist. A tiny dagger wreathed in smoke. This charm was powerful and Fate did not want to waste it. Looking up, he watched as the Tutor took the tray of food from Madam Carletta and laughed at something the enormous man at the bar said to him.

People liked the Tutor. Indeed, Fate liked the man himself, but he had a difficult choice to make.

He was fairly sure he would be able to pay Veleno, but he was not *certain*. And as for the Kane twins...

If he and the Tutor returned to Blackfell House he could protect them both, but if the Tutor refused to come then he would be at the mercy of the twins and not even a demon hunter could defeat two such powerful sorcerers.

As for himself, there were only two ways that Fate could be *certain* of surviving. One was to work for Veleno and the other was to kill the Tutor and cut the tattoo from his chest. All other choices came with an element of risk and Fate had just moments to decide before the Tutor returned from the bar.

Finally he made his decision.

Reaching out casually, he held the dagger charm over the Tutor's drink. Then, with a pinch of his fingers he crushed the charm and it crumbled into a fine powder that quickly disappeared in the golden liquid of the Tutor's ale.

'Roast lamb with parsnips and crusty bread,' said the Tutor as he got back to the table and took his seat. 'Are you sure you won't join me?'

'I'm sure,' said Fate and he watched as the Tutor picked up his tankard.

'To the shadows of the past,' said the Tutor. 'Maybe Abbess Shimitsu is right. Maybe men like us deserve a second chance.'

'Maybe we do,' said Fate. He raised his own tankard and his eyes glittered with gold as the two men drank to the Tutor's toast.

'Well,' said Fate. 'If I can't convince you to come back to my home, then I will leave you in peace.' He rose from the table and was about to leave when the doors to the inn opened and a dark-haired woman rushed into the room. It was Countess Cévaro.

Fate and the Tutor frowned as the countess hurried over to their table.

'They're coming,' she gasped, and Fate's eyes narrowed in concern. 'They said they would be coming tomorrow, but they're not. They're coming tonight.'

'Who?' said the Tutor. 'Who's coming?'

'The sorcerers,' said the countess. 'Two sorcerers, pale as ghosts… They're coming for you tonight.'

Putting a hand on his sword, the Tutor looked at Fate, but Fate was staring at the Tutor's drink. He knew the dagger charm would work, but he did not know precisely how long it would take to work. As the Tutor invited the countess to take a seat, Fate glanced around the inn. Everyone was looking at them, but he was not concerned with their attention. He was searching the darker recesses of the room, looking for a shadow that seemed out of place, a shadow that might be following the movements of the Tutor.

'I heard them talking,' the countess told the Tutor. 'They're coming to kill Lord Fate and to cut the tattoo from your chest.'

'Is something wrong?'

The Tutor looked up to see Madam Carletta standing there with Viktor looming over her shoulder. 'There might be trouble,' he told the landlady.

'We should leave,' said Fate.

The two men stood up from the table and the Tutor turned to the countess.

'You should go,' he told her. 'You took a risk in coming to warn us, but you should leave.'

'Cévaro thinks I'm still at the monastery,' said the countess. 'But my horse is exhausted. There's no way I can get back before he finds out the truth.'

The Tutor gave nod of understanding and turned to Madam Carletta. 'Is the light carriage still in the courtyard?' he asked and Madam Carletta gave a smile.

'Don't worry,' she said. 'I'll make sure she's home before sunrise.'

'Thank you,' said the Tutor before turning to Fate. 'Maybe it *would* be a good idea to spend the night at your house.'

'It's too late,' said Fate as the room filled with the smell of burning stone. 'They're here.'

28
Demons, Daggers and Debts

The Tutor watched as a fiery rift suddenly appeared in the room. Stretching from floor to ceiling, the rift pulsed with an orange light and the heat radiating from it was so strong that people backed away, coughing and gagging on the foul smell that now permeated the room. To them it was new and unsettling, but the Tutor knew it only too well. It was the smell of the underworld, the stench of the Daemonaria.

Beside the Tutor, Fate stared at the rift and then his dark eyes narrowed as two figures emerged. Tall and ghostly white, the Kane twins looked around the dimly lit room before their gaze settled on Fate and the Tutor.

Almost instinctively, the Tutor took a step forward, placing himself between Fate and the two pale sorcerers. Madam Carletta did the same, stepping in front of the countess as her hand moved to the handle of a dagger concealed in her skirts. The shocked customers backed away from the sorcerers. Victor drew his shortsword and Divorian looked at the enormous man as the Guillotto sisters swept in through the front door. Meanwhile, Tilluvian raised an arm and pointed a pale finger at Fate.

'We have come for Fate and the demon hunter.' His eyes were on Fate, but it was Madam Carletta who answered.

'Not here,' she said in a surprisingly calm voice. 'The customers of this establishment are under my protection.'

Tilluvian's eyes slid across to her and the landlady of the Fool's Hope raised her chin in defiance.

'So be it,' said the sorcerer.

'I think it's time you gentlemen left,' said Viktor.

211

The doorman spoke politely, but he was so huge that his very presence seemed like a threat. As he started towards the twins, Tilluvian extended his arm. From the palm of his hand there came a pulse of orange force and Viktor was thrown back into a group of customers standing around a table. Victor's face and clothes were singed, and the table gave off the smell of scorched wood.

Even as Viktor was sent sprawling, a dagger came spinning from near the door. Thrown by Gizelda, the dagger was heading straight for Tilluvian. However, before it could strike, Divorian raised a hand, conjuring a magical barrier that flared for an instant as the dagger was reduced to a shower of hot fragments.

Alarmed by this show of magical force many customers scrambled for the exits, but more than a few held their ground. Over to the left a burly man grabbed a chair and made to throw it. However, before he could let go, the strands of an energy whip flicked towards him and the man howled as the magical thongs branded the skin of his hands.

Far from intimidating the remaining customers, these magical attacks seemed to galvanise their courage. Drawing various weapons, they started forward then stopped as the twins produced several small silvery orbs and threw them into the room.

Time seemed to slow as the glowing orbs sailed through the air. People followed them with their eyes then recoiled in shock as they hit the floor and burst open to unleash the demons trapped inside.

'Lacerabi!' growled the Tutor as five enraged demons began attacking the customers.

Standing almost five feet tall, the demons were vaguely humanoid with skin like the dark crust that forms over lava. With piercing shrieks they sprang forward, slashing at customers with curved blades that were actually an extension of their arms.

'Don't touch them!' cried the Tutor as a man burned his hand when he tried to grab one of the lacerabi. 'Aim for the heart! Steel in the heart will kill them!'

Seeing the customers struggling he rushed to help, leaving Fate to face the two pale sorcerers alone.

Dark eyes met those of turquoise and blue, but the Kane twins seemed uncertain as if they expected Fate to unleash a magical attack of his own. For a moment they hesitated, but then they smiled. The rumours were true. The great feral mage no longer used magic. Decimus Fate was no longer to be feared.

With renewed confidence, the Kane twins drew their swords and advanced.

All around the room, the fight was raging and Fate stood at the centre of the storm. He drew his dragon-handled daggers, but he knew that without his magic, he was no match for the twins. The Tutor could probably defeat one of the sorcerers, but not both of them together. As the Kane twins came closer, Fate wondered again how long it would take for the dagger charm to work. His eyes flicked towards a dark corner of the inn.

Was that a shadow there, a sinister darkness in the form of a cowled figure?

Whatever the case, he had no time to look more closely as the coils of a blue energy whip lashed out towards him. Wielding his black-handled dagger, Fate sliced through the whip and the severed strands began to turn black as their light was extinguished by the lethal magic in Fate's blade.

With an audible hiss, Divorian cleansed the weapon with a surge of magical force. Fate might no longer wield magic, but he still possessed items that had magical

213

properties of their own. As the lacerabi continued to cause havoc, the twins attacked in earnest.

Fate fought with surprising skill, deflecting whips and sword strokes with his daggers, but he soon found himself attacked from two sides.

Tilluvian's whip flicked out towards him and Fate blocked it with his white-handled dagger. However, the magic of this weapon had no effect on demonic forces and so the glowing coils wrapped around the blade and snatched it from his grasp.

At the same time, Divorian attacked from the opposite direction and Fate ground his teeth as the strands of the blue whip wrapped around his wrist. Divorian sent a surge of power through the whip and Fate's legs almost buckled. That amount of force would have been enough to render a normal person unconscious, but the innate power of Fate's feral magic offered him some protection, even if he never tried to use it.

He tried to swap the black-handled dagger to his free hand, but Tilluvian caught his other arm with a flick of his own turquoise whip. Fate sank to one knee as his arms were pulled out to either side then he threw back his head and mouthed a silent scream as the Kane twins channelled their hateful power into his flesh.

Fate's body shook with the force of it, but still that core of feral magic held death at bay. The Kane twins grew impatient and Tilluvian was actually raising his turquoise sword for the kill when a fighting star zipped through the air before biting into the flesh of his upper arm. A moment later, the Tutor darted forward and slashed the cords of the sorcerer's whip. So clean was the cut that Tilluvian actually staggered backwards, and it was only this movement that saved him from the Tutor's second attack.

As one of his arms came free, Fate collapsed to the floor as the Tutor took the fight to Tilluvian. The pale sorcerer was clearly a trained fighter, but he was no match for an experienced demon hunter. He blocked a downward blow then gasped as the Tutor's sword whipped across his stomach. The sorcerer hunched over a shallow wound and would have died had his brother not relinquished his hold on Fate.

Wrenching his energy whip from around Fate's wrist, Divorian reached into the Daemonaria and flung out a mass of burning stone. Tilluvian was saved as chunks of red-hot stone hammered into the Tutor's side and a bloody gash appeared on his cheek as one of the larger pieces struck him in the face.

The Tutor swayed from the impact as Divorian moved in with his sword. The blue-eyed sorcerer was about to strike when Gizelda leapt onto his back. The Guillotto sister managed to stab him once in the shoulder before Divorian's body burst into blue flame. The cold flames did not harm the sorcerer but they burned Gizelda with an icy fire and with a cry of agony she was forced to let go.

As she fell to the floor, Megan leapt in to defend her as Tilluvian attacked them both. With a sweep of his sword he unleashed an arc of fire that threw the sisters backwards, smashing them into tables and chairs. Gizelda's body went limp as she struck her head while Megan's hair and clothes were set on fire.

Twenty feet away, Madam Carletta saw the two sisters being struck down. Still trying to shield the countess from harm, she watched in horror as one of the lacerabi turned its attention to the sisters, one of whom was unconscious. The landlady of the Fool's Hope was too far away to help, but her enormous doorman was not.

'Victor!' she cried.

With a stool in one hand and his sword in the other, Victor was trying to subdue another of the demons when he heard Madam Carletta's shout. Looking round, he saw the Guillotto sisters sprawled on the floor with a lacerabus bearing down on them. The slender demon was silhouetted against a window that looked onto the street. Without hesitation, Victor charged straight at the creature. Discarding the stool, he dropped his shoulder as he drove the demon straight through the lattice window, taking out a sizeable chunk of the wall in the process.

Victor and the demon went sprawling into the street, but the demon was quicker to get back to its feet. Victor had lost his grip on his sword and even as he reached for the weapon, the demon slashed down to deliver a burning wound to the big man's shoulder. Still on his knees, Victor growled, pulled in his arm and looked up as the demon aimed another blow at his face. The curved blade would have cloven his skull had it not been blocked by a slender sword that seemed to appear from nowhere.

The big man watched as a cloaked figure avoided another attack from the lacerabus before severing the demon's arm at the elbow. The attack was so fast that Victor could barely follow it, and it was followed up by a second attack that bit into the demon's neck.

'The heart!' gasped Victor. 'Go for the heart!' This information was clearly heeded as the stranger lunged forward to bury the point of their sword in the demon's chest.

The lacerabus let out a high-pitched scream as it burst apart in a shower of cindered flesh.

Flinching from the explosion, Victor looked up to see that his saviour was a woman; a young woman who stumbled now as if she was nursing an injury of her own.

Putting a hand to her belly she braced herself on Victor's shoulder before limping away towards the hole that now gaped in the wall of the Fool's Hope Inn.

Retrieving his sword, Victor struggled to his feet and followed after the woman as she swayed on her feet and slumped against the shattered frame of the window. It was clear that the woman was wounded and Viktor reached out to catch her before she collapsed. He winced as she leaned against his injured shoulder then he looked down to see her leather trousers soaked in blood. Still the woman tried to continue.

'Wait,' said Viktor. 'It's too dangerous.'

'I need to see,' said the woman, her voice stiff with pain.

'See what?' said Viktor.

'Fate,' said the woman. 'I need to see him die.'

Viktor just stared at the woman then glanced inside to see the customers struggling to defeat the remaining demons while the Tutor was fighting both twins at the same time.

Striking at one and then the other, the demon hunter prevented them from coming close to Fate. However, each time he closed the distance on one, the other would snag him with a whip or strike him with some attack from the demon realm. They could not defeat him with swords so they concentrated on magical attacks.

With each attack, the tattoo on his chest would glow as it absorbed some of the magical harm, but slowly his strength began to fail and the sorcerers' attacks began to burn more deeply.

The Tutor lunged at Tilluvian only to find his free arm caught by Divorian's whip. Gritting his teeth he tried to pull the blue-eyed sorcerer within reach of his sword, but at the last minute Divorian opened a rift around the

217

Tutor's arm and then let it snap shut, trapping the Tutor's arm in a glowing manacle of fire.

The Tutor tried to pull himself free, but the rift held him fast. He was trying not to imagine what creatures might be drawn to his human flesh when the thongs of a turquoise energy whip wrapped around his neck. The pain from the burning cords suddenly became more intense as the twins combined their power to subdue the demon hunter.

Still reeling from the energy that had almost killed him, Fate retrieved his black-handled dagger. Stumbling forward, he tried to sever the turquoise whip, but he was knocked off his feet by a blast of energy from Divorian. His head struck the edge of a table and his vision swam as he tried to stand, but then he too felt the choking grip of an energy whip as the blued eyed twin stood over him. The coils of Divorian's whip were now so short that it looked as if the sorcerer was holding Fate on a leash.

The eyes of the twins shone with triumph as both Fate and the Tutor were brought to their knees. With a shake of his head, Divorian dismissed the rift that was holding the Tutor. The demon hunter sagged a little as his hand came free then reached up to try to relieve the scalding pressure around his neck.

Fate's vision began to fade as the constriction of the whip cut off the flow of blood to his brain. Deep in his heart a part of him was screaming.

'*Kill them!*' the screaming cried. '*Let me loose and we can kill them both!*'

It was the sound of his own magical power raging to be free, a power so great it could eclipse that of the Kane twins combined.

The screaming was so insistent that it seemed impossible to refuse. And yet Fate refused it. It had taken many months and all his willpower to silence that screaming, and now it was using the threat of his own death to test the strength of his conviction. Was he the master of himself or was he forever doomed to be a slave to magic?

Even as the room darkened around him, Fate smiled. The Kane twins might kill him, but he would die a free man. Finally he knew that he had won.

Nearby, the Tutor showed no such acceptance. He clung to life with the strength of a man who did not know how to give up. He tried to pull Tilluvian's whip from around his neck, he tried to reach the sorcerer with his sword, but slowly the vitality was being squeezed out of his body.

Fate could see that the Tutor was doomed, but even as Tilluvian raised his sword to kill the demon hunter a dark shape appeared behind him. At first, Fate was not sure if it was a cowled figure or just another shadow heralding the onset of death. But then he saw the cold glint of a steel dagger, a dagger that closely resembled the charm he had crushed into the Tutor's drink.

All these years he thought he would use that charm to save his own life, but now he had used it to save the life of another. Even as Tilluvian's sword began to fall, the shadowy figure caught his arm. Tilluvian's body tensed with surprise, but before he could even think about casting a spell, the figure reached round to slit the sorcerer's throat.

The turquoise light went out of Tilluvian's eyes. He dropped his sword and the coils of his energy whip vanished. For a moment the Tutor could only gasp as oxygen flooded back into his brain but then, as Tilluvian's body collapsed behind him, he swept up his sword and dived in the direction of Fate.

Divorian stared in horror as his brother's body crumpled to the floor. For a few seconds he was stunned with disbelief, and that was all the Tutor needed. Coming out of a roll, he killed the sorcerer with a single thrust that took the sorcerer under the ribs.

Divorian's pale blue eyes faded to white as the Tutor rose to his feet with the sorcerer still impaled on his sword. Lowering the weapon he allowed the lifeless body to slide off his blade. Behind him, Fate coughed and choked as the strangling cords vanished from around his throat.

Struggling to his feet, Fate looked across at the shadowy figure that had killed Tilluvian. He could not see the assassin's face but he could just make out the eyes of a woman. There was recognition in that unyielding gaze, but also surprise. A life-saving kill from *her* order was a priceless gift. Using it to save another person's life seemed unthinkable, but it was not the assassin's place to question how the gift was used. She had done her duty and repaid the debt they owed to Fate. With the merest of bows, the cowled figure took a step backwards and seemed to melt away into darkness.

Around the room people stared at the Tutor and the man in the charcoal grey robes.

'Well,' said Fate as he touched the burn marks on his neck. 'That was a little too close for comfort.'

Hardly able to believe the sorcerer's glib comment, the Tutor turned his blue eyes on Fate. The questions were just beginning to form in his mind when four purple-robed figures stepped in through the hole that Viktor had made in the wall of the inn. Before Fate or the Tutor could utter another word, the four mages made sweeping gestures with their hands and both sorcerer and demon hunter were thrown across the room and pinned against the wall by magical force.

Two more robed figures entered the room followed by a mage that Fate knew all too well. His left arm was covered by a long black glove and the dark skin on the left side of his face appeared to be made of glass. It was Xanda, Veleno's personal mage. Xanda quickly assessed the situation. He made sure that Fate and the Tutor were securely held before stepping aside for his employer.

There followed the crunch of broken glass as Master Veleno entered the Fool's Hope Inn.

'My, my!' said the self-styled Lord of the City. 'This party seems to have got a bit out of hand'.

29
Until Tomorrow

Looking around the room, Veleno spotted Madam Carletta still shielding the countess as they stood close to the wall. 'I take it you are the mistress of this fine establishment.'

'I am,' said Madam Carletta with a touch of defiance.

Veleno gave a shallow bow before shifting his eyes to the countess and repeating his bow. He might not know every noble woman from out of town, but he recognised a woman of high standing when he saw one. Straightening up, he looked around the room, shaking his head in disbelief.

'What a frightful mess,' he said to Madam Carletta, and still he did not look at Fate or the Tutor. 'I have no idea what might have caused such a ruckus, but I will gladly pay for the damage if you will allow me a quiet word with two of your guests.'

Despite herself, Madam Carletta's eyes moved across the room to where Fate and the Tutor were being held against the wall by an invisible force.

'Ah, the very chaps!' exclaimed Veleno. 'I wouldn't be at all surprised if these two miscreants were the cause of all this commotion. Am I wrong?' he asked, turning back to Madam Carletta as he crossed the room to stand beside Fate.

Veleno removed his fine leather gloves as his eyes flicked up towards the sorcerer. Seeing how Fate's face was being squashed against the wall, he gave an impatient gesture and Xanda instructed the mages to relax their hold.

'I must admit to being a little hurt,' said Veleno. 'Someone tells me you've been playing with new friends.'

As Veleno said this, two more figures appeared at the hole in the wall. One was young and wiry of build. The other was hunched and slightly crooked of limb. Fate gave a sigh as he recognised his housekeeper and the wayfinder known as Weasel. Veleno glanced at Motina and Weasel before turning to look at the two pale sorcerers lying dead on the floor.

'Oh dear,' he said. 'It looks like you and your new friends have had a falling out!'

Fate raised his eyebrows as if to say, '*These things happen,*' and Veleno nodded as he pursed his lips.

'But I will be most annoyed if this affects our agreement.'

'It won't,' said Fate. 'I can settle our agreement tomorrow.'

'Tomorrow?' said Veleno, with a dubious frown. 'From the look of you, I think you'd have difficulty getting out of bed tomorrow, never mind taking on the difficult job I have lined up for you.'

'I never said I would work for you,' said Fate.

'Forgive me, old friend,' said Veleno. 'But you don't appear to be in a position to negotiate.'

'I don't need to negotiate,' said Fate. 'We have an agreement. And everyone knows the Lord of the City is a man of his word.' Fate raised his voice to make sure everyone in the room heard his words.

Veleno gave a little laugh and forced a smile onto his face.

'Quite right,' he said as he turned to address the room. 'Never let it be said that Master Veleno would renege on a deal. 'So...' he continued. 'Will you call at my residence tomorrow or shall I be forced to come and find you at Blackfell House.'

'The Western Gate at the seventh hour of the morning,' said Fate. 'We'll meet you there.'

Veleno slapped his fine leather gloves into the palm of his hand. He did not think that Fate was lying, but the sorcerer was altogether too slippery.

'Very well,' he said at last. 'The Western Gate at seven of the morn. But there are to be no more shenanigans!'

'You have my word.'

'Until tomorrow then,' said Veleno and with that, he gave a click of his fingers.

Veleno's mages removed their magical force field and Fate and the Tutor collapsed to the floor.

'My ladies,' said Veleno offering Madam Carletta and the countess another bow as he left through the hole in the wall.

As Veleno and his mages moved off into the night, Motina climbed in through the hole and rushed to her master's side, while Madam Carletta and the countess went to see to the Tutor. Both men were sporting multiple injuries but neither appeared badly hurt.

'Are you all right?' asked Motina as she studied the burns around Fate's neck.

'I'm fine,' said Fate.

Beside him, the Tutor was worrying about Viktor and the Guillotto sisters.

'They'll be all right,' said Madam Carletta. 'A few cuts and burns, and Viktor's got a nasty gash on his shoulder. But they will be all right.'

Sighing with relief, the Tutor turned to Fate.

'So,' he began. 'Are you going to tell me what the hell just happened?'

'I will,' said Fate. 'But first let's get back to Blackfell House. I don't think these good people will be happy with you staying here tonight.'

The Tutor did not like the idea but Fate was right. After causing so much trouble, it would not be a good idea for him to remain at the inn. He would hear what Fate had to say, but he would be glad when he could put the sorcerer and this whole mess with Veleno behind him.

Slowly the drama of the night began to subside. Madam Carletta's staff began clearing up the mess as Fate and the Tutor got to their feet. They were just starting towards the door when Fate felt the unsettling sensation of being watched. Turning to scan the room, he saw a hooded figure slumped against the edge of the hole that Victor had made. The figure's face was cloaked in shadow but Fate knew who it was.

It was Sienna Blade, daughter of the friend he had killed. As Motina led the way out of the inn, Fate put a hand to the letter in his breast pocket. The Tutor was not the only one who deserved some answers.

30
The Rich Man in the Forest

It was an hour before dawn when the countess arrived back at the Cévaro estate. Feeling sick with fatigue, she settled Volatore in the stables before making her way to the kitchens where her maid was dozing in a chair. With no time for explanations they set about returning the countess to her chambers before any of her guards returned from their drunken night in town. Moving quickly through the house, they made their way up to the first floor landing. They were just turning towards the countess's chambers when the count's voice drifted up from the dining hall.

'Why haven't they returned?' Cévaro shouted. 'What's taking them so long? What if they failed to kill Fate?'

He paused.

'Do you think Fate will come for me?' The count asked. 'If he finds out I sent the Kane twins... Do you think he'll come for me?'

'You should get some rest,' said the voice of Lorden Sole. 'I'm sure there's nothing to worry about.'

Nothing to worry about.

The countess had no idea if Fate would go after her husband, but she felt a surge of wicked satisfaction. For the first time in their married life, her husband was afraid.

The countess and her maid turned to continue. However, as they passed one particular door they heard a muffled sound coming from within. It sounded like a sob. Despite the fear of being discovered, the countess stopped. Her maid stepped forward to open the door but found that it was locked. However, the key was still in the lock and upon opening the door they found one of the serving girls tied to a bed and crying from the pain of a leg that was clearly broken. At first she did not see who had entered the room and she shrank away begging them not to hurt her.

'It's all right,' whispered the countess as her maid went to calm the young woman.

'Don't let them take me,' sobbed the girl when she saw who it was. 'Please mistress! Don't let the pale devils take me.'

The countess did not know what had happened to the girl, but she could guess who the pale devils were. Checking the coast was clear, they untied the girl and helped her out of the room. With no other servants around, they struggled to get the girl to the countess's chambers.

The countess laid the girl down on a couch while her maid went to run a bath for her mistress. There was no time for hot water so the countess bathed in cold. She scrubbed the mud from her face, and brushed twigs from her hair before retiring to bed with her heart hammering in her chest. There was little chance of sleep, indeed she almost felt as if the night's adventures had been nothing but a dream.

When the sun rose she gathered her courage and went down from her bedroom. As she reached the bottom of the staircase, her husband emerged from the dining room looking anxious and gaunt.

'Good morning, my lord,' she said while her husband could only stare.

'I... I thought you were at the monastery.'

'Abbess Shimitsu was not at the monastery so I decided to come home early,' said the countess. 'I would have greeted you last night but I heard you talking and didn't want to disturb you. Besides,' she added. 'I was tired from the long ride.'

The count looked as if he were trying to gauge how much she might have heard.

'I can take breakfast in the parlour if you still have business in the hall.'

'That... would be appreciated.'

'Oh,' said the countess as she stopped at the parlour door. 'The serving girl who broke her leg on the stairs...' The count looked suddenly pale. 'I've taken her to my chambers until a physician can be called.'

'Of course,' said the count. He attempted a smile, but it was the smile of a man who had spent the night playing high stakes poker... and lost.

*

Back in Guile, the city was coming to life as two men waited on horseback beside the West Gate of the city. The road was busy and yet people moved aside as Master Veleno approached the gate with a retinue of five mages and a six armed guards.

'Are you sure about this?' said the Tutor as they watched the Lord of the City approach.

'Fairly sure,' said Fate.

The Tutor rolled his eyes. He had spent the night in the guest apartment of Blackfell House where Fate had explained the appearance of the mysterious cowled figure.

'They're known as the Informis Umbra,' said Fate as they sipped a mulled tonic that Motina had prepared for them.

'The Formless Shadow,' said the Tutor. 'I thought they were a myth.'

'Most myths have some basis in reality.'

'And *they* owed *you* a favour?'

'It was more of a promise,' said Fate. 'The settling of a debt.'

'Some promise,' said the Tutor. 'So why use it on me? We were both in danger. Why not use the promise to save your own life?'

'A simple calculation,' said Fate. 'If I used it to save my life then both of us might have died because I could not have killed even one of the Kane twins. But if I used it to save your life there was a chance that you might save mine in return.'

The Tutor seemed to accept this, but then he frowned. 'But you used the charm before we knew the twins were coming.'

'No,' said Fate. 'I knew they were coming.'

'Yes,' said the Tutor. 'But you thought they were going to attack the following night, when I would have been on my way to the mountains.'

'Perhaps,' admitted Fate. 'But you would have been in the open, while I would have had the relative safety of Blackfell House.'

'So you *did* use it to save...'

The Tutor was cut off mid sentence as Motina placed a hand on his arm.

'Best just to leave it,' said the housekeeper as she took the Tutor's empty glass. 'You're not going to say thank you, and he's not going to say you're welcome.'

Fate arched an eyebrow, but the Tutor's frown remained. The Decimus Fate of legend would never waste such a powerful charm to save the life of another. He had always thought the sorcerer was acting in his own self interest, but maybe he was wrong. Maybe the great feral mage really had changed.

Slowly the drama of the evening, and Motina's potent tonic, had begun to work on both men and they slept in their chairs until Motina woke them with bowls of sweet porridge and bergamot tea.

'All right,' said the Tutor as he finished his breakfast. 'I'm finally convinced that you don't plan on cutting the tattoo from my chest. So exactly how do you plan on paying Veleno?'

Fate told him what he had in mind and the Tutor shook his head in disbelief. More calculations that may, or may not, work out the way Fate hoped.

Now it was morning and the Tutor's misgivings remained as Veleno brought his black stallion to a stop. Behind him was Xanda, his eyes filled with hate as he kept his expression neutral so as not to crack the smoky crystal skin that formed the left side of his face.

'So,' said Veleno. 'Are you going to work for me, or are you going to carve the tattoo from this poor man's chest?'

'Neither,' said Fate.

'Then what?' asked Veleno and it was clear that his patience was nearing its end.

'We're going to pay someone a visit.'

'Oh,' said Veleno. 'Who?'

'A rich man who lives in the forest,' said Fate.

If Veleno had been annoyed when they left the city, he was positively fuming when he finally realised where Fate was leading them.

'I hope you don't intend to pay me with my own gold,' said Veleno as they turned into the driveway of Lord Cardini's estate. 'I'm warning you, Fate. If you've done anything to interrupt Cardini's production I will not be pleased.'

The Tutor glanced at Fate. It was unnerving the way Veleno's talk of displeasure conjured up images of thumb racks and branding irons.

As they reached the house, Fate knocked on the door and the tension mounted until Cardini's manservant answered.

'You!' he exclaimed when he saw Fate. 'And you, my lord!' he added when he saw Veleno standing beside him. His tone changed from accusation to fear as he looked from Fate to Veleno. 'It's not my fault,' he cried in a high, wheedling tone. 'I only let him in. I had no idea that he meant the master harm.'

'What do you mean, *harm*?' said Veleno as they moved through into the reception hall where the remains of the security golem still lay on the marble floor tiles. Veleno stared down at the broken statue and his expression darkened as he looked at Fate.

'He's done something to the master,' said the manservant.

'And where is your master now?' asked Veleno.

'He's in the workshop, my lord.' The manservant motioned towards the phase door. But he hasn't come up for food or drink, and he never stays down there so long.'

Veleno turned to look at the enchanted door, the tiles of which formed the image of a sloping tunnel.

'Don't touch it!' said Fate as Veleno moved to stand before the door.

'What have you done to Cardini?' asked Veleno. 'Did you kill him?'

'He was alive when I left him.'

'Then, what?'

'We'll find out soon enough,' said Fate. 'But first you must make a promise.'

'You are in no position to make demands.'

'And you will never get past that door unless I open it for you.'

The muscles in Veleno's jaw bunched.

231

'Very well,' he said. 'What is this promise?'

'You can take whatever you want from Cardini's workshop... except for two particular pendants.'

'And what is so special about these pendants?' asked Veleno with a dangerous glint in his eye.

'One is of sentimental value and the other is dangerous.'

Veleno did not like making 'blind' deals but he was desperate to see that his gold supply had not been interfered with.

'Oh, very well,' he sighed. 'But no more tricks.'

'No more tricks,' said Fate. 'Now, stand back. I will only get one chance at this.'

Veleno and his men backed away, while the Tutor hovered at Fate's shoulder.

'I hope you're right about this,' he said in a low voice.

'So do I.'

'And what happens if you fail?'

'I will be burned alive and you will need to explain to Veleno that his gold supply has been cut off.'

'Then please don't fail,' said the Tutor as he also backed away.

Standing in front of the tiled door, Fate closed his eyes and took a breath. In his mind he recalled the image of Cardini touching the various tiles of the door. He needed to remember the sequence precisely or die. Finally he opened his eyes and then his hand began to move.

The others in the hall watched as Fate's fingers touched one tile after another. He must have touched more than twenty tiles when the image of the door fell away to form a downward sloping tunnel.

'Impressive,' said the Tutor as he returned to Fate's side.

'Thank you,' said Fate as Veleno came to stand with them.

'Is it safe to proceed?'

'It is, so long as I accompany you,' said Fate. 'I opened the door, so it will accept those who enter with me. But it will close if someone tries to enter alone. Your mages will need to hold it open or risk losing access forever.'

Waving his mages forward, Veleno walked down the passageway, calling out to the alchemist as he went.

'Cardini, my friend... are you there? Lord Fate has treated you in the most beastly fashion and I can only hope...' Veleno's words were suddenly cut off as he entered the alchemist's workshop.

'What is it, my lord?' said Xanda, giving Fate a poisonous look as he moved to follow his master.

Fearing the worst, the Tutor put a hand to his sword as he and Fate moved down the passage. He expected to hear cursing and threats, so he was surprised when the first sound he heard from Veleno was laughter... soft, deep and highly amused laughter.

More curious than ever, the Tutor walked beside Fate as they moved into the workshop. The centre of the room was dominated by a large device formed from interwoven hoops of brass and silver. The Tutor stared at the complex machine until he noticed Veleno standing beside a figure who appeared to be operating the device.

'It's Cardini,' said the Tutor.

'Yes, it is,' said Fate.

'But he appears to be made entirely from...'

'Gold!' said Veleno, finishing the Tutor's sentence. 'The poor alchemist has worked so hard that he has transformed *himself* into gold.'

Once again, Veleno laughed as the Tutor looked on in horror. Fate had told him that the talisman would have compelled Cardini to keep producing gold, even to the point of death.

'You knew,' he whispered to Fate. 'You knew he would end up like this.'

'I suspected,' said Fate. 'I saw his handprint on the tankard and I saw that he had already lost the ends of his fingers. I just didn't know how long the chrysopoeian cascade would continue after his mind gave out.'

'Oh, my dear Lord Fate.' Veleno's voice was full of warmth as he walked around the perfect gold statue of the man who had once been Lord Cardini.

Clothes, hair, teeth and eyes; every part of the alchemist had been transformed into perfect gold. Only two things remained unchanged: one was the ornate talisman that hung around Cardini's neck. The other was the heel of his right boot, and the stone floor of the workshop was stained with the blood that had leaked from the last remaining chunk of human flesh.

'Oh, Fate, but you are a wonder!' Hands on his hips and a smile on his face, Veleno stepped back in admiration. 'This is more gold than Cardini could have produced in a lifetime. Ha!' he exclaimed, laughing at his unintended joke. 'More gold than he could produce in a lifetime! Haha!'

Beside him, Xanda appeared to be torn between frustrated rage and professional awe. In all his years as a mage, he had never seen anything like this.

'Oh, he will look wonderful in my bedroom,' said Veleno. 'No!' he corrected. 'I will make him the centrepiece of the ballroom. People will come from miles around to admire the latest addition to my collection. I will call it... The Alchemist.'

'So can we call our agreement settled?' said Fate.

'But of course,' said Veleno with that dismissive wave of the hand. 'Indeed, I might even go so far as to say that I am in your debt.'

Fate knew better than to rely on such a statement, but he was satisfied that their current issue with the Lord of the City was resolved.

'And the pendants?'

'What? Oh, yes… take them,' said Veleno.

'But my lord,' said Xanda. 'These pendants might be more valuable than he has led us to believe. Maybe I should examine them before we do anything hasty.'

'If you must,' said Veleno who was clearly struggling to think of anything other than his new statue.

With a satisfied sneer, Xanda crossed the room as Fate lifted the monastery's pendant from a nearby work bench.

'One moment,' said the mage.

With a sigh, Fate allowed him to examine the Shīku pendant.

'And what is its purpose?' asked Xanda.

'It is a religious relic,' said Fate. 'Designed to enhance the effects of meditation and prayer.' He made no mention of it being a 'good luck' charm.

'And why would Cardini want such a thing?'

'He thought it might help focus his mind, but I suspect he was too self-centred to benefit from the aura of such a passive relic.'

Still holding the pendant, Xanda's eyes narrowed with suspicion. 'And the other pendant?'

'Is this,' said Fate, walking over to Cardini.

'Careful!' said Veleno as Fate reach up to remove the Talisman of Dreams from around the statue's neck.

Even as he took hold of it, Fate could feel the malignant force of the talisman trying to coerce his will.

'And what does this one do?' asked Xanda, his expression more intense because he could feel power radiating from the talisman.

'This one holds a spirit from the Daemonaria,' said Fate. 'It offers riches but leads to ruin. Here,' he said, holding out the talisman. 'Try it for yourself.'

Xanda instinctively recoiled. Fate would only offer such a thing if he knew it would do him harm. And Cardini had been wearing the pendant when he transmuted himself into gold. 'I will take your word for it,' said the mage as a small crack appeared in the crystal skin of his cheek.

'So, are we free to go?' said Fate as Xanda wiped a trickle of blood from his face.

'What? Yes, yes…' said Veleno. With an effort, he tore his eyes away from Cardini. 'I will find someone else to carry out the job I had planned for you. And as for the tattoo,' he switched his gaze to the Tutor. 'I've survived this far without such protection.'

'Indeed you have,' said Fate.

'But I haven't given up on retaining your services. I will just have to dream up a new way of persuading you.'

Fate sighed at the implicit threat and he realised that satisfying Veleno was only a temporary state of affairs. With a shake of the head he turned to the Tutor.

'We should go,' he said quietly.

'What about the pendants?'

'I'll take care of this one,' said Fate, looping the chain of the talisman over his head before slipping it under the neck of his robes.

'And the monastery's relic?'

'I thought we might return that one together.'

Once again, the Tutor just stared at Fate as he walked back up the tunnel where Veleno's mages were now holding the phase door open with walls of magical force.

Outside the house they mounted their horses and for the first time since meeting him in Blackfell House, the Tutor felt comfortable in Fate's presence. Back in the mansion, they could hear Veleno barking instructions on how they might remove the enormously heavy statue from the alchemist's workshop.

'And if you break so much as a hair on his head, I will have your hide!'

Fate and the Tutor exchanged a smile as they turned their horses and set off for the monastery of Tan Jit Su.

31
The Monastery and the Mound

Fate and the Tutor were greeted with joy as they returned to the monastery, but the joy was tempered by sadness. Freed from the harmful effects of the talisman, the monks had begun to recover. However, the recovery had came too late for Sister Myuko. The female monk never woke from her coma and while her death filled them all with grief, there was one monk who found it particularly hard to bear.

While most of the monks had gathered in the courtyard to greet them, Nawashi had hidden himself away. It was almost dark and the Tutor could just make out his broad-shouldered figure standing in the shadows of the vegetable garden.

'Will he be all right?'

'In time,' replied Abbess Shimitsu with a sigh.

It was later in the evening, as they watched Fate play a game of Hokaku with Master Ganjin, that Abbess Shimitsu asked the question he knew would come.

'Did he kill Cardini?'

The Tutor did not answer at first. He knew the return of the relic would be tainted if it had been achieved through murder.

'No,' he said at last. 'The alchemist was caught in a trap of his own making. In the end it was his greed and his lust for power that killed him.'

'Such is the downfall of many a powerful man.'

'Indeed it is,' said the Tutor as Master Ganjin finally defeated Fate in a game that had lasted almost three hours.

They stayed just one night at the monastery and the following morning was bright as the monks came out to bid them farewell. Abbess Shimitsu said an emotional goodbye to the Tutor, standing on her tiptoes to kiss the tall black man on the cheek. And then she turned to Fate.

'You have shown yourself to be a good man, Decimus Fate.' she said, but Fate seemed unconvinced.

'One good deed does not a good man make.'

'Is that so?' said Abbess Shimitsu with a smile. 'And how many 'good deeds' does it take?'

Fate laughed.

'That remains to be seen.'

For a moment, Abbess Shimitsu just looked into his gold flecked eyes, then she reached out to shake his hand.

'Goodbye, Lord Fate,' she said with a knowing smile.

'Goodbye, Revered Mother,' he replied with a bow.

With that, Fate and the Tutor made their way down from the escarpment and back into the forest valleys below. They made good progress and Fate assumed they would make camp before continuing on to the city together. However, as the light began to fade, they reached the mouth of one particular valley and the Tutor drew his horse to a stop. It was the valley that Abbess Shimitsu had referred to as Tearmann; the valley that shone with the faint light of Faerie.

'Is something wrong?' asked Fate.

'Nothing wrong,' said the Tutor. 'Just something I want to do.'

Fate pursed his lips and gave a nod. 'Then I will see you back in Guile.'

'No doubt,' said the Tutor, his tone subdued and distracted.

'The guest apartment in Blackfell House is yours if you want it,' said Fate. 'Until you find another place to stay.'

'Thank you,' said the Tutor. 'I'll consider it.'

'Then I'll bid you farewell, for now.'

'Farewell,' said the Tutor.

They did not shake hands, but their expressions conveyed a sense of mutual respect and the Tutor watched as Fate continued along the main forest road. As the sorcerer disappeared around a bend in the road, the Tutor turned his horse up the smaller track leading off into the valley. It was three years since he had passed this way, but the pain still felt raw. As he urged his horse forward he wondered if he would have the courage to visit them tonight.

Fate waited until he was out of sight before doubling back to the mouth of the Faerie vale. Being careful to stay well back, he followed the Tutor as the demon hunter travelled further and further along the winding road. It was dark when the Tutor finally came to a stop and only the light of the moon allowed Fate to see anything at all.

From a safe distance, he watched the Tutor tie his horse to a tree before making his way off the path and into the forest. Fate quickly led his own horse off the path and tied it up. Then, moving as quietly as possible, he cut through the forest at an angle that would allow him to shadow the Tutor's progress.

He was just beginning to wonder how far the Tutor intended to go when he noticed a change in the level of darkness beneath the trees. Just ahead of the Tutor, the forest seemed to be illuminated by soft white light. Fate moved closer and the light grew stronger as a clearing came into view.

This clearing was obviously his destination, and yet for some reason the Tutor seemed unwilling to go any further. Peering through the trees, Fate watched as he bowed his head and clasped the circular pendant that hung around his neck... a sapphire set in a circle of silver, which in turn was set in a vibrant disk of jade

He stayed like that for a long time and Fate remained silent until the Tutor finally raised his head. Tucking away the pendant, he wiped his face on the sleeve of his doublet before bending down to pick two silver anemones from the forest floor. As he straightened up, Fate noticed the shimmering forms of several sprites moving through the trees above him. Looking down, they stopped in hushed respect as the Tutor kissed the flowers before laying them gently on the ground. Then, squaring his shoulders, the demon hunter turned and walked away.

Once again, Fate waited until he was out of sight before making his way towards the clearing that glowed with an ethereal light. Overhead, the Faerie sprites followed, surprised by his presence, yet curious to see what he would do.

Moving through the trees, Fate saw autumn give way to spring as rusty bracken and fallen leaves were replaced by green grass and early season flowers. He moved beyond the point where the Tutor had stopped and passed through the final ring of trees until he saw a grassy mound crowned with several moss covered boulders.

Still confused, he entered the clearing. The whisper of the sprites grew louder as he circled the grassy mound then he stopped, and even his jaded heart grew tight with sadness. There, lying on the green grass, were the perfect forms of two humanoid figures; one a tall Faerie woman with raven black hair and smooth alabaster skin, the other a beautiful human child with the same black hair, but with skin the colour of honey. A mother and daughter lying together in death, their bodies perfectly preserved by the power of the Hidden Realm.

So this was why the Tutor had come to the clearing. And this was why he could not bring himself to enter. It was one thing to visit the grave of people you loved. Quite another to look upon their faces and to be reminded of all that you have lost.

Oh, but the Fair Folk could be cruel, thought Fate.

Looking closer he could see that the veins of both mother and child shone like silver threads of the finest silk.

Fate closed his eyes. The silvery veins were a sign of what the Fair Folk called *bás álainn*, a beautiful death. Faced with some unthinkable horror, the mother had used her power to take the life of both herself and her child. The Fair Folk were entranced by such tragedy, and so they had merged the worlds, preserving the moment of ultimate sacrifice forever.

Fate was pondering the perverse sentiments of Faerie when the luminous sprites grew quiet as a stronger light now bloomed beside him.

'He only entered once,' said the voice of a woman.

Fate drew a breath and closed his eyes as he recognised the voice. He did not turn, but he knew who it was… silver hair, emerald eyes, and clothed in a gown of dragonfly wings. It was Lonrúil Croí, a queen from the realm of Faerie.

'He rushed to them, that first time,' Lonrúil Croí continued. 'He stroked their faces and tried to gather them into his arms.'

Fate was a tall man and yet the Faerie woman who stood beside him was at least a full head taller and her body shone like moonlight and fire.

'He did not realise that they could not be moved,' she went on. 'Not from this place.'

'You wouldn't let him take them? You couldn't give him even that relief?'

'The pain of grief is a thing of beauty,' said the Faerie queen. 'This mound has become a place of pilgrimage for our people.' She looked up at the ghostly forms of the lesser faeries hovering in the trees. 'That a woman of the Greater Realm could love so deeply a man from the Dimming Wold.'

She paused, her head tilting as she looked upon the Tutor's wife and child.

Fate turned to look at the queen and despite her apparent detachment, her emerald eyes glistened with tears. With a sigh, Fate turned to leave.

'Take care old friend,' said Lonrúil Croí.

'Friend?' queried Fate and the queen's laugh was like the tinkling of broken glass.

'I would hope so,' she said with a smile.

'Forgive me,' he said. 'It's been a trying few days and I am eager to get home.' Fate did not mean to be rude, but he was still wearing the Talisman of Dreams and the malignant aura of temptation was growing stronger by the hour. He offered the queen a bow then paused as she spoke again.

'I hear that you still share your crimes on the night of the Penance Moon.' Fate looked up at the tall and beautiful woman. 'You have done more than enough to earn your passage along the Lanes. You can cease your sharing with the Moribundium.'

'I will decide when the sharing ends.'

'Even though it causes you pain?'

'Even then,' said Fate.

Lonrúil Croí looked at Fate as if he were a creature she did not quite understand.

'As you wish,' she said with a shrug that made her gossamer gown shimmer.

'Good night, your Majesty.'

'Goodnight, Lord Fate,' said the Faerie queen, her eyes lingering on the sorcerer as he made his way back to his horse.

As Fate disappeared into the gloom, a second figure appeared in the clearing. Dressed in a full length tunic of Autumn leaves, the male Faerie moved to stand beside the queen.

'Why *did* he ask for passage along the Lanes?' asked the man, his voice echoing deeply as if he spoke inside a great hall.

'I do not know,' said the queen. 'He is Fate…Who knows what he sees when he gazes down the river of time.'

'And he still ignores the brightness at his heart.'

'He does.'

'Then he is a fool.'

'Yes,' said the queen. 'But we do so love a fool.'

Fate spent the night beneath the bows of an ancient oak tree. In the morning he shook the dew from his bed roll and took a drink from a spring before continuing on his way. As he drew closer to Guile he passed through the Opal Fields where the forest floor was riddled with pits and covered with large conical mounds of excavated earth. It was a notoriously dangerous place, but it was here that Fate now stopped.

Tying his horse to a nearby tree he headed off into the forest, treading carefully lest he fall through the rotting planks that covered many of the pits. He continued until he found a particularly large mound of earth. The pit beside it was ten feet wide and certainly more than a hundred feet deep.

Looking down into the seemingly bottomless pit, Fate reached up to remove the Talisman of Dreams from around his neck. The muscles in his forearm were tense and his hand trembled as he stared at the turquoise stone at the centre of the pendant. Angry flames seemed to burn in its depths and an insistent voice was screaming at him to put it back on; promising riches and power, and all manner of good fortune if he would only put it back on.

The force of the demon spirit was incredibly powerful, but it was nothing compared to the temptation to use magic, and Fate had overcome that. He had thrown off the shackles of one controlling force. He would not submit to another.

Staring at the pendant, he held it out over the yawning abyss. He felt his muscles spasm with one last effort from the demon spirit and then he let it go. The tempting aura quickly diminished as the talisman disappeared into darkness. He heard it 'tink' and clatter off the walls of the pit and then it was gone.

Fate gave a sigh as the screaming temptation faded from his mind. With a stamp of his foot, he dislodged some of the earth from the edge of the pit then scrambled back as more of the ground gave way, and the Talisman of Dreams was buried forever. With that task completed, Fate headed for home, but there was one more thing he needed to do before he returned to the sanctuary of Blackfell House.

32
A Father's Love

Sienna was beginning to feel more like herself. Sitting in the upper gallery in the Temple of Abnoba, she watched a small flock of goldfinches pecking black seeds from a brass dispenser. The birds flitted back and forth from the branches of a walnut tree that grew up from the main body of the temple below. It was now four days since the incident in the Fool's Hope and the injury to her stomach was finally starting to heal.

The wound had bled badly after she tore the stitches, but now she was feeling stronger and had begun to eat with more enthusiasm. The sun was getting low in the sky and its warm light cast a filigree of shadows from the canopy of copper branches that formed the domed roof of the temple.

She was just beginning to think about an evening meal when she heard the sound of someone coming up the steps to the balcony. Turning, she saw one of the Scions ascending into the gallery.

'Pardon, mistress,' said the Scion. 'There is someone here to see you.'

Bowing her head, the Scion retreated down the stairs as another person stepped onto the landing.

'Hello Abigail,' said Fate.

Sienna instinctively reached to her waist, but her sword was not there. The peaceful Scions had insisted that she leave it in her room.

'What the hell do *you* want?' she snapped.

'I only wish to talk,' said Fate as he moved a step closer to the bench on which she sat.

'That's close enough,' said Sienna. 'Another step and I'll throw the both of us over the balcony.'

'I'm sure you would,' said Fate. 'But I assure you that won't be necessary.'

Sienna appeared unconvinced.

'I know that you hate me,' said Fate. 'And I do not blame you for the way you feel.'

'How farting gracious of you,' said Sienna with a scornful sneer.

Fate raised an eyebrow at her choice of words. 'It sounds like you've been mixing with folk in the cruder quarters of the world.'

'You're right,' said Sienna. 'And it was those 'crude folk' who taught me the things that my father never would.'

At this, Fate gave a sigh. 'If only you knew how much he loved you,' he said and Sienna's face flushed with fury.

'Don't you dare mention him,' she growled as she rose awkwardly from the bench. 'He never had time for me. Even when my mother died he hardly gave me the time of day.'

'He tried,' said Fate. 'But you were filled with such anger.'

'Of course I was,' said Sienna. 'I wanted to kill someone and he wouldn't show me how!' Turning from Fate she waved a hand in the air. 'But he had time for everyone else,' she cried. 'He would teach the soldiers and nobles' sons, but not his own daughter. Not once I took up a sword and showed some promise.'

She turned on Fate, her face contorted with pain.

'You should have seen his face when I first bested my instructor,' she cried. 'Was he pleased? Was he proud? No! He looked shocked and frightened. Was he scared that I might become better than him? That a skinny girl might be a better swordsman than the great Arturo Blade!'

She was raving now, but Fate could only look at her with sadness in his eyes.

'You are right,' he said as Sienna's chest rose and fell with emotion. 'He was afraid that you would follow in his footsteps; that you would become a killer of men like him. He did not want you to feel the guilt that he felt from taking the lives of fathers, husbands and sons.'

'But he only killed when it was right.'

'No,' said Fate. 'He did not. He killed for many reasons and only some of them could be described as *right*.'

For a moment Sienna seemed lost for words. 'And why didn't he tell me this himself?'

'He wanted to,' said Fate. 'He tried to, but…'

'You killed him,' Sienna interrupted him. 'And now he can never tell me anything.'

For a few moments they just looked at each other.

'It's true,' said Fate. 'I killed your father, but it is not what you think.'

'Oh, don't try and weasel your way out of it, you snake.'

'I would never try to deny it,' said Fate. 'For many years, your father was the closest thing I had to a friend.'

'Then why do it?' Sienna cried. 'I suppose someone made you an offer you couldn't refuse?'

'That's true,' said Fate. 'And the payment they gave me has saved my life.'

At this he reached inside his robes and pulled out a piece of creased parchment.

'I always intended to show you this, but I never imagined it would happen like this.'

Sienna's eyes narrowed with suspicion as Fate held out the parchment, but finally her curiosity got the better of her. Snatching it from his hand she unfolded it and her heart lurched as she recognised her father's 'AB' mark, written with the flourish of a rapier's cut. She put out a hand to steady herself as she sat back down on the bench.

Something in her eyes made the faded words shimmer as she began to read.

'*Old friend*,' the note began…

After many years of keeping an enemy at bay, I find myself in a bind from which I cannot withdraw. I have dodged the fatal thrust of death so many times that I do not fear for myself, but this particular enemy has also threatened the life of my daughter, and that I cannot abide.

No payment or entreaty will stay the party's hand, and there is nothing I can do to prevent it. The only way to stop him killing me is if someone equally powerful kills me first.

And so, my friend, I have added my name to a list of people who wish to see you dead. I know that you will find out about the list, and I know what you do to people who conspire against you. In essence, I have taken out a contract on myself. Now all we need to agree on is payment.

You have no shortage of money, and I have nothing in the way of magical items that would impress the likes of you. So the payment I offer will be in the form of information. I have a secret that I would share with you; something I have suspected for many years and yet never told you.

*So if our friendship counts for anything, then I would ask you to do this for me, and to do it swiftly. If **you** kill* *me then my enemy might overlook the life of a wayward child. Forgive me, my friend, but it is the only way I can think of to save her.*

Sincerely yours

AB

As she read the letter, Sienna felt as if she were getting smaller and younger. Sounds echoed strangely in her ears and she had the strangest feeling that she was watching the scene from a point somewhere near the domed roof of the temple. Finally she lowered the parchment into her lap.

'How do I know this is true?' she asked without looking up.

'You know it is,' said Fate.

'And what was the payment he made for his own death? What was this secret he had to share with you?'

'He told me that I was a slave to magic and that it would destroy me if I did not give it up.'

'That's it?' said Sienna with disbelief. 'And you believed him?'

'No, I didn't,' said Fate. 'Not at first. But then I made the mistake of trying to prove your father wrong. Only when I tried to live without magic did I realise he was telling the truth.'

'You gave up power because Arturo Blade told you to?' Fate acknowledged this with a shrug. 'Then you're a fool as well as a murderer.'

'That I may be,' said Fate. 'But at least *Abigail* Blade now knows why her father was killed.'

'The name is Sienna.'

Fate smiled at this and turned to leave, but then he stopped.

'Do you know what the name Abigail means?'

Sienna gave a snort of derision.

'It means Father's Love.'

With that, Fate disappeared down the stairs, leaving Sienna sitting on the bench with the faded letter clenched tightly in her lap. She now had the gallery entirely to herself, and all that could be heard was the flutter of twilight birds and the muffled sound of a daughter's grief.

33
Just For a While

Fate was accustomed to various looks and stares as he made his way about the city, but this evening there were more than normal. Taking a detour past the Fool's Hope he caught the attention of tradesmen who paused in repairing the broken window to watch him pass. Further on, he overheard a small group of wayfinders heading back to their makeshift home.

'That's him, I tell ya,' one of them whispered to the others. 'That's Weasel's friend.'

Fate arched an eyebrow and the frown on his hawkish face fell somewhere between amusement and irritation. But there was one particular encounter that made him pause. Crossing a bridge he saw a group of people pulling a pale and bloated body from the river. They carried out the task with quiet solemnity, while along the bank a woman began to keen.

'The Butcher,' Fate heard one man say. 'It's the Butcher done for Eleanor Todd's boy.'

The Butcher was the name given to a killer who had evaded the authorities of Guile for years. Targeting the poor and homeless, he had the grizzly habit of dismembering his victims before dumping their remains in the river.

However, it was not the Butcher's latest victim that made Fate pause. It was two figures on the far side of the bank. One was a well known vagrant. Unwashed, insane and dressed in the filthy robes of a pilgrim, he walked the streets of Guile preaching about a 'Great Reckoning' that would cleanse the city of all its ills. He called himself a 'servant of the divine' but people simply ignored him, or laughed at him, or moved him along to be rid of the smell. But now, it seemed, he had a friend.

Standing beside the so called servant was another figure. Younger and taller, but bent at the hip and shoulder as if his body was somehow misshapen. Together they watched the townsfolk retrieving the body from the river, but then the younger of the two looked up. Noticing Fate in his sorcerer's robes, he leaned over to say something to the servant who then pointed a bony finger at Fate.

'Your time is coming, sorcerer,' cried the vagrant. 'Magic is heresy. Only the power of the divine is pure.'

The threat rolled off Fate as water rolls off waxed cotton. Cities like Guile were never short of mad old fools pronouncing doom. But it seemed that this mad fool had a disciple. And that was a much rarer thing.

Still, neither of them posed a threat to a man like him and so Fate dismissed them from his mind and continued on his way.

A few more streets and Blackfell House came into view. It was dark now and the house might have appeared forbidding were it not for the flicker of light coming from his bedroom on the first floor, and from the kitchen on the ground. It would seem that Motina had warmed his room before going down to prepare some food. She obviously knew he was coming and Fate was not surprised. After all the recent excitement she probably had birds out watching for his return.

Fate's boots crunched on the stones of the driveway as he walked down the avenue of leafless trees. Stepping up onto the porch, he opened the front door and paused. There were voices coming from the kitchen.

'That doesn't prove the point,' said the deep voice of a man.

'Oh, but I think it does,' replied the familiar voice of Motina.

Fate gave a sniff of amusement and smiled as he hung up his long-coat. He did not catch the next part of the exchange and then the conversation suddenly stopped as he opened the door to the kitchen.

The Tutor was sitting at the large wooden table while Motina tended something on the stove. Both turned to look at him as he entered the room then...

'Boots!' snapped Motina before anything else could be said. 'I know you like to keep them on, but it would be nice if you could wipe them on the mat before you go walking mud through my kitchen.'

Fate rolled his eyes and it was clear from the Tutor's expression that he had recently been given a similar lecture.

'Well, your supper's ready,' said Motina, ladling lamb stew into a bowl before adding a sprinkle of chopped mint and two slices of crusty bread. 'I'll warm some beds while you welcome your new tenant.'

The Tutor began to correct her, but Motina raised a hand to silence any objections. Gathering up a basket of clean laundry she hobbled out of the room, leaving Fate and the Tutor alone.

'What were you talking about?' said Fate as he sat down at the table and poured himself a glass of red wine from a carafe that was sitting on the table.

'Power,' said the Tutor as Fate reached over to top up the demon hunter's glass.

'And what was the contention?'

'The old adage that power corrupts,' said the Tutor.

'And you believe it does?'

'Of course! Just look at Veleno, or the Emperor, or the priests of Guile's largest church.'

'But Motina disagreed,' said Fate, his dark eyes gleaming with gold as he took a sip of wine.

'That she did,' said the Tutor. 'She says that one only needs to look at the thousands of families in Guile to know it isn't true.'

Fate's smile suggested that he had heard Motina's argument before.

'She says that, in these households, the parents hold all the power and yet most do not abuse it. They use their power to protect and nurture their children.'

'And what do you say to that?'

'I would say your housekeeper's wisdom extends beyond the mysteries of cooking and cleaning.'

'Indeed it does,' said Fate and silence followed as they began to eat their food.

'I'm glad you decided to take me up on my offer,' said Fate.

'Just for a while,' said the Tutor. 'Just until things settle down.'

Fate raised his glass. 'Until things settle down,' he said, and the two men clinked their glasses.

Finishing their food, they sat back and Fate smiled to himself. For years, Motina had kept the guest apartment in a state of readiness. Fate had often told her she was wasting her time, for he had no intention of sharing his home with anyone other than her. He should have known better than to doubt her, but in his wildest dreams he never imagined that he would be sharing his house with a man like the Tutor.

The two men sat in companionable silence until Fate spoke again.

'Last night,' he said. 'In the forest... I followed you to the enchanted glade.'

'I know,' replied the Tutor and Fate winced like someone caught in the act of stealing.

'The Fair Folk don't mean to be cruel,' he told the Tutor. 'They only wish to honour something that moved them.'

The Tutor bowed his head and Fate could think of nothing else to say. The soft crackle of the fire was the only sound in the kitchen until...

'Aoife,' said the Tutor and Fate recognised the Faerie name, which in the common tongue would be written as Eefa. The name could mean warrior or beauty, or both.

'That was my wife's name,' said the Tutor.

'And your daughter?' asked Fate and the Tutor shook his head as a sad smile pricked his eyes.

'We called her Caoimhe.'

'*Keeva*,' thought Fate as another log popped and fizzled in the fire. He instinctively converted the name into common, but he spoke the meaning out loud.

'Beloved,' he said.

The Tutor nodded and, in the quiet kitchen of Blackfell House, the sorcerer and the demon hunter sipped their wine as they stared into the flames.

Dear Reader

Thank you so much for buying Decimus Fate. If this is the first time you have read one of my books then it is a pleasure to meet you. And if we have met before, then thanks for joining me once more.

My last book, Battle Mage, was a big epic fantasy and it was always intended to be a single complete story. By contrast, Decimus Fate is intended to be an introduction. If people like the world I have created then I have more adventures in mind for Fate and the Tutor.

And even though Battle Mage is a stand-alone book there is scope to expand upon it and my mind has been exploring the threads of that world to see if they are strong enough to follow Falco's tale. But whatever I write next it will be with you, the Reader, in mind.

If you enjoyed Decimus Fate I would be immensely grateful if you could spare a few minutes to leave a short a review on Amazon.

And if you have any comments, or would like to get in touch, you can say hello on Twitter: @TheFlanston

Or via my website: www.peter.flannery.co.uk

Either way it would be great to hear from you and thanks again for buying the book.

With warm regards
Peter

Printed by Amazon Italia Logistica S.r.l.
Torrazza Piemonte (TO), Italy

12948141R00160